East Union High School
Textbook
1700 N. Union Rd., Manteca, CA 95336

901057

☆ ♡ ☆   ☆ ♡ ☆   ☆ ♡ ☆

"Splendidly imagined and written . . . TEEN ANGEL maps out a territory of peculiarly modern adolescence. . . . Sexual frankness is taken for granted—the teen-age girls in these stories drape Barbie dolls in diaphragms 'like a hoopskirt.' "
The New York Times Book Review

"Gingher captures both perspectives: teens rushing hopefully toward adulthood, their parents and older siblings looking back with a certain wistfulness. . . . She remembers what it's like to be a teen-ager, and she makes us remember, too—the restlessness and confusion but also 'the dumb luck and magic.' "
The Orlando Sentinel

"These warm, insightful stories portray adolescents at touching moments of infatuation, awareness and recognition of the many guises of love. . . . Gingher has provided the reader with a gift of closely observed, deeply felt stories that shimmer with truth "
Publishers Weekly

"Not simple tales of sweet romance, these stories deal with love of a textured, more genuine kind."
Booklist

Also by Marianne Gingher
Published by Ballantine Books:

BOBBY REX'S GREATEST HIT

TEEN ANGEL

and other stories of young love

Marianne Gingher

BALLANTINE BOOKS • NEW YORK

Library of Congress Catalog Card Number: 88-1368

ISBN 0-345-35783-3

This edition published by arrangement with Atheneum Publishers, an imprint of Macmillan, Inc.

"The Kiss" appeared originally in *South Carolina Review;* "The Magic Circle" in *McCall's;* "Wearing Glasses" in *Redbook;* "The Hummingbird Kimono" in *Seventeen;* and "No News" in *The American Review.*

Manufactured in the United States of America

First Ballantine Books Edition: May 1989

LOVE TO BOB, RODERICK, SAM,
AND TO FRED CHAPPELL—
GENEROUS TEACHERS ALL

CONTENTS

☆♡☆ ☆♡☆ ☆♡☆

THE KISS   1

TEEN ANGEL   15

THE MAGIC CIRCLE   42

WEARING GLASSES   54

THE HUMMINGBIRD KIMONO   72

AURORA ISLAND   90

CAMOUFLAGE   118

TOY PARIS   142

NO NEWS   157

MY MOTHER'S CONFESSION   190

The author wishes to thank the North Carolina Arts Council and the National Endowment for the Arts for the co-sponsored award of a North Carolina Fellowship in Writing during which time several of these stories were revised or written.

Praise and thanks to Rod and Betty Jane Buie, Jennifer L. Hofmann, Mary E. Morris—and they all know why.

THE KISS

☆ ♡ ☆   ☆ ♡ ☆   ☆ ♡ ☆

One year it seemed to Nicodine that the familiar Carolina hills lay magic with winter and did not look the same. They took on live and slumbering shapes, bristling spiny backs against the wind like big old porcupines. The magic changed Nicodine's ears, too. The cold blue lips of January piped the chimney for her like a flute: whole, bright little tunes that made her dance with her mop or broom and stir the corn cakes faster. Her hands moved almost too quickly for her chores, flapping like chased crows about the house; and she felt a tender power in them that made each thing she touched seem shaped to her, loved by the very blood that sang beneath her skin. She brought a little pig into the house and taught him to dance on his hind legs.

And after she had spooned Mama Dear the nighttime cup of honeyed tea with the one old wrinkled prune at the bottom that Mama Dear liked to gum when the tea was gone, after she had waited for her to spit the prune pit into the palm Nicodine held open like a small pink china saucer, after the pillows had been plumped and fluffed and Mama Dear's silvery wig removed and hung like a sleepy possum on the bedpost, then, as Mama Dear began to doze, Nicodine crept barefoot into the attic where she kept a candle and the Roebuck wishbook and the books that had been her brother's before he went off to war and got killed.

She had discovered the books accidentally. There were twelve—one for each of her years. Squinting in the dust-colored light, she had read each one at least that many times, so that if she was sleepy she could close her eyes and turn the soft, worn pages; her memory urged simply by the feel of the books got the stories told. Often as she read, she would recall her brother's face, rowdy with dreams, his eyes roving the distant hills of their farm. And she would wonder if in all his travels he had seen the ocean or walked a blazing desert or hidden from tigers and panthers like the ones that prowled the jungles of his books. She read tales of cowboys and pirates and thieves, of soldiers and sailors, murderers and kings. But her favorite book was a love story. Its cover showed a dark, handsome gentleman kissing a lady whose face glowed white and round as a cotton boll. Her bright yellow glory of hair looked like a hat covered with buttercups, and she smiled from heart-shaped lips that parted to show teeth white and sharp as stars. This was a lady who wore crinolines, who pinned brooches to a soft pink bosom and dusted herself with violet sachet. And if Nicodine did not know what a crinoline was or a brooch or sachet, she hunted in the wishbook until she usually found a picture. She kept a list of the things she would need in this world to become a lady, for she had learned to write as well as read before Mama Dear got old and sick and the mule that had carried her down the road eight miles to school each day had died.

Sometimes she read until cockcrow. But if she fell asleep, awaking in the middle of the night to the bawling of a calf or the scream of the old barred owl who hunted the moon-bleached garden for a small fat rabbit or mouse, she would lie pretending it was a man in the yard who called her with

a voice secret and dark as an animal's. Sometimes she thought
that if she did not kiss someone soon, her lips would turn
inside-out with wishing and stay, stuck that way, so that no
man would look at her twice. Ever.

At sunrise, when it seemed to her that the clouds flaunted
themselves red and sassy as valentines across the sky, she
rose from her dreams not sulky with regret but happy for a
day in which anything might happen. The pale January air
hummed in her nostrils with all the clear, cool expectations
of space, and, sucking it deeply, her head felt like a flower,
cloudy with bees. She did not know what he would look like
when he came. It would seem a long time, like waiting for
the kettle to boil, but he would come. He would probably
arrive on horseback, and she might first glimpse him out the
kitchen window as she peeped through a droop of leaves
sprouting from the sweet potato she'd put in a Tube Rose
can. As he rode up the drive, he'd have to duck the limbs of
the horse pear tree or lose his hat, which she knew would be
the tall, black silk hat of a gentleman. She wondered what
she would say to the stranger. If she could not think of any
words, she would fetch her little pig to dance, and they would
laugh together.

It seemed to Nicodine that the land waited for him, too:
dreamy and wide and blank as a page in the winter sunlight.
Where no tree grew and no house sat it waited to be filled
with the surprise of shadow.

She did not tell Mama Dear about the books she kept in
the attic. The only book Mama Dear cared for was the Bible
that rested beside her bed on a pink lace doily. Each night,
before she brought the tea and prune, Nicodine read to Mama
Dear from the little white Bible that looked prim as a tea cake
but old and crumbly as if someone had nibbled it around the
edges. It had a sky-blue, grosgrain ribbon sewn into its binding that always marked the spot where Nicodine had left off
reading the night before. And on Sunday evenings, the first

thing Reverend Mr. Benbow did when he paid his weekly visit to all shut-ins was open the Bible to the page where the slim blue ribbon lay and check how far Nicodine had read.

Mary Magdalene was about to bathe Jesus' feet on the Sunday Reverend Benbow came and told them about the circus. He was a short fat man with skin dull and dark as coal. His black morning coat, fastened neatly with half-hidden safety pins, parted to show a cheerful orange vest that stretched across a stomach as round as if he held a pumpkin in his lap. He wore a clump of nandina berries in his lapel and on three of his fingers, the wedding rings of the wives he had outlived.

He sat at the kitchen table by the hearth and talked with Mama Dear through the bedroom door that Nicodine propped open with the old black iron. Mama Dear always felt better when the preacher came. She fastened her wig to her head with big mother-of-pearl haircombs and powdered the shine from her face with cornstarch. After she and Reverend Benbow had taken tea and said a prayer (they always blessed Nicodine for her industry and kindness), the two of them gossiped like jays, Mama Dear giggling and hooting and slapping at her throat as if it were on fire with so much talk.

That night Reverend Benbow had the circus on his mind, but he waited until he and Mama Dear were finally talked out, and before he commenced to tell his story he turned to Nicodine and out of politeness said, "I be wanting to see that little pig of yours now."

Nicodine was proud of the little pig. She whistled it inside, and they all watched and clapped as it jigged about the room. Then, because entertainment made her thirsty, Mama Dear panted for another cup of tea. Nicodine poured four fresh cups. One cup she set on the floor for the pig, who did want a drop after dancing so hard. The Reverend praised her for her gentleness with God's creatures.

They sat quiet for a spell while the Reverend sucked down

the last of his tea through the hole where two teeth should have been. Then, he told them all about the circus.

"They don't have no dancing pig," he said, "but they's a man who hammers nails up his nose and a alligator lady and a full-growed baby they got pickled in a jar."

"Jesus have mercy!" called Mama Dear from the bedroom.

"Amen, Sister."

"Amen," said Nicodine.

"They got a midget man rides a goat and a lady eats glass and razor blades and live bees. I seen it." Reverend Benbow smiled at the pig and the pig smiled back.

"Do you reckon they got a handsome man in a tall black hat?" asked Nicodine. She didn't know how the words got out. They came alive by themselves and hopped from her throat, sparrow-quick. She felt giddy and light with their leaving. She slapped a hand across her mouth too late.

"They got a magic man," Reverend Benbow said. "I didn't see no hat, but a magic man has got to have hisself a hat somewhere, I s'pose. *You* know"—and he winked—"for keeping rabbits. Why you ask, Nicodine?"

But she never answered because just then the little pig of his own notion began to dance and dance around the kitchen, and Nicodine had to put him on her lap and whisper in his ear to quiet him.

"My, my," said Reverend Benbow, scooting back from the fire. He winked at Nicodine again. "I believe I feel a warm spell coming on not natural. Two weeks till Groundhog's Day but I got me a taste for Easter Bunny pie." He shook from one trouser pocket a red bandana broad as a flag and mopped his shiny face. He looked at Nicodine with his wise old wrinkly elephant's eyes. "Mr. Pig feels the sap rising in his toes."

"You stay close by your Mama Dear," he told Nicodine

at the door. "They's gypsies and ruffians following the circus got feathers in their hats for every young gal they stolen."

And after he had been gone a long while, Nicodine still stood on the front porch, holding the door wide open and feeling a strange warm wind on her face and arms. Overhead the sky boiled reckless with stars and the January moon throbbed hotly in the horse pear's limbs like a piece of fruit ripe for picking.

Just inside the door Nicodine stopped and caught a cricket, and she carried him with her to bed so that he might sing to her all night. For she could not sleep. The patience that had made waiting seem like nothing better and whole days quick and dream-lazy as the yawns and stretches of a cat had left her. Outside the crazy weather answered her own restless sighs with big winds warm as March.

In the morning her brain burned with the fever of purpose. And after breakfast and the flurry of chores, when Mama Dear began to doze into that dreamless daze of sleep that would last until suppertime, Nicodine crawled quietly into the attic to fetch from her wishbook the secret list.

A lady needs shoes. Downstairs she found in the cupboard two empty flour sacks, pretty and white and not very wrinkled. She tied them on her feet with scrappy red twine that she looped into nice neat bows.

A lady needs a pocketbook. She took two biscuits from the piesafe and some slices of dried apple that she tied into a handkerchief. Then, carefully, she unhooked the egg basket that hung by the kitchen door and placed the bundle of food inside, because a pocketbook should never be empty.

A lady wears a hat with a long bright ribbon. Quiet as could be, Nicodine tiptoed into Mama Dear's bedroom. Her brow felt rainwet as if she stood under a leaky spot in the roof, and for a moment she stopped still and hardly breathed, thinking lightning from out of nowhere might pounce and strike her dead. But the fever that had started in her head had worked its way to her fingers. Trembling, she opened the Bible to where the sky-blue ribbon lay and gently tore the ribbon from its binding. Then, she tied it to the pink lace doily, which she set atop her head.

A lady needs perfume and lipstick, rouge, a petticoat, gloves and silk stockings. She slipped through the little house, opening drawers and peering into chifforobes to gather what she could. But oh she would look silly with clothespins on her ears for earbobs and socks on her hands instead of gloves! And she was about to cry for not having all the things a lady should have when she suddenly touched, deep within Mama Dear's cedar chest, the raggedy black umbrella that Papa Dear had carried on his arm to church. She lifted it out; it smelled sweet enough to eat. She felt like doing a little dance, because more than anything else a lady needed a parasol. For what would happen when the sun beat hot on a lady's face? Her skin might shrivel hard and dry as an old pecan, and she would not look beautiful in spite of the finest clothes in all the world.

Finally, although it was not written on her list, Nicodine knew that a lady needed someplace to go when she was all dressed up: a shimmering ball or a wide green park filled with lily ponds and live oak trees with skirts of shade where a lady might sit and be cool and eat herself a picnic. But a circus will do just fine, thought Nicodine. A circus will do me just fine.

There she stood, looking at herself in the hall tree mirror, smiling at her hat and the basket on her arm and the flour sack shoes out of which her legs sprouted thin but firm as young plum trees. And she smiled for the umbrella that she wouldn't dare open until she got outside for fear of evil luck. And she was about to turn and walk outside, up the narrow road eight miles to town, when somebody whistled and tapped at the door. It was not the wind.

Nicodine didn't know what to do. First she grabbed off

her hat; then she stuck it back on. She tossed the pocketbook basket on the hall tree bench; then she snatched it up again. She spun around in the mirror and checked her skirt hem for loose strings. All this motion in the blink of her own two eyes. Her heart fluttered up and down the insides of her ribs, shy as a butterfly. The whistling came again and a rat-a-tat-tat and a rat-a-tat-tat. "That you, Reverend Benbow?" she whispered. And she half-hoped it was so that somebody who knew and loved the old Nicodine could forgive her for being so brand-spanking new that she didn't know what to do with herself. But it couldn't be Reverend Benbow because today was Monday.

Mama Dear turned over once in her bed, and the mattress springs sounded like an angry hen fussing. Nicodine almost ran into the bedroom until she remembered the blue ribbon in her hat.

Slowly she crept across the parlor to the window and peeked through the frilly curtain she might have tied around her waist for a petticoat if she had thought about it earlier. Outside, parked under the horse pear tree, she saw a fat white horse hitched to a wagon. On the side of the wagon in big gold letters was written: OTIS SUNSHINE CIRCUS. When she saw what sat on the wagon seat, she giggled and gasped all at once. At first she thought it was a monkey. But when it drew a cigar from its pocket and struck a match across its knee and bent its tiny perfect fingers around the flame, she saw it was a little man no bigger than a blackbird.

She pressed her face to the window and tried to see who stood on the front porch, knocking and whistling. All of a sudden the blackbird man started laughing and pointing and before she could think to let the curtain drop, a face on the outside drew near to her own with just the pane of cloudy window glass between them.

"Oh!" cried Nicodine.

"I see you," said the man. "You come out on the porch.

I want to ask you something, darling-pie.'' She could hear him easily through the glass, and his voice poured cool and clear as creek water into her ear.

On the way to the door, trembling and happy, Nicodine decided what she would do. She would do it gracefully, and if he were a gentleman she would find out soon enough. She turned the doorknob carefully. It felt like an egg. Then, moving dreamily to the rhythm of that January wind that waltzed into the house, she lowered her eyes, dropped one knee in a deep deep curtsy and held out a limp, small, delicate hand to be kissed.

''Looky there at her foots! What's she got there on her foots?'' screamed the blackbird man from the wagon.

''My goodness, are you a clubfoot, darling-pie?'' said the man on the porch, reaching for her outstretched hand. ''Steady now. Don't fall.''

Nicodine looked at him. He was the whitest man she had ever seen. He was so white that her eyes hurt to look at him, and his hand closed over her own, cold as frost. ''There now,'' he said, dragging her upwards from her curtsy. ''I'm Otis Sunshine himself, ma'am,'' and he tipped his hat. A black hat it was and tall, but burnt-looking as an old piece of stovepipe. ''Am I addressing the lady of the house?'' His eyes were small and red as a rooster's, but his voice warbled gentle and low, and Nicodine wasn't afraid when he spoke.

''I knowed you'd come,'' she said. ''Why, it's a miracle.''

Otis Sunshine laughed and ran one long white hand through a crackly zigzag of hair. Nicodine blinked. His hair was the color of lightning. ''Yeah,'' he said, ''we're miracles all right, ain't we, Mr. Bub?''

From his perch on the wagon Mr. Bub cawed and stomped his feet.

''You ever seen a man so little?'' Otis Sunshine asked.

''No sir.''

''Mr. Bub's fingers is skinny as shoestrings, and he can

sleep down inside one of my socks. I'll bet you never seen a man white as me neither."

"No sir. You white as sun on snow," she said dreamily, half-blinded by the sight of him.

"White as *nothing*," said Otis Sunshine proudly. "If I was any whiter, I'd be invisible."

"For sure," said Nicodine.

"You ain't afraid to touch me, are you? Go on. Take a holt of my skin."

Nicodine lowered her eyes and touched the bare extended arm with one shy finger.

"Poke on it," he said, laughing. "I ain't no snake. It won't fall off."

"It's normal skin except the color," Otis Sunshine said matter-of-factly.

"Go on and ast her," Mr. Bub called impatiently. "Ast her what we come for."

"You must be kindly parched," said Nicodine, remembering that a travel-weary gentleman always took refreshment. "Would you like some tea and a biscuit?"

"Well now. That's right fine. Mr. Bub, would you like a taste of tea?"

"Go on and ast her!" Mr. Bub said. "What's them bandages wrapped around your foots for missy-girl?"

"Mr. Bub don't see too good," Otis Sunshine told Nicodine. "They're flour sacks, ain't they?"

She lowered her eyes at the flour sacks that looked silly to her now. "Shoes," she said.

"Forget it. They're only shoes," he called to Mr. Bub. "Pretty shoes," he added. "Practical for walking. Come up high so the mud don't get on your ankles. And, by the by, that's a fancy hat, too."

"Thank you, sir," said Nicodine. "I made it up all by myself."

"I'd say it was a fancy churchgoing hat what with that pretty ribbon hanging down your back."

"Ribbon come out of the Bible," she said.

"I knew it," Otis Sunshine said. "I told Mr. Bub we'd come to the house of a lady. Anybody else at home 'sides you, darling-pie?"

Nicodine shook her head. "Only Mama Dear who's fast asleep and feeling poorly."

"What's she look like, your mama?"

Nicodine wrinkled her brow and thought for a long moment. "Old," she said.

"She got any great big ugly birthmarks?"

"No sir."

"Got any hair growing on her face?"

Nicodine giggled. "Mama Dear ain't even got hair growing on her head!"

"You hear that?" Mr. Bub called excitedly, flapping his tiny black arms. "I told you we just got to get out and beat the bushes."

"You mean, darling-pie, that your mama's a baldheaded lady?"

"Oh, she don't let nobody see her without her wig on."

"Well then," said Otis Sunshine, scratching his head. "You got any menfolk with extra arms or fingers or their eyes different colors?"

"No sir. Menfolks is all dead."

"Do you got any odd-looking critters around this place?" His voice had grown loud and husky. He put his hat back on and stood with one hip out of joint, looking suddenly full of business and in a hurry. "Got any two-headed chickens?"

"No sir," said Nicodine, feeling dizzy with so many questions.

"I got a dollar bill has your name on it," Otis Sunshine said. He rummaged in his pocket and pulled out a dollar. "And there's other dollars where I got this one."

"Where's that?" she said, her eyes large.

"At the getting place, that's where." He laughed. "You ever been to a freak show?"

She shook her head.

"She seeing one for free right now in her own front yard," whooped Mr. Bub.

"Well, I got a dollar says you're hiding two belly buttons under that dress or maybe them feet is all wrapped up because you were born without your rightful number of toes. Huh?"

"No sir," said Nicodine. "I got all my toes for sure."

"Don't be shy now. You got a little deformity you can show Mr. Bub and me why it would just about make us kinfolks."

She shook her head, truly sorrowful.

Otis Sunshine sighed. "Sorry to take up your valuable time, then, ma'am. Folks normal as apple pie stay poor." And he put the dollar back in his pocket. Her head spun like a spool as he turned to go.

"You ain't even had refreshments yet!" she cried.

"Good-day, darling-pie. Bye-bye."

"But you ain't even . . . you ain't even . . ." She closed her eyes feeling the words in her mouth so hot that they would melt her tongue if she did not get rid of them. She grabbed hold of the porch railing for fear she would faint. "Why, you ain't even *kissed* me yet," she said. And she wished she could will her lips to turn inside-out and stick that way forever if that was what Otis Sunshine was looking for.

It seemed to her that she kept her eyes closed a very long time, afraid to look after the bold words had been spoken. When, at last, she peeked, she saw him whispering with Mr. Bub. The fat white horse pawed the ground and whinnied like a horn.

"You come along here," said Otis Sunshine, wiggling a finger long and white as Mr. Bub's cigar ash.

The yard had thawed to a soft red mush, and Nicodine felt the dampness seeping through her new sack shoes as she crossed to the wagon.

"Mr. Bub here says we need us some dancing ladies," Otis Sunshine said. "Do you know how to dance?"

"Oh!" she gasped, her face suddenly brightening. "You just got to stay so I can show you my little pig."

Years later, when Nicodine sat on the porch of her own snug house, telling the stories of her youth and how she had come to marry the Reverend Mr. Benbow, she never forgot to mention her rescue from Otis Sunshine, who had carried her and her little dancing pig away to join the circus that January spring. For it was Reverend Benbow who met them on the road to town, who later said he would not have known her save for the ribbon fluttering at her back. Who for punishment made her leave the little pig behind in Otis Sunshine's wagon, because anyway Otis Sunshine said he'd paid a dollar for the pig, and sure enough he had. When they got home Reverend Benbow built a big fire in her yard and burned the books and sent her inside to wash her hands and arms for touching man-flesh, which is something a lady wouldn't do unless it was her husband or kinfolk. And then, because she looked so sad, still dreaming of the circus and the big, bright world of Otis Sunshine, whose name would have rhymed with her own, Reverend Benbow took her inside and they finished the story of Mary Magdalene together, whispering so as not to wake Mama Dear.

It was a warm night, a dancing night, and she missed her little pig. A fly, warmed from its crack in the ceiling by the crazy weather, buzzed drowsily about the room. She never forgot how Reverend Benbow snatched it from the air with a motion quick as light, and from his trouser pocket he took a toy he had made: half a pecan shell fitted with toothpick legs. Gently he plucked off the wings of the fly and set the fly under the pecan shell. Magically the shell came alive, swirling across the tabletop, and Nicodine had to laugh. Everything good in the world was in her laugh. And the Reverend Benbow turned to her then and kissed her on the forehead. It was her very first kiss.

TEEN ANGEL

☆ ♡ ☆   ☆ ♡ ☆   ☆ ♡ ☆

"If memory never failed us and if we were always willing to tell the truth, wouldn't we be able to anticipate our problems?" my friend Becky Reece asked. She picked an Opera Creme apart to lick the filling. "Who'd need psychoanalysis?" It was Saturday morning, early in the summer of 1962, and we were lolling around Becky's kitchen doing one of our philosophy gigs, watching her mother roll out piecrust.

"We'd have to get into the habit of thinking backwards," I said.

"*Yes!*" Becky agreed. "Spontaneously and with precision. Thinking backwards. I *like* it, Jennifer." She chewed her Opera Creme thoughtfully. "It's like this," she said. "All of today's problems have the equivalent of family trees, *ancestral* problems."

"Please," Mrs. Reece said, stirring something. "You girls are giving me a headache."

Becky said, "Mom, if we could think backwards, miscry might reverse itself. Sort of like when the universe collapses, time will run backwards."

"If the universe collapses, who'll hang around to reset their watches?" Mrs. Reece said tiredly.

15

She said this at the exact moment her husband barreled into the kitchen and slammed her around. I remember because it broke her watch. Actually he didn't slam her—I was only fifteen and memory is prone to exaggerate—but he shoved her aside, brutishly, then he threw a sack of oysters at the sink, which missed, hit the drainboard, and broke several dishes.

"And in front of *you*," my mother said later when I told her. *"Company!"*

Well, I was hardly company. I came closer to being a piece of furniture with all the time I logged at the Reeces'. We lived at opposite ends of Dogwood Drive, and Becky and I had been friends since first grade. I was drawn to their house as if to great adventure. It was cluttered and squabbling; but Mrs. Reece understood me in a way my own mother didn't, and Becky had an older sister, Rita, who was heartily sexual and told us every detail of her exploits with a kind of flat-faced erudition while she gooed on her makeup. At the Reeces' I got to smoke cigarettes and eat crème de menthe parfaits and play strip poker unabashedly. You could lounge around on the living room furniture and put your feet on the coffee table. Best of all there was the thrilling unpredictability of Mr. Reece's fury to reckon with.

"Yikes!" Becky said, swooping a protective arm around her mother as her father blew past. "Should we feel like simpletons?"

I didn't know what she was talking about. I was too horrified to try to guess. I stooped to pick up all the Opera Cremes, which had somehow loosened and scattered themselves.

"Mom," Becky said patiently. "Think backwards."

Mrs. Reece gawked at her. "He's a maniac!" she shouted. "Think *backwards*? Okay, he was a maniac yesterday, the day before, last year. He was a maniac in 1942 when we got married. He was a maniac in high school. I knew every girl who dumped him and why. *Why?* Because he was a maniac. He was a maniac at birth—a breech. It almost killed his mother. Is that far enough back? I'll take him right back to the Garden of Eden, if you like. To his slimy perch in the Tree of Knowledge.''

I had no idea what the fight between Mr. and Mrs. Reece was all about. I supposed it had something to do with the sack of oysters. I was straining to think backwards, even though I had the barest facts and observations. I'd seen some of their other fights, and none of them ever seemed to make sense. I always felt as if I'd entered the movie late, that the high drama had already happened offstage and the ragtag exchanges I'd come upon were an effort at patching up rather than dismantling their scarecrow marriage. Once I'd watched them fling shoes at each other. Once I'd seen Mrs. Reece dig what she called a grave in the backyard and bury her wedding album.

On the whole the Reeces seemed more quirky than violent, and I was going through a stage where I was infatuated with quirkiness. My own home was bland and regular. Everyone was soft-spoken and polite. If I wasn't well behaved I got sent to my room. My parents, although never openly passionate, were kind and deferential toward one another. If you want to know the truth, we all kind of treated each other like company. When I think back on my childhood, I see a tidy beige home filled with Coke bottles dressed in little terry cloth sweaters so as not to leave rings on the furniture. I recall a perpetual, calming sound of sloshing: clothes in the washer, dishes in the dishwasher, toilet brushes churning the water of our toilets, keeping us clean. The rhapsodic scent of Airwick sweetened every room.

The very air at the Reeces' house roiled overhead, sparky and volatile. Everybody smoked, including Rita and Becky, but that's not what I'm referring to. It felt like atmospheric conditions over there, emotions gusting up on you that, like severe weather, were always beyond your control. Everybody seemed to place high value on argument. Argument had as much shape and volume and independence as any member of the family. It came and went as easily as I did.

Later, on the afternoon of the thrown oyster sack, Mr. Reece appeared in the kitchen wearing the sort of docile-looking house slippers that have always made me think of hound dogs. Maybe it was their innocuous, shuffling sound that implied a doggy contriteness. He padded about the kitchen like nothing had happened, whistling and gathering utensils. He concocted a dip of horseradish, ketchup, and lemon, which he poured into a saucer. He pried open a dozen of the oysters and tried to cajole us into learning how to eat them raw. He ended up eating all twelve oysters himself in a gluttonous, show-offish way, smacking his lips and delighting in our chagrin. Addressing Mrs. Reece, his voice had a teasing quality, intending more to wheedle than insult. Once he kissed the nape of her neck. Becky and I discussed the kiss later, cringing. It seemed like a mating ritual.

Maybe that was the night we heard them making love or thought we did because Rita had told us that oysters were aphrodisiacs. I can't really believe we were fifteen and did what we did, because it seems that we would have felt too ashamed or fearful. But I vividly recall our snaking down the dark hallway toward their bedroom and lying on the threshold, flat on the floor, listening to the rush and tumble of their sheets.

"One, two, three, *push*," Mr. Reece said, and Mrs. Reece laughed her smoker's throaty laugh.

Were they really making love or simply, as Becky preferred to think, trying to fix a broken bed?

There was a vaguely comic side to whatever sorrow persisted between Mr. and Mrs. Reece, and although I couldn't explain this to my parents, who were forever questioning my devotion to such a family, I was bedazzled. I suppose, look-

ing back, that I observed far more of their spectacle than
their pain, and that they were really more private than I gave
them credit for being. Becky and I, with our blithe philosophy, reduced her despair about her parents by always finding
something to laugh about. That's what I remember most about
our style of philosophy: we philosophized until something
made us laugh. Once, in the wake of one of Mr. Reece's
outbursts, Becky and I invented curse poems. We called them
voodoo haiku and planted them like bad-luck fortune cookies
in the innersoles of Mr. Reece's shoes.

Becky's sister, Rita, was a day student at a local college
and madly in love with a senior named Howard Cox. We
loved to pester her on weekend nights when she was getting
ready to go out. We followed her from her vanity to the
bathroom, back and forth, observing her ministrations, and
I suspect that we learned everything there is to learn about
grooming one's body for romance. Rita shaved her legs to
the hipbones and daubed drops of Estée Lauder on the insides of her thighs and the plush well of her navel. She
plucked her eyebrows into graceful, wispy arches and applied this miracle makeup you could only buy at McFall's
Drugstore and which transformed even the most rocky com-
plexion into peachy, placid terrain. It was called Liquimat
and was manufactured in San Antonio, Texas, out of probably the same mud they used to build adobes. She ratted her
short, bleached blond hair until it surrounded her head like
a dandelion puff, then she patiently tamed it into a volumi-
nous, smooth bubble and attached a velveteen ribbon to one
side of her bangs.

She waited to dress last, parading around in her underwear, which was lacy and scant and unquestionably see-
through. She had fabulous, perky breasts and she talked about
what it felt like for Howard Cox to touch them. She showed
us through her brassiere how she could make the nipples hard
by touching them herself, but she said that Howard could

make them harder. She relished showing us and loved to shock us. Once she parted her legs and showed us what she called her "love bud." She told us everything about Howard's anatomy, too, only she called him "How hard" in a breathy, lunging voice. She told us that once they'd done it in a phone booth while he was talking to his mother long-distance.

I don't mean to suggest that Rita was crude or that I ever came away from our gabfests feeling offended. I came away feeling informed and inspired. Her detached manner of delivery was almost scholarly. Her sexual discoveries filled her to the brim, and what we learned from her was like an overflow she couldn't contain. She talked with similar zest about the books she read in college. She loved reading. She loved finding things out. I've often thought that it was only her curiosity that was promiscuous. And I've never been certain of any clear difference between promiscuity and the sort of enthusiasm that is so wholehearted you simply abandon good judgment.

She was reading Ayn Rand the evening I witnessed Mr. Reece attack her. I can see the books even now, stacked together on her vanity, dog-eared paperbacks she obviously cherished. RITA LOVES HOW HARD was inscribed on the front cover of the topmost book. Years later I would read these books, I'm embarrassed to say, searching for the salacious passages that I'd always believed prompted Rita's reading selections.

Becky and I were sitting on one of the twin beds, watching Rita get ready for Howard and trying to listen to "Louie Louie" on the record player. Rita wanted us to hear the dirty lyrics and you had to slow the record down to 33 rpm to hear them, she said. Becky and I weren't having much luck; the words still sounded garbled to us at the slower speed. But Rita, in tune with that vibrant netherworld that so enthralled and eluded us, laughed at the music and slapped her knee with bawdy apprehension.

She was wearing only her panties and brassiere when Mr. Reece blasted, unannounced, into the room. He had a lit cigarette in his mouth. In one stride he reached her vanity and with a ferocious swipe of one arm he scattered her makeup, hair curlers, and the two books across the room. He looked wall-eyed with rage. But as if he'd realized that he hadn't done enough damage yet, hadn't realized his revenge, he began to grasp and crush things indiscriminately: a pack of Rita's Newport cigarettes, a dried souvenir corsage. He snapped an emery board in two. He grabbed a pair of her nail scissors and surveyed the room until his eyes locked upon the chair where she'd laid out her garter belt and stockings. Swiftly he seized the stockings and cut them in two at the ankles. It was horrible; I tucked my feet up under my bottom. Finally he dug a little plastic case from his pocket, flipped it open and removed a white rubber disk. I recognized it as the diaphragm Rita had shown us. Mr. Reece regarded it bitterly. He held it away from himself with two fingers, wincing as if it were something dead. Then, quickly, he took the cigarette out of his mouth and burned a hole in the center.

I sat there quaking after he stomped out of the room. "Louie Louie" was stuck on a scratch, and Becky finally unfolded herself from our huddle on the bed and turned off the record player. She picked up the perforated diaphragm and handed it to Rita. Rita had often referred to it as her "joy toy." It had seemed a whimsical device. Now it just looked evil. It made me think of rape. Seeing it convinced me that Mr. Reece was a maniac and that the Reeces were all trying to fool themselves with philosophy and their easy-come, easy-go theory of domestic unrest. Eventually somebody was going to get killed; I knew this in my heart.

I glanced sympathetically at Rita, but she wasn't even crying. There was a kind of radiance about her, a look of ultimate triumph. She picked herself off the floor and scooped up Mr. Reece's smoldering cigarette where it had rolled under her bed. "Just look at this mess," she said with a tone of dismay. She stepped over the rubble of makeup and spilled perfume to the record player. She removed "Louie Louie" and slipped the record into its jacket. She paused a moment, thinking, looking out the window into a far-reaching night, and then she put on "Teen Angel."

We all listened for a while. It was a chance to catch our breaths, maybe to think about a truer victim of disaster. "You know," Rita said finally, "the girl in this song is a real jerk. But somehow I really love her."

I just sat, still stunned, watching as Rita and Becky straightened up the room. Eventually they got to laughing about the diaphragm. "Have a donut!" they said, laughing, flipping the diaphragm back and forth. They took down one of Becky's old Barbie dolls and put the diaphragm on her like a hoopskirt. They said she had a heavy date with Ken.

I began to see what Mr. Reece's rage was all about: he simply didn't count. He was exiled. They had decided long ago and for reasons I couldn't determine that he was unnecessary to their happiness and utterly dismissable. He was fighting them for access.

One of the neat things about Mrs. Reece was that you could talk her into practically anything. She enjoyed Becky's and my company and, eager to be included, she'd offer to drive us anywhere we liked. On Friday and Saturday nights we liked to choose the Boar and Castle.

The Boar and Castle was a drive-in hamburger joint that specialized in deep-fried foods. There wasn't a menu, just the Boar and Castle's reputation for specialties like skillet bread and onion rings. They sold a soft drink called the Esther Williams. It was the aquamarine color of a swimming pool and turned your tongue blue. In our town blue tongues had become sort of a status symbol, proof that you'd been whooping it up at the good old B and C.

The most popular high school kids hung out at the Boar and Castle. They liked to try to outcool the carhops. The carhops were old, garrulous black men who wore white coats and hats. They'd worked there for years, a real fraternity of raconteurs. They'd seen just about everything there was to see at least twice and they liked to jaw with you about it. They'd cultivated raspy, obliging voices like Rochester's on "Jack Benny" and the sort of flattering banter that guaranteed them good tips. They'd do anything for a tip. Rita told us that once Howard Cox sent one of them across the street to the Bi-Lo service station to buy him a rubber.

Behind the Boar and Castle, under a lush grape arbor, there was a parking area known as the Passion Pit. It was an unspoken rule that you didn't park in the Passion Pit unless you were committed to getting passionate. If you parked there with your date, you made your reputation. Everybody treated the Passion Pit with respect. If you parked anywhere close by, you tried to be discreet. You'd signal the carhops by flashing your headlights rather than honking.

Becky and I were still young enough to squander our pride, and so we always talked Mrs. Reece into parking in the Passion Pit. She'd protest, assuming it was her duty as a mother to protest, but she'd end up doing it. She got a real kick out of our bossing her around, and she was a good sport. She'd dated at the B and C when she was a young girl, and she could still call most of the carhops by name. Something about the way the grape arbor smelled in the summertime turned her face sweet.

After we'd wolfed down our supper, the main business of the evening began. Becky and I would take out our compacts and position the mirrors at various angles so that we could

spy on the inhabitants of nearby cars. Sometimes Mrs. Reece
would take out her compact, too.

We rarely observed anything other than an arm or a leg
unraveling from the dusky interior of a car. Occasionally a
girl would rise up and start to cry. Once somebody threw a
class ring out an open window and it shot into Mrs. Reece's
car and bounced into my lap.

I don't really know what we were watching for. It seems
unlikely that Mrs. Reece would have indulged such shame-
less perversion, even joined it, yet she did. And what a peculiar comfort to have her along, holding up her own compact
and giggling alongside us. Whenever she lit a cigarette, the
match illuminated her plump, girlish face. In the pinkish
gold flare she looked fifteen herself: mischievous, sly. Her
charm bracelet tinkled as she extended a hand to flip an ash.
She seemed at deep peace with whatever disappointments
she'd suffered. Even to the point of returning to the scene of
what she often referred to as her original sin: falling in love
with Mr. Reece right there in the Boar and Castle Passion
Pit back in 1942. She could return with her daughter Becky,
who was most likely on the verge of making similar mis-
takes, and she could flip open her compact and pretend to
powder her nose as if nothing ruinous was happening all
around her.

Once we'd screeched off to the Boar and Castle after one
of her fights with Mr. Reece. It had something to do with the
way she sorted and balled his socks. She'd been cooking
supper, but after the fight she took a balled-up pair of socks,
lathered them with mustard, and sandwiched them between
two pieces of rye bread. She smacked the whole package on
a plate with a garlic pickle. "Your dinner's ready!" she called
to Mr. Reece, then hustled Becky and me out the back door
and into her car. We zoomed in the direction of the Boar and
Castle without our even suggesting it. When we arrived at
the Passion Pit, she cut the ignition and slumped in her seat;

her posture suggested relief. She breathed deeply, thrust her face out the car window into the lush, sleepy scent of grape leaves. Then she rummaged in her purse, not for a Kleenex, but to find and withdraw her compact.

"Mom," Becky said sympathetically.

"Shhh," Mrs. Reece cautioned, gazing steadily and tearlessly into the mirror. "I'm thinking backwards, dear."

I noted, then, an eerie lack of anger in her voice. Thinking backwards provided her neither solace nor insight. It seemed more a trick of erasure. Her eyes glazed with forgetting. When she lit a cigarette, the match illuminated a calm, remote girlishness. She thought backwards perhaps to imagine herself making different choices. She could have been anybody; it was a miracle to see her believing it.

That summer, between eighth and ninth grade, middle and upper school, Becky and I lived at the neighborhood swimming pool. We took a transistor radio and beach towels with beer logos, and we camped out all day. For lunch we bought hot dogs and Zero bars at the Snack Shack. We took a thermos of lemonade that we alternately drank and poured over our hair to lighten it. We rubbed our darkening skins with baby oil and Coppertone.

We'd been tomboys and bookworms together, and boys had never paid much attention to us, but that summer things started changing for Becky. Not that she was *looking* for a boy to like. When we weren't practicing our jackknives off the high dive, we were reading under the straw sombreros that we'd bought at the Family Dollar Store along with flip-flops and Holly Golightly–style sunglasses with big black round lenses.

Becky loved horror stories and had checked out this real tome from the public library called *Supernatural Omnibus*. It had a skull and crossbones on the cover, and she looked formidable reading it.

I tended to engross myself with science magazines. Since I thought I wanted to study medicine and become a dermatologist like my father, I took his *New England Journal of Medicine* to the pool. I admit I was a bit of a show-off about it. It delighted me for Pansy McBride, the voluptuous high school girl who was lifeguarding that summer, to ask me what I was reading and for me to flash her a nauseating full-color shot of *Pemphigus vulgaris*.

As Becky's first romance developed, I often wondered that if I'd been reading *Supernatural Omnibus* with unselfconscious fervor whether I might have been the one he spoke to—the tall, pale boy with glasses Scotch-taped together at the nosepiece. Becky and I were practically twins in our hats and sunglasses and tank suits and brownish, lemonaded hair—except for our books.

I was first aware of his shadow, and then he squatted down beside Becky, so sudden and graceless that she jumped. "Have you read 'The Beckoning Fair One'?" he asked. " 'The Monkey's Paw'?" He shuddered dramatically. "Never read them alone late at night," he cautioned.

Becky, immediately intrigued, invited him to sit on her beach towel. As soon as I found out that he was a philosopher type as well, I knew Becky was a goner. His name was Randolph Lake. All afternoon he regaled us with his theory of objective expressionism.

As best as I can remember it was the theory that objects hate people. "You're getting out of your car with a heavy bag of groceries," Randolph said with ominous glee. "Inside the house, your phone starts to ring. On your rush to the back door, you trip over the garden hose. Your keys are all scrambled up and you have trouble making the right one fit. Inside the house, your phone rings a fourth, a fifth time. You're really starting to sweat. Finally you jam the proper key in the door and dash inside. On the way to the phone, you fall over the footstool. You reach the phone on the seventh ring and—'' he paused, reared his head back and laughed a laugh resonant with jeerful recognition of human folly—''nobody's there!''

''Whose side are you on anyway?'' Becky said.

''It was a conspiracy!'' he whispered. ''The phone rang all by itself to excite you. The garden hose positioned itself in your way. The keys tangled themselves deliberately. The footstool leaped into your path. Want to bet that the groceries in the grocery bag were laughing their labels off?''

Before the afternoon was over, Becky was rubbing Coppertone on his shoulders.

Most afternoons, after she'd gotten home from summer school and he'd been released from his summer job at the A&P, Rita and Howard Cox would show up at the pool for a dip. Rita wore a scandalous string bikini that she'd ordered through the mail and Howard a pair of white French-style briefs that, once wet, might as well have been Saran Wrap. All the mothers at the pool cut their eyes at them. Pansy McBride put on a pair of dark sunglasses to better observe them undetected. Once they stayed underwater so long that Pansy blew her whistle and initiated lifesaving procedures. Out of *spite*, Rita said later. She'd gotten jealous, peering down from her lofty, prick-teasing tower. Rita said this in front of Randolph Lake, and he blushed.

I noticed a strange new brittleness in Rita. She seemed arrogant and impatient. I'd always thought of her as rambunctious, but now she seemed wild in a weary, hostile way. She wore a pouty, self-absorbed expression. She told us she was bored. She did cannonballs off the side of the pool that splashed our towels and got us all wet. She borrowed our Coppertone, wasted it, made fun of my medical journals, said our sombreros looked dumb. She'd try to pick fights with Howard, but he'd have none of it and dive into the pool.

"What's wrong with Rita?" I asked Becky.

But Becky was too preoccupied with Randolph and didn't seem to notice. She'd only shrug and say, "Maybe she's got her period. What do you mean?"

I didn't know what I meant. Just watching her made me feel restless, made me know that summer was ending and it was time for it to. By the first of August I was usually fed up with the wasteful, goofing-off feeling summertime gave me. I started anticipating my return to the rituals and habits of the school year weeks in advance. What excuses can I make? It was my upbringing: an irrepressible penchant for order, the beige tidiness of a classroom with a certified teacher in control. Deep down my parents had me, all my genes in their death grip.

In a week's time, Becky and Randolph Lake had become a real item. They enjoyed all the same things: Planetarium shows, listening to opera, playing Clue and Scrabble. They read H. P. Lovecraft stories to each other by moonlight. They invented this new theory called Layered Life.

"Imagine that you're driving down a highway with your parents," Randolph said to me cheerfully one afternoon at the pool.

"Do I have to?"

"Okay, then, with your boyfriend."

"I don't have a boyfriend," I said pointedly. "Let's say I'm driving down the highway with *Becky*."

I saw Becky and him exchange a look that told me they pitied me behind my back. I hardly listened after that. Basically the Layered Life theory was something about a Mack truck hitting Becky and me head on. At the moment of impact, I transcend death, move into an advanced time frame, the continuity of my life upheld, layers of existence working much the same as a roll of film passing through a sequence of exposures in a camera. In the old time frame, Becky may find me dead. Actually I've merely been shot forward into a new exposure and am waking up in the rubble of a wrecked car. I have no knowledge of my death, which really only occurred in Becky's time frame. Perhaps we're out of sync, now, the real Becky and the real me. But we've both been granted "duplicates" of each other, either alive or dead, to convince us of our separate realities. What I remember most about the Layered Life theory was that despite its crackpot, labyrinthine nonsense it was ultimately a theory of deathlessness.

I watched Randolph Lake's face as he tried to explain the theory. His eyes were milky blue behind his smudged, taped-together glasses. The rosy flush of earnestness crept up his neck and spread over his cheeks. The freckles scattered across his nose looked as sweet as brown sugar. I found myself leaning toward him, comforted in spite of my feelings of exclusion. In another time and place, another life—the life behind the book I *should* have been reading at the pool the day he came along, the life that awaited me after a tragic car wreck, possibly—I might have taken his face in my hands and kissed him on the mouth.

I turned fifteen and a half on August 19 and qualified for my learner's permit. It was something constructive to do. I could actually drive a car now as long as I was accompanied by a consenting, licensed adult. When I turned sixteen I would have access to my own car—the 1952 Chevrolet bequeathed to me by my grandmother before she went to live in a nursing home. The car was stored in our garage. It was finless and it had no radio, but its upholstery was in mint condition and certain gizmos, the cigarette lighter, for example, had never been used. Needless to say the car was beige.

To celebrate my obtaining the learner's permit, my parents, in a rare burst of enthusiasm, cranked the old Chevy up and let me take her for a spin. My mother even tied a festive balloon to the hood ornament. But this seemed an indignity my grandmother's car would not endure; she stalled out before we reached the corner, and my father had to fetch his jumper cables.

I was spending less and less time at the Reeces' house. There didn't seem much point in my hanging around with Randolph camped out on the doorstep, teaching Becky how to chart stars and make bottle rockets or explaining the wall theory we'd learned in science in such a way that would calm her heart. The wall theory had just about driven us crazy all year. It you drew a line near a wall and divided the distance between the line and the wall in half, then divided the distance in half again, and so on and so forth, you would never reach the wall in an eternity of division. *Never reach the wall!*

One night late in August, Becky phoned me. She sounded muffled and far away as if she was calling long-distance. I could tell she'd been crying. "You've read all those medical journals," she whispered. "You know stuff. Help me, Jennifer."

My heart fluttered. I felt a Layered Life experience about to occur. "What stuff do you need to know?"

"Like how do you get . . . oh, God, I can't say it—"

"Becky!" I cried. "Tell me."

She was sobbing. "An abortion," she said. "It's not what you're thinking. It's not me, Jenn."

"It's Rita," I said, thinking backwards to everything.

"She says she and Howard are getting married. She told the maniac tonight."

"Oh, God."

"It's like she has this death wish. You should have seen him. He ran her out of the house and chased her halfway down Dogwood Drive. When he came back inside, he started ripping her clothes out of her closet and piling them up and carting them to the Sternberger Elementary School dumpster. He yelled out the front door to whoever was listening that she was dead to him from that moment on, his daughter Rita Jane Reece was *dead*. Oh, God, Jenn."

"Oh, God," I repeated softly. "I don't think you can get a safe legal abortion in this country," I said. "You have to go some place like Puerto Rico, and it costs a fortune."

"Jennifer Anne!" my mother cried, peering around the doorframe, aghast. "Who on earth are you talking to?"

While my parents watched "Gunsmoke," I slipped out the back door and ran down to the Reeces'. The night felt wicked and indulgent, the sky like a twirling black skirt, lifting to show you too much. A rich, weedy fragrance thickened the air and mixed with the aroma of somebody's outdoor grill. Perfume floated out opened windows. Patios glimmered with those Japanese-lantern-lit, murmurous backyard parties that my parents were never invited to. The trees looked heavy and swashbuckling, undulating against the dark sky.

I had almost reached their yard when I saw Mr. Reece. His arms were loaded with clothes, and he hurried toward the open trunk of his car. I remember thinking with horror: that could be a body. The maniac could have done his deed, murdered Rita, murdered all of them, and me, *company*, practically an eye-witness. He slung his burden into the trunk and slammed the lid. I crouched behind some boxwoods in a neighbor's yard until he drove off.

Inside, Becky and Mrs. Reece flopped morosely across

the twin beds in the room that Becky shared with Rita, the room where Mr. Reece had taken Rita's diaphragm to task. Every few minutes one of them would rally and go telephone Howard Cox. He didn't answer. They couldn't bear not knowing where she'd gone or what she was planning to do. She'd screamed that she was getting married, like it or lump it. She was twenty goddamn years old. Just try to stop her, maniac, and she'd call the police. She'd thrown a book at him, *Atlas Shrugged*, and he'd picked it up and ripped it in two.

It seemed to me, after I'd heard them describing Rita, that they were crying because she'd turned into a maniac, too. They didn't know her anymore. Mr. Reece still wasn't able to make them cry.

I couldn't stay long to comfort them. I felt awkward and inadequate, the outsider I'd always been, really, dutifully checking my watch to make certain "Gunsmoke" wasn't over yet and that I'd been missed, checking my watch almost grateful for the first time in my life that my life was so circumscribed. I could just leave all this like a bad movie and go home.

In the days that followed we learned that Howard Cox had quit his summer job at the A&P and vacated his apartment. But nobody knew where he'd gone, and nobody had seen Rita. The community college resumed fall classes and neither of their names appeared on any class rosters.

Rita's disappearance felt like a death in the family. Becky and Mrs. Reece dragged around with pathetic, tear-swollen faces. Mother and I made them a spaghetti casserole, but they wouldn't eat. Only Mr. Reece seemed content. Every day when he came home from his hosiery mill, he'd slip on old clothes and putter around his garden until dark. He hummed vigorously, tunelessly to himself. Becky and I called him Farmer McGregor behind his back. Once I saw him snip a butterfly in two, midair, with his garden shears. When he saw me staring, he made the excuse that it was only a moth, the kind that eats holes in leaves, a pest like the Japanese beetle. I didn't believe him, and I let him see that I didn't. It seemed like the most dangerous commitment I had ever made.

The last week of our summer vacation, Becky and I spent almost every night together, endlessly speculating about Rita's fate. Were they already married? Had they flown to Puerto Rico for an abortion? What was she doing for clothes? Money? Were they doing it all the time now that they were constantly together? Or had the novelty paled? Could you even do it when you were pregnant? I tried to find out from my father's medical textbooks, but the only chapters on sex I could locate were about disease.

I prayed to fall in love some day like Rita: the sort of love for which you'd hurl yourself into the night, leave family and friends, vanish without a trace. The pain of it all created its beauty, the heart's descent like a meteor, burning itself up in such an inexorable plunge. I lay in bed and thought such thoughts until I felt feverish. I moved my top sheet up and down, pretending it was Howard Cox.

I thought about sex all the time, and in some of the most unlikely places: church, Girl Scouts, taking the mail our postman, Mr. McBee, handed me, wondering when he and Mrs. McBee had last done it, trying to imagine the same businesslike hand that sorted and delivered our letters fooling around with a breast.

It was a blessing when school started after Labor Day, although high school wasn't like anything I'd expected. Ours was an enormous, consolidated high school, and I felt dwarfed rather than exhilarated by its offerings. On the first day of school I found myself looking down at my feet all the time rather than meeting people's eyes. Roaming the vast, uncharted corridors, my loafers felt as unwieldy and conspicuous as canoes. I'd put bright new dimes in their slits for good luck, and some upperclassman cheer-leader, standing in the cafeteria line at lunch, had pointed and laughed. Or maybe I *thought* she did. But in high school it was only what you *thought* that mattered anyway.

When my last class let out, I headed toward the parking lot to meet Becky. I recognized Randolph Lake standing near a school bus. He was wearing a short-sleeved seer-sucker shirt decorated with rocket ships and planets; it looked like a little kid's pajama top. His glasses were still taped together, only the tape looked yellow and brittle. He'd crooked pencils behind each ear and was reading this cinderblock-size physics manual and chuckling to himself as if it were a book of jokes. Impulsively I headed toward him, glad to see a familiar face.

"Pssst!" somebody whispered. "Jennifer!" It was Becky, crouched behind a nearby trash can.

"What on earth are you doing?"

"I don't want Randolph to see me."

"Why not?"

She rolled her eyes heavenward. "Because this is *high school*, Jennifer," she said. *"Tabula rasa."*

"Are you dumping him?" I asked. "I thought you were in love."

She shrugged sadly. "Not like Rita," she said.

We sneaked away from the parking lot and started walking home, though it's possible that we got hit by a school bus and never realized it. Maybe we were killed on our very first day of high school, collectively ignorant of our deaths, and passed, unremorseful, into the next layer of our lives.

When we arrived at Becky's house, everything looked the same, but everything felt different. Mrs. Reece greeted us at the back door, smiling broadly, doing this jivey little shuffle. I could hear Connie Francis on the radio singing

"Where the Boys Are." Mrs. Reece had just gotten home from the beauty salon, where she'd had her hair newly frosted and her fingernails manicured. She wore a crackling linen dress, two-toned maroon and white like my father's Buick. It had a matching two-toned straw hat with a veil. She said she'd just clipped off the price tags. "Mother of the bride!" she exclaimed radiantly, striking a pose. "I've got big news, girls!" Then she hugged the breath out of both of us.

Rita had called. She was staying in Goldsboro, a mere hundred miles away, with Howard Cox's grandmother. The wedding would take place this Saturday afternoon, weather permitting, in old Mrs. Cox's backyard. Everything was all arranged.

My first reaction was feeling strange about knowing where Howard Cox was from, Goldsboro, and that he had a grandmother feisty enough to provide him a wedding. Howard Cox had not seemed very real to me before.

Becky was worried about logistics. "Everything's all arranged except our escape," she told her mother gloomily. "Don't forget that the maniac is supernatural. He's going to know."

"Why, he won't suspect one thing," Mrs. Reece chirped. "We'll get up Saturday morning, put on some normal-looking clothes, and tell him we're going out shopping. *Meanwhile*," she said slyly, "the car will have been loaded up with all our wedding paraphernalia, locked in the trunk for days." Mrs. Reece clasped her hands together over her heart, and her eyes sparkled. "Oh, this is so exciting!" she cried, twirling around. It was as if she were the one eloping. She linked arms with Becky and they promenaded around the living room.

I couldn't sleep at all Friday night. I kept getting up to stare back at the round-faced Peeping Tom of a moon. It was a hot, dry September night and the trees, filled with scorched-out insects, made a sound like frying. Overhead stars wheeled and sizzled like the sparks from a bonfire.

I wished I were going with Becky and Mrs. Reece to the wedding, but I wasn't. Mrs. Figg, our next-door neighbor, had asked me to baby-sit. But also the true nature of their Goldsboro mission was top secret, and I wasn't capable of concocting the sort of elaborate lie that might have duped my parents into freeing me to accompany them. My one request was that Becky bring me a slice of wedding cake so that I could sleep with it under my pillow and dream of the man I'd marry.

When I finally fell asleep, the insects had calmed down but the birds were starting to twitter. I slept until almost noon. What finally woke me, I think, was the sensation of an empty house. My parents had already left to visit my grandmother who lived at Green Willow Nursing Home and didn't know us anymore. Normally I was expected to go with them to visit her. It took up an entire Saturday and I always left her feeling depressed. I was glad to have the baby-sitting job lined up as an excuse not to join them. My grandmother had been such a sweet, genteel woman, and now she spat her food at us and glared. She took out her dentures and worked them like a hand puppet while she talked. Once, when we'd gone to visit, we found her and her roommate, Mrs. Wiggins, dancing together in their underwear. They'd picked out a rock-and-roll station on the radio and turned it up full blast. My father shook his head sadly and diagnosed my grandmother as having gone backwards in time, reverting to adolescence. Of course I doubted that she'd ever behaved that way during her teenage years, and I wondered what was so awful about dancing around in your underwear anyway. She was in her own room, wasn't she? She had the door closed. The radio wasn't on *that* loud. It wasn't even a boy she was dancing with.

My parents wouldn't return from the nursing home until late afternoon, so I indulged myself. How pleasant to dawdle about the house in my nightgown on Saturday. I flipped on the television and watched "Mr. Wizard" for a while, then I poured myself a bowl of cereal and sliced some peaches. My baby-sitting job wasn't until three: Mr. and Mrs. Figg were going to play golf and have supper at the country club.

I turned on the radio and WCOG was playing "Teen Angel." Somebody over at the station really loved that song. It had never had much appeal for me; I thought it was sappy. Since it was not a favorite of mine, I don't know why my mother crusaded against it so, but she did. She was riveted to it with disgust, the way people driving past wrecks couldn't help staring. Whenever it came on the radio within her hearing, she'd listen intently with a down-turned mouth until the song was half over. Then she'd pounce on the volume control knob and switch it off. "Teen Angel," she'd say with derision. "That's a contradiction in terms."

I can't say that I blamed her. The lyrics were appalling. The souped-up grief going on in that song oozed over you, shamelessly seductive. But as a *love* story, as something contagiously sexy—the sort of music that got banned in those days—the song was pretty thin. It morosely documented the aftermath of one fateful night when two teen-aged lovers stalled their car on a railroad track. As the train bore down upon them, the boy jumped from the car and yanked the girl to safety. Then, inexplicably, seconds before impact, the girl broke free from the boy and dove back into the doomed car while he looked on in horror. Of course a girl so mysteriously impetuous was bound to haunt the memory of the boy who loved her. At sweet

sixteen she was an untimely angel. And while he be-
seeched her to love him beyond the grave, he puzzled over
her fatal haste to return to the car. What was she searching
for? She was searching for his high school ring that the
authorities found clutched in her poor dead hand.

I remembered Rita listening to "Teen Angel" after Mr.
Reece burned the hole in her diaphragm. She'd gazed into
the night, admiring the dead girl not for her bravery or
loyalty, but for her consumptive foolishness. She'd regarded the girl in the song as an ally. As I listened closely
to the lyrics, I heard them as if for the first time and I felt
shocked. Teen Angel had lost her life because she went
back to hunt for a ring that belonged to a boy she'd obviously decided to dump. Why else wasn't the ring on her
finger? And what had made her change her mind and run
back for the ring? Was it love? Dying for love didn't seem
nearly as tragic as dying for guilt, wasting yourself out of
some spellbinding sense of obligation. Her boyfriend singing the song sounded bereft, but wasn't he ignorant not to
figure things out, not to figure out that, as much for the
loss of her, he should be wailing for her change of heart?
His sorrow was uninformed.

I let the song run its course without switching stations,
only because, with Mother gone, it was the chance of a
lifetime. It depressed me, though, to strive so hard to make
sense out of nonsense. It's as if I believed that was how
you reached maturity: by being able to explain things.
When the doorbell rang, I leapt up guiltily and raced to
find my robe and slippers. I thought it was probably one
of the Figg kids, but when I opened the door, there stood
Becky and Mrs. Reece, panting and disheveled. Mrs.
Reece had lost one earring, and runs streaked her stockings. They were dressed up as if to go shopping, only they
were barefooted and didn't have their purses.

"What's happened?" I asked. "Where are your shoes?"

"Oh, Jennifer! Thank God you're here," Mrs. Reece said, leaping inside the doorway. "When we didn't see your parents' car in the drive—"

"He's locked us out of the house," Becky cried. "He's taken Mother's car and *hidden* it."

I'm certain my jaw dropped.

"I swear to you, this is *it*," Mrs. Reece said. "I can't live another day like this. He's done it now. This is the limit."

"He ought to *die*," Becky said, wild-eyed and through clenched teeth.

"But how did he find out about Goldsboro?" I asked. "Who told?"

"Because he's the goddamn Devil," Becky said. "He knew the plan before we ever thought it up."

"But it's impossible that he just found out on his own," I argued. "Somebody spilled the beans. Who knew besides the three of us?" But they didn't really seem concerned about *how* he knew; it's what he'd done about it that mattered to them now. They had no car to take them to Rita's wedding. They collapsed in each other's arms, sobbing. "Calm down, we'll think of something," I said to them. "Think backwards."

Becky looked at me like I was a lunatic. "No more *thinking*, period," she said. *"Action,"* she said, and the way she said the word made it seem as dangerous as a live grenade. "You've got to help us, Jenn."

I guessed I knew what was coming: the end of my life as I'd always known it and taken it for granted. Dreamy with fright, I lay on the pavement of some uncharted highway and watched the encroachment of a Mack truck. I felt that excruciating pause before impact during which I recalled, in a flash of beige scenes, the sensible shelter of my upbringing. What was I doing out here in the middle of nowhere? I loved Becky and her mother, but was that

sort of love worth dying for? Becky and Mrs. Reece were
driving the Mack truck, and if I didn't leap out of the way
they were going to ask me to help them murder Mr. Reece.
And I was going to do it.

Then Becky hugged me and she said, ''You've got your
grandmother's car, Jenn. We want you to drive us to
Goldsboro.''

I will never forget our exhilaration, and I will honor and
cherish my wickedness, if that was what it truly was, until
death I do part: backing my grandmother's unlicensed
Chevrolet down the driveway, running over my mother's
chrysanthemums, waving at Mrs. Figg and all the little
Figgs out watering their yard, never stopping to explain
that I would not show up at three, stopping at the Bi-Lo
where they all knew my father and charging a tank of gas,
dragging the Boar and Castle once and even honking as
we sailed past the Passion Pit.

Once on the Interstate we rolled all the windows down.
and I watched Becky and Mrs. Reece light their cigarettes
from my grandmother's virginal cigarette lighter and drop
their ashes on the car's unblemished upholstery. I hunkered over the steering wheel, awash in wind, an opulence
of sunshine, high-toned with purpose, heroic, deft, singing because we had no radio, harmonizing, making up
naughty lyrics to ''Louie Louie'' in honor of Rita, on my
way to a bad girl's wedding, on my way to life.

Mrs. Reece leaned back in her seat looking dreamy and
smoked one Newport after another. She had runs in her
stockings, no purse, no shoes, but God she looked happy.
She sang the loudest of all, her face abloom with the satisfactions of survival. We couldn't have guessed that she
would go back to him and live on Dogwood Drive as his
wife for twenty more years until he finally died of emphy-
sema, not murder. Just as we couldn't have guessed that

it was she who had told Mr. Reece about the trip to Goldsboro, Friday night after they had gone to bed and she was feeling at peace with him, believing that, like his passion, his understanding and forgiveness were possible. The looming disappointments of our lives were not what we imagined when we viewed the sun-spangled horizon. We rode within that shimmering dimension between departure and arrival as if entitled to our joy, empowered by as much unhindered delusion as anyone could invent.

THE MAGIC CIRCLE

☆ ♡ ☆   ☆ ♡ ☆   ☆ ♡ ☆

Dobie Rhinehart was on a definite roll. Take Friday, for example. He'd broken the school track record, run a mile in 4:30. Coach just about squeezed his neck off, and the rest of the Cheetahs pounded his back, whooping like maniacs. All Dobie could think to say to them was, "I just went wild."

He could have never explained how it really happened, how during the last tenth of a mile he'd *become* a cheetah. The guys would have howled with jeerdom. He didn't understand it, but something had happened: something like an out-of-body experience, something transcendental.

And afterward there came a supernatural moment when Meredith MaGraw agreed to be his date to the Midwinter's Dance. He'd asked her, still sweating, right after gym class. How had he gotten up his nerve? He was rolling, that's how. Bobby Flynt, his best friend, had said to ask her while he was still experiencing an adrenaline high. And there she was as if summoned, lingering at a nearby locker: available, easy. It was as if he'd walked into a dream queen convenience store. *Meredith MaGraw!*

News of pursuit and conquest traveled fast. He'd gone back to gym class to pick up his biology textbook and had run into

Ladd Ferrell, Meredith's ex-boyfriend. "Congrats," Ladd said, shaking hands. Dobie thought he meant congrats about the mile in 4:30 until Ladd said, "Don't think I don't miss her. The trouble was she got so possessive it was love without air." Then Ladd volunteered all these arousing details about how nice Meredith always smelled and how she kissed and where she liked to put her hands and what she did with his. Ladd sat on a bench, a towel slung over his shoulder. He looked dizzy with memories.

"She seems to go for Cheetahs," Dobie offered. The Cheetahs was what Coach Weaver called the sprint team.

"Fastest animals on earth." Ladd winked in an exaggerated way, then bent to unlace his track shoes.

Dobie imagined Meredith whispering in his ear, "An endangered species," petting him as if he really was. He imagined flexing a muscle beneath her touch. "Survival of the fittest," he would tell her, winking boldly the way Ladd had winked. Winking like a school big shot, a connoisseur of gazelles.

"So she's really going out with you?" Bobby Flynt asked, feigning disbelief. "Roll on, Dobie, roll on." Then Bobby reminded him of the old "Twilight Zone" episode they'd watched together once about the man who had everything he wanted and thought he was in heaven but he was really in hell.

They were in biology class and it was still fabulous Friday. Bobby was always goofing around and today he'd brought his little sister's Barbie doll clothes to put on the frog they were dissecting. Their teacher, Miss Blondell, had laughed like crazy when she saw the frog. She was fresh out of college, unmarried, and she thought everything high school boys did was funny. Since he was Bobby's lab partner, Dobie got credit for the Barbie doll prank, too. The whole class laughed admiringly, and Dobie grinned and held up the frog for everybody to see. It was wearing a polka-dot bikini and sunglasses

and carrying a little canvas beach bag. Bobby Flynt was singing ''Surfer Girl'' in a falsetto voice. Things couldn't get
much better.

On Saturday it rained. Well, it had to, didn't it? Dobie
opened the car door for his mother and she ducked in quickly,
despite the fact that he held an umbrella over her head and
that she was wearing one of those plastic, accordion-style
rain hats. She was in the sort of mood where she'd go berserk
if one droplet of water touched her. She and Dobie's father
had quarreled at breakfast, and now he towered in the driver's
seat, his posture of anger monolithic. They were on their
way to the marriage counselor's again. They went every Saturday morning, but nothing seemed to get any better. And
sometimes it seemed to Dobie that they had a big argument
on Saturday morning on purpose. Just so they would have
plenty of stuff to talk to the counselor about. They both hated
to waste time.

They were giving him a ride to Bobby Flynt's house, and
nobody spoke. Dobie's father drove without flicking on the
wipers. It was a strange habit. Sometimes he left the wipers
off on purpose, whether he was mad or not. He used a floor
button that swept the windshield clean about once per minute. It was like some sort of irritating and dangerous exper-
iment.

Dobie's mother finally said, ''Wipers.''

''I can see,'' his father said.

''How can you possibly see?''

''Trust me.''

''You can't see one thing. Do you want to wreck the car?
Do you want to kill us?''

Dr. Rhinehart turned on the wipers. ''Sometimes,'' he
said quietly.

Of course his father didn't mean it. Later he'd apologize
to everyone. But even before his father's apology, his mother

would come to Dobie and tell him not to be upset, that his father didn't really *mean* that terrible comment in the car about wanting to kill them. He'd only meant it as a kind of metaphor, wanting to kill what they were *then*, wanting to kill the anger and wrongness of the moment. It's our time of life, Dobie, she'd say vaguely. Growing pains, she'd say. As if nobody ever grew up permanently. Maybe we love each other too much? she'd say in a wondering voice. I believe that there can be too much love, Dobie. She was deeply into paradox, his mother. She could explain everything, one way or another. She'd gone back to school and was studying to be a psychologist.

His father worked too hard; she was always saying that, too. He was an internist with a private practice, but he also taught classes at the University Medical School. Miss Blondell, the biology teacher, had takén anatomy classes at the university, and she knew of Dr. Rhinehart. Her face sort of bloomed when she found out Dobie was his son. "Everybody knows Dr. R.," she told Dobie. "He's a love." He'd thought of Miss Blondell's remarks when his father wouldn't turn on the wipers. He thought of how nobody really knew anybody. Maybe it was the single blessing on humanity that most assured its survival. Who in their right mind would ever marry and have children if they knew all there was to know about the person they thought they loved? Who, for that matter, would ever write a love song or a poem that promised tenderness forever? Why on earth did he want to go out with a flowery girl like Meredith MaGraw? What would it amount to in the end?

He and Bobby Flynt spent Saturday afternoon at the movies. They wore paper 3-D glasses and watched a triple feature of sci-fi movies. The movies were absurd but zapped Saturday and moved him one day closer to graduation and leaving. After the movies, Bobby wanted to go over to Sally Robinson's house and let her spike his hair and play her new album by some group called Legal Evil. So Dobie went home to study for mid-terms.

Exams were scheduled for the next week, followed by the Midwinter's Dance. He dreamed of nuzzling Meredith MaGraw. Thank God for goals. It was difficult to study. When he opened his biology text, a tiny polka-dot bikini fell out.

At supper his parents spoke genially, as if nothing had happened that morning. His mother had baked a pecan pie, his father's favorite.

"Have you got a date tonight, Dobie?" she asked.

"No," he said, "have you?" He didn't know why he said that; it made his heart feel pinched.

"When is the Midwinter's Dance?" she asked cheerfully. She was almost too good at turning the other cheek. He supposed it had something to do with psychology.

"*Next* Saturday."

"Are you going?"

"Maybe," he said. It felt good to act vague about something he was truly looking forward to. He felt powerful, acting noncommittal. It seemed a way of avenging himself, of making them pay.

"You should go out more with your friends," his father said. "These are the golden years, Dobie. Raise a little hell— that's what youth's all about."

"Want some pie?" his mother asked him.

"No, thanks, I'm full."

"Well, I'll have some more," his father said.

"Another piece? You're going to get fat," Dobie's mother chided.

Dr. Rhinehart sighed and put his fork down.

"It's just that I thought we were going out to a movie later, and you always like to get popcorn," Dobie's mother said hopefully, touching her husband's sleeve.

"Forget the pie," he said, scooting back from the table.

"Forget the movie, too. I've got to go back to the hospital tonight."

Dobie studied until midnight, and then he went out to run. The rain had finally stopped, but the January air felt raw and icy. Each breath of it that he took seemed to bolt itself to his lungs. It was a pitiless, gaping night all around. The suburban streets looked like tunnels leading to houses that seemed huddled forlornly around their secrets. He heard the vacant, lonely sound of dogs barking, the sinuous wail of an ambulance. The miles seemed to roll effortlessly beneath him; he didn't feel them. There was no ardor or enchantment, only a bleak kind of persistence. Cheetah! Cheetah! He ran past the high school, the stadium and track, his father's office, the East-Meets-West Massage Parlor that the guys were always talking about. He ran past the condominiums where Miss Blondell lived. The cold was splitting his chest. He imagined himself a criminal, a spy with a bullet in his heart. Cheetah! Cheetah! He raced himself all the way to University Hospital, and when he saw his father's Volvo in the parking lot, he made for it like a hurdle and jumped the breadth of its hood.

He never expected anyone to be inside the car, but someone, a woman, cried out as he sailed across the hood. He had a fleeting glimpse of white—a nurse's uniform. He didn't look back and he didn't break stride. Cheetah! He just kept running, boiling, a streak of steam in the night. He supposed he could go on running until he just evaporated.

He and Bobby Flynt were double-dating to the dance. Bobby had rented a neon-blue tuxedo and was wearing a Hawaiian print shirt underneath with a skinny white tie. He had on white bucks and Day-Glo orange socks. His date Sally would love it; she'd promised to wear her mother's leather mini-skirt and fishnet stockings from the sixties.

Dr. Rhinehart made a big deal over Bobby's tuxedo and shirt. "The humor!" he said over and over. He slapped

Bobby on the shoulder fondly. "You boys headed in the same direction or have you got a funeral to attend first, Dobe?"

Dobie wore a black wool suit and a woven red tie that his mother considered "spiffy."

"I think Dobie looks divine," she said, straightening the tie. "He looks like Richard Gere." She and Dobie exchanged looks. He hadn't wanted to catch her eye. Ever since he'd seen the nurse in his father's Volvo he'd avoided meeting her gaze. It was almost as if he thought she might be able to read the events of that night, an engravure of shock, in his eyes. But glancing at her just then he felt relief. She knew nothing but her steadfast approval of her son at this moment. She sighed. Then she gave Dobie's father an intimate, misty look. *"Déjà vu,"* she said.

"Here, Dobie," his father said, whipping out his keys. "Take my car tonight."

Impulsively Dobie waved the keys away.

"Hey, we're talking luxury," his father said. "We're talking reclining front seats." He winked just like Ladd Ferrell.

"I might wreck it or something," Dobie said.

"I insist," his father said, pressing the keys into his hand. They felt hot. "Live a little, Dobe. Enjoy."

Loving his father made him some weird kind of traitor, didn't it? The love seemed to go against everything everybody had tried to teach him all his life. If only he could have said to his father: Hey, set me straight. I saw something the other night, and it scared me. It messed everything up. And then his father would say: All right, ask me anything. I'm listening, and I want to make sense of it all for you. But that would never happen in a billion years. It would be silly if it happened. There couldn't be any happiness conjured out of that kind of talk anyway. Only embarrassment. Exposure rather than solution. There wasn't any sort of talk for it because there wasn't any sort of understanding.

He remembered the magic circle his parents had stood in when he was much younger. Nobody ever talked about the magic circle; it just *was*, wordless and theirs. His father would arrive home from work and hurry into the kitchen where his mother was cooking. There he embraced her and kissed her, enfolding her in a way that made her seem frail and reckless. There was an inviolate aura about their greeting. Nobody talked about it or ever tried to describe it, but it was there, a given. The passion between an adult man and woman had seemed a pure and remote privilege. Back then he'd had no words for it, just as he had no words for its opposite now. Their bitterness excluded him as much as their passion had. All of what happened between his mother and father was ultimately beyond him and always would be.

It was snowing by the time he and Bobby Flynt arrived at Sally's. Dobie waited in the car and listened to his father's Bruce Springsteen tape. Alone, he noticed the car's luxurious perfumy smell, and his heart beat faster as if he were eavesdropping.

"Hi, Dobie," Sally Robinson said, kissing his cheek as she scurried into the backseat. "I'm so glad you're driving tonight so that Bobby's hands are free!"

"Hohoho!" said Bobby, and Dobie laughed.

He heard them kissing then. He liked the twinkly sort of girl that Sally was. For Sally nothing seemed a very big deal. Her parents were divorced and she made jokes about it. As he pulled away from Sally's house, the snow seemed hurled, eerily, with aim. He turned on the wipers high speed.

Meredith MaGraw didn't scoot close to him and lay her head on his shoulder like Ladd had predicted. She wore a long white dress and a red cape and, instead of gloves, she carried a white fur muff. She reminded him of an old-fashioned ice skater, the kind you see on Christmas cards.

Her long blond hair was scooped off her neck with glittering combs. She'd worn high-heel boots because of the snow.

He couldn't see Sally and Bobby in the rearview. He turned up Bruce Springsteen so that Meredith wouldn't be offended by their sounds. He didn't know why, but he assumed she would be. Maybe because she hadn't scooted close. In an odd way he felt pleased if, indeed, she was offended. She sat tall in her seat with her hands inside the muff. She peered out into the snow, alert, concerned for their safety. "There's a stop sign, Dobie," she said, pointing.

Dobie glanced at her profile: elegant, intense, *spiffy*. He could imagine falling in love with her. Not just lusting but the real thing, the swooning stuff, the sort of consuming love that ate holes in everything else worthwhile, that ruined you for everything else, but you didn't care. He could even imagine, in time, making love to her in this very car. It could happen. It was not so impossible as he'd thought before gathering courage to ask her to the dance. Here she was, wasn't she? She'd done her hair and dressed herself up and sprayed herself with cologne all for him, and he barely knew her. What power men had! He saw himself walking with her along some beach at sunset, writing her a sonnet. He imagined their wedding, the lace of her trousseau. Then, the nuts and bolts of marriage: jobs, cars, houses, children, discord, yearning, half-hearted reconciliations, faithlessness. And there, oblivious to his destructive flame, sat Meredith MaGraw, pristine and perishable as a snowflake. He could save her.

At the gymnasium he held himself apart from her when they danced. But her hands felt warm and slender, and if he squeezed them, she squeezed back. They danced almost every dance, except the ones when Ladd Ferrell broke in. Once, after dancing with Ladd, there were tears in her eyes. Then, Miss Blondell asked Dobie to shag.

Miss Blondell closed her eyes while she danced and

mouthed the lyrics. She'd worn a red mini-skirt to the dance and he could see the older teachers shaking their heads at her. People were always encouraging you to be yourself; then, when you finally broke out and acted who you thought yourself to be, they disparaged you because it wasn't their version. He felt sorry for Miss Blondell because she seemed to miss high school so much.

Now the dance floor throbbed with an oldie, Jimi Hendrix's "Purple Haze." Bobby Flynt flailed his arms to the beat. "Why doesn't anybody today write music this good?" he shouted.

Sixties music made Dobie think of his parents, of how whenever, say, an old Dionne Warwick song came on the radio, his mother sang right along. Sometimes his father would sidle right up to her and do the harmony, and they'd look so enraptured that Dobie had to turn away. It was as if the love between them only existed in fixes of memory. It seemed as detached as an old wedding gift, an ornamental paperweight. They were *maintaining*. That's just the way it was. That was the Future. All the endless-seeming mush dried up in time; it turned to concrete. You could walk on it, stomp on it. Hearts were nothing but baby rocks.

Maybe he was going crazy: transforming himself into a cheetah that day was only the beginning. He took Meredith's elbow and steered her toward the coatracks.

"What are we doing?" she said.

"I don't know," he said. "You don't have to come if you don't want to."

She hesitated. Ladd Ferrell was watching.

"I'll come," she said.

He slipped her red cape over her shoulders, and she took his hand as they treaded the slippery parking lot. The snow gusted dizzily around them, wind belling her skirt. He unlocked the Volvo and they slipped inside. He started the engine and turned on the heater. After several minutes they were still shivering.

"Look," he said, "this is crazy. I'll take you back in."

"I like it," she said, settling back, closing her eyes. The red cape slipped from one of her shoulders, but she didn't bother to readjust it. Her shoulder glowed like a pearl.

"Did you see Ladd's face when we went out together just now?" she said. She laughed in a burst and clapped her hands together, but Dobie saw tears in her eyes. "Can we listen to a tape?"

He opened the glove compartment where all the cartridges were stashed.

"Prince," she said. "Have you got any Prince?"

"I don't know," Dobie said, looking. "No, I don't think so. These are my dad's."

She selected a Beatles tape and popped it into the tape player. "It's incredible how much Julian Lennon sounds like his old man," she said, "only better."

"They didn't like each other very much," Dobie said. "I read that somewhere."

Meredith shrugged. "What do you expect? They were father and son," she said lightly. "Maybe when everybody got grown up they would have been better friends. Who knows?"

"I think Ono was the real problem between them," Dobie said.

"So, what was Julian supposed to *do* about her?" Meredith adjusted the reclining seat a notch backwards. "It's funny about love."

"Funny?"

"If love's supposed to be the greatest thing in the world, why does it cause so many problems?" She was talking to herself, maybe trying to cheer herself up, it seemed to Dobie, because she didn't wait for an answer. "It's the greatest thing in the world because in one form or another it's always around." She settled back in her reclining seat. "Gosh, this is nice, Dobie. Good music, the snow . . ."

A stunning silence fell between them like invisible snow. He'd thought his mouth held words to say, but it felt frozen shut. Don't be shy, spill your guts, Bobby Flynt was always telling him. Girls love it; it turns them on. They start out mothers and end up lovers. But the truth was he knew he'd scare Meredith MaGraw to death if he told her all he wanted to tell her. There was such an urgency within him to betray. Not just the secret of his father's affair, but the wicked impermanence of love itself. He wanted to warn her, he supposed, that love was a sprinter, a cheetah. Hunted for all its thrills, dying in captivity, the most endangered thing of all.

"Earth to Dobie," Meredith MaGraw said, touching his hand. Then, silkily, she removed her red cape. She took the combs out of her hair and lay them on the dashboard. She leaned toward him. She smelled like honey. "Well?" she said.

He opened his arms to her. He didn't understand how he could feel so powerless.

WEARING GLASSES

☆♡☆ ☆♡☆ ☆♡☆

I was fourteen then, and maybe when you are fourteen you expect more out of life than at any other time. It has something to do with being so unreasonably hopeful that the world can't touch you with its shadier truths. I didn't just expect a lot, I expected everything. Maybe I'd watched too much of the Anderson family on "Father Knows Best," where everyone neatly resolved their problems and ended up chuckling warmly and twinkling their eyes at one another. My family wasn't like that at all; my family was disintegrating.

My father had recently moved out of our house and taken a room at the Shady Lawn Hotel downtown. There was no great fuss. He simply disappeared one morning along with his books and rickety old typewriter. He needed to get away by himself and write, Mother told my sister Lolly and me calmly. Since Father was on leave from the university that semester anyway, at first we thought of his departure as a sabbatical. Occasionally he dropped us all a postcard.

We mostly fretted about the Shady Lawn Hotel, which didn't have a lawn at all, but a concrete porch painted bright lime green. And the nearest tree grew across the railroad tracks—a lone, haggard cedar about as shady as a feather. It was a dumpy, penal-looking place that only charged a few dollars a night and attracted all sorts of unsavory characters. Lolly and I were forbidden to visit him. And of course we all worried about Father staying there; he was a clean-shaven, mannerly college professor who had no experience whatsoever in living among the down-and-out. Mother frequently mailed him little CARE packages filled with such things as rolls of toilet paper printed with flowers, refrigerator magnets—items she hoped would make a scedy, loveless place like the Shady Lawn more homey.

On top of everything, I had to get fitted for my first pair of glasses. I was impossibly vain, and wearing glasses made me feel irrevocably handicapped. Any potential I'd had to be pretty seemed wrecked. I tried to think up somebody famous who was attractive *because*, not in spite, of their glasses.

"Name one famous person who looks wonderful in glasses, Dr. Clutts," I asked my optometrist. I was about to burst into tears.

Thoughtfully Dr. Clutts removed his own monstrous bifocals and cleaned them with a special, premoistened tissue. When he put them back on, it was as if they helped clear his mind as well as his vision. "I thought of somebody," he said. "Harry Truman."

I finally selected a pair of powder-blue harlequins. Dr. Clutts felt so sorry for me that he threw in a special glasses chain that hooked to the stems with jaunty little gold musical notes.

I wondered what my father would think about my glasses. He'd always said my eyes were my best feature. Once, when Mother had been about to cut me some shaggy, sheepdog-style bangs, Father became almost passionate about bangs hiding my eyes.

"It's just a little change," Mother said, trying to calm him. "It's the latest craze."

"I like her hair just as it is," he said. "Why are you always trying to modernize everybody?"

Mother glared at him, but he ignored her. "Cutting bangs to hide pretty eyes like yours," Father told me, "is just about as sensible as hanging curtains in front of stained-glass windows."

"A new hairdo has nothing to do with being *sensible*," Mother said. "If we were sensible, we'd shave our heads and never worry about hair at all."

I was the only one who laughed.

Of course glasses changed the looks of my eyes much more than sheepdog bangs. I had the strangest feeling when I put them on that I was betraying my father somehow. I doubted he would recognize me if we passed each other on the street. Wearing glasses made me feel homesick even though I wasn't the one who'd left.

The Friday after I got my new glasses, I spent the night at Doris Hattaway's. Through Doris's open window we could hear the stadium noises—the pep squad and the cheering. It was the first football game of the season. There we sat: dateless, Noxzema all over our faces, hair rolled up for nobody.

"I hate myself for being so vain," I said finally. "I didn't have a boyfriend *before* I got glasses, so what difference will having them really make?"

"I hate myself for even wanting a boyfriend," Doris said.

We turned out the light and made up ideal boyfriends. For herself Doris concocted Teddy Jessup—winsome, freckle-faced, joke-a-minute, star quarterback. Mine was a tall poet with violet eyes and thick black lashes that languished on his cheeks whenever he gave me one of his frequent lovelorn glances. I gave him a brooding disposition and dark, wind-swept hair. I imagined that he enjoyed wearing flamboyant clothes like paisley ascots and hats with droopy feathers. He carried walking sticks. Of course he wrote sonnets—all dedicated to me—and was considered "weird" by cheerleader types. I named him Alexander Roundtree. My father would have liked him, and I felt glad about that.

"Mr. Blue" was boohooing on the radio when Doris and I finally said good night. Were boys ever *really* blue? I wondered, thinking of my father at the Shady Lawn Hotel.

I loved my father dearly. If it seems that I was overly preoccupied with vanities and trifles rather than with the deterioration of my family, it was because, in the beginning, I didn't believe his departure was permanent. Lolly called his leaving a "goofy fling," something Rock Hudson did all the time to Doris Day in the movies. Mother hinted that the book he'd gone off to write was of great consequence to his future at the university. She implied that we were all distractions. Doris Hattaway speculated that he'd come to a point in his life where he needed a little adventure. Once, right in the middle of filling her tooth, Doris's dentist had run off to Europe with his hygienist.

Our school bus rumbled past the hotel each morning, and Lolly and I got goose bumps as we observed some of the residents already lined up in their lawn chairs for the day. Our favorite wore a patch over one eye and had fangy teeth and looked mean enough to spit nails. We named him Spike Crawley. To think that Father was surviving at the Shady Lawn, *preferred* it, at least temporarily, to our snug, safe house on Chestnut Street with its picket fence and birdbath, made him seem like some hero in a book rather than our quiet, serious-minded father.

We might have been more distraught over his leaving had Mother acted more disturbed. But she seemed almost relieved, as if the worst thing she could have imagined had happened and she didn't have to dread it anymore. She seemed much younger without Father in the house. She went around in bobby socks and sandals, gypsyish scarves, and full, bright skirts I'd never known she had. She chewed bubblegum and consulted Tarot cards. She went out to movies a lot and stayed up late watching television. She took a part-time job at Mr. Sandman's Toyland, and she did not act lonely at all.

We talked about Father a lot, especially at meals, when his absence seemed most conspicuous. "Wonder if he still carries Dentyne gum in his pockets," Lolly said. "I hope he has a TV in his room," Mother said. "I hate to think of him missing Groucho." "Wonder if he can get Spike Crawley to play chess with him?" I asked.

Our house had begun to smell vacant without Father's pipe smoke. There was no Saturday afternoon opera on the radio anymore, nobody to read from *Arabian Nights* after supper on Sundays. I missed seeing him shuffle about in his maroon smoking jacket. Nobody else's father wore a smoking jacket. Nobody else's father kept a diary or sprinkled sherry in their scrambled eggs. I began to realize that I'd not just lost him, but lost those habits and rituals that distinguished him and helped define my love for him, habits and rituals that structured my life more than I'd ever realized. I felt the lack of him. I found myself lighting the candles at dinner the way he always had, trying to maintain the kind of order he'd established.

There had been no arguments between our parents, no volatile accusations. In recent months Father had acted more beaverish, more preoccupied with scholarship while Mother had seemed slightly restless, eagerly lured away from his dusky academic world by whatever was glittery or current. She'd whisk his Chopin preludes off the hi-fi and put on her Perry Como. She was always trying to drag Father off to see a Jerry Lewis movie or have a potluck supper with the neighbors. Because Mother and Father never openly opposed each other's evolving differences, neither Lolly nor I noticed just how irreconcilable they'd become. We never thought to look for unshared glances, unheld hands, unaccompanied laughter—those arid spaces in a marriage that can broaden into wastelands.

I couldn't help wondering, after I got my new glasses, if I might have detected things going awry between my parents had I been able to see more clearly. That thought alone was enough to make me overcome my initial vanity and start wearing them regularly. But I didn't want to seem too dependent on them. So at school I wore them only when I needed to read a blackboard. I tried to act as casual about them as some girls acted about drastic new hairdos. Maybe, I decided, if I acted matter-of-fact about them, I could pass them off as a mere cosmetic whim.

Despite everything I managed to sink myself into the almost comforting routine of school. English had always been my favorite subject, and that year I'd been lucky to draw for a teacher Miss Goodman, who was not only young and beautiful, but fun and easy, too. She always passed out cake and ice cream whenever it was some famous author's birthday. She made up games like Literary Bingo and gave jawbreakers for prizes. But after the first week of school, Miss Goodman eloped with Mr. Kelly, the guidance counselor, and we were assigned a new teacher.

We all determined to despise the new teacher—except for the class brain, Olivia Walters. The morning he was due to arrive, Pip Rogers borrowed Mindy Lee's clear fingernail polish and dipped all the chalk ends in it so they wouldn't write. Olivia, however, had made this clever room deodorizer in Girl Scouts out of an apple studded with cloves. She left it on the new teacher's desk with a little note that read: WELCOME!

It was a sunny fall day, but he strode into class with an umbrella hooked over his wrist. He wore a dull black, wrinkled suit, already vaguely chalk-covered. His shoes were great black boxes that squeaked, and he wore an unstylish string tie. He was pale and thin, and his jerky, angular stride made me think of a praying mantis. He had mud-colored hair that was plastered backwards and needed cutting. Olivia Walters said, "Oh, my lord!" and put her head down on her desk. She refused to take credit for the apple-and-clove deodorizer.

I kept staring and staring at him. What struck me most was that he looked as though he could have resided at the Shady Lawn Hotel. He was just shabby and lonesome-looking enough to have lived down a ramshackle hall from my father. They might have been friends, shared coffee together, talked about books! I couldn't help feeling a sudden flush of warmth toward the stranger.

He shrugged off his coat and unburdened himself of a leaning tower of books. Then, he plucked a piece of chalk from his briefcase (so much for Pip Rogers's chalk prank) and wrote on the blackboard: GRACE.

"Grace," he said, "That's me."

Olivia Walters looked mortified.

Of course he meant his *last* name, but he didn't seem aware of what anyone might be thinking. He told Mindy Lee to put away her nail polish. But he wasn't gruff or kingly about it; his voice was a kind, mild tenor. It seemed to orchestrate rather than rule over us. There was nothing flashy or modern about Mr. Grace as there had been about Miss Goodman. He possessed an earnestness that seemed almost obsolete.

"How would you like to read about two teenagers, passionately in love, who commit suicide?" he asked. "Do you object to a few obscenities?"

"Hell no!" Pip Rogers shouted, and everybody laughed except Mr. Grace.

But by the time he'd passed out his battered copies of *Romeo and Juliet*, I was in love.

At first I kept my feelings secret. Then, one day, after

Doris and I had been listening to Johnny Mathis records all afternoon at my house and I was in a gushy mood, I told her.

"Not Mr. Grace the English teacher!" Doris gasped. "You need new glasses."

"Love is usually blind," my mother said, overhearing us.

Lolly was less judgmental. Since she didn't yet attend high school, she'd never seen Mr. Grace. But she was intrigued by the notion of an "older" man and said so.

"I fell in love with an older man," Mother said.

"Who?" Lolly and I asked together.

She looked briefly startled, then smiled tenderly at us. "Why, your father, of course," she said. Of course. We knew that. Why had we expected someone else? She'd met Father when she was a student at the university where he still taught. He'd been twelve years older than she, her teacher when she was eighteen.

"What made you fall in love with Father?" I asked her later. We were in the kitchen baking Open Sesame pie, which we always baked for special occasions and holidays. The next day would be Lolly's birthday.

She didn't hesitate to answer. "He had such *style*, your father! You should have seen him then. He *swooped* into class, very dramatic. He wore a mustache, and he smoked a huge French horn of a pipe. I think sometimes he even wore a cape."

"Father?" I said, incredulous. "That sounds like Rhett Butler."

Mother slid the Open Sesame pie into the oven, so slowed by memory that she burned her finger.

The pie turned out beautifully, meringue so lush and curly that I couldn't resist pinching off several warm ringlets for myself. Open Sesame pies were very tricky to make; you needed special luck for one to turn out as well as that one had. I decided it was a sign. Suddenly Mr. Grace seemed truly possible.

I couldn't sleep that night. Long past midnight I got up and wrote another sonnet to Mr. Grace and hid it in my "Songs of the Soul" notebook where I also kept a large collection of his handwriting clipped from the margins of my tests and papers that he'd corrected. I liked to pretend they were love notes. After I'd written the poem, I wrote a letter to my father.

Dear Father, I wrote. *What made you fall in love with Mother? Did she try to get you, or did it just happen? How long did it take? Did she do anything special like stay after class to ask questions or turn in stuff for extra credit? Please tell me why she stood out. Please please please write soon. I miss you. I will love you till Niagara Falls. Claire.*

At school it was announced that there would be a Christmas dance. Everyone skittered about excitedly, making plans. The air tingled with the threat of snow, and the radiators clanked and chuckled merrily. It was the best time of the year. Even when the school bus passed the Shady Lawn Hotel, my dauntlessness prevailed. Somewhere inside, my father was finishing up his book and tiring of his vacation from us all. Surely he'd begun to contemplate what Christmas would be without us.

Mother seemed happy. Three weeks before Christmas she already had the tree decorated and mistletoe hung in the hallway. And just as I would have never begged to open my presents before Christmas Day, I didn't dare ask her why she whistled and hummed and twirled her bright skirts and laughed so gaily at nothing. I believed that she was saving her knowledge of Father's homecoming as our biggest Christmas surprise.

Only Doris Hattaway seemed glum. "You're so gushy lately," she told me in the girls' bathroom at school. "Did somebody ask you to the Christmas dance?" I guffawed.

"What do you take me for, Doris, a traitor? You know we'll go together, same as we did last year to the eighth-grade sock hop."

But she did not seem reassured. She blotted her lipstick briskly on a paper towel. "It won't be the same. You *know* it won't be."

"What are you talking about?" I cried. "Wallflowers together, until the Twelfth of Never." It was our motto.

"*He'll* be there," she said mournfully. "He'll be there because the faculty has got to be there, and you'll be mooning all over the place. You realize, don't you, that you'll probably get to dance with him. It's girls' choice."

Of course I'd realized it. I'd thought of nothing else since Mindy Lee had told me it would be a girls' choice dance with little dance cards all the girls would tie on their wrists with blue and orange ribbons—our school colors. A little variety would do everyone some good, said Mindy, who'd just broken up with her steady boyfriend.

"Well, I may not go," Doris said flatly. "I don't have an ally anymore. You've changed, Claire. You don't need me as much as you used to."

"I need you more than ever," I protested. "I need you to help me not chicken out of getting him to sign my dance card. I need you to be my *eyes*, Doris."

"Your eyes."

"I just can't wear my crummy old glasses to the Christmas dance."

"Why not?" Doris said. "He's seen you in them about one million times.

"But he never really sees *me*."

"Good grief," Doris said, "you're beginning to sound like one of your poems." But finally she agreed to go.

I kept waiting for Father to answer my letter. At first I pined for a long explicit letter. But as the Christmas dance grew nearer, I would have settled for a postcard that listed just a few tips—something as detached and specific as a recipe. When I didn't hear from him, I began to worry that the letter had never reached him. Maybe the postmen were all afraid to deliver mail to the Shady Lawn. Maybe somebody like Spike Crawley had swiped it from my father's mailbox.

The Friday of the Christmas dance, Doris and I got ready at my house. We rolled each other's hair and painted our fingernails with a lavish new color called Rock 'n' Rose. We ate supper in our slips. Before we put on our dresses, Lolly solemnly presented us with four leaf clovers that she'd picked and pressed in her diary over the summer. We were to tuck them inside our brassieres for good luck.

I unrolled my hair, hoping it would stay curly despite the rain outside. Why didn't it snow? It seemed that snow would make the night truly special, lacy like a valentine. I imagined how romantic it would be for Mr. Grace to see me rushing into the gym with spangles of snow melting in my hair. I would not be wearing my glasses either; and if I did not quite look beautiful, maybe I would look unencumbered and that would be enough. Father hadn't answered my letter. I had not found out how Mother had so entranced him years ago. I knew that she had never worn glasses, and I assumed that she had simply been the most beautiful girl in his class.

At seven Doris and I were ready. I heard Mother rummaging in the hall closet, and when she came into the living room where we were sitting, she carried something.

"Mink!" Doris gasped.

"It's only squirrel," Mother said, holding the little cape out to me. "But it will look so dressy and grown-up." She smiled at me. "Your father gave this to me years ago. The moths are beginning to eat it."

I unbuttoned the wooden barrel buttons of my drab old car coat. I slipped the cape around my shoulders and shivered.

It felt lighter and cooler than my coat and had a lush, dank, perfumy smell.

"Look at you!" my mother said. Her eyes glimmered.

I looked at myself in the hall mirror and the cape seemed to make me taller and sterner-looking.

And then Mother said a very odd thing for such a cheery person to say: "You look so . . . brave."

"Brave?" I said. It didn't seem the right word at all. It made me think of Joan of Arc.

But she didn't answer. "Let me run upstairs and put on my face and we'll be all set. A friend is coming by to take me to the movies. We'll drop you at the high school on the way, okay?"

I stared critically at myself for a long time in the mirror. I wished I could do my hair in another style besides a ponytail. I wished I didn't look so stiff and serious when I got all dressed up. Finally I took off my glasses and stuck them in my purse and pretended I looked perfect.

"Ready?" Mother called at last. "I just saw him pull into the driveway, let's go."

"What?" I cried. I gawked at Doris for confirmation of what I thought I'd heard. *"Him?* Did you say *him?"* Doris was staring at her dyed-to-match turquoise spike heels.

Mother looked at me deeply. "It's only Mr. Sanders from the toy store," she said.

"Is this a *date?"* I cried.

She searched my face for a glimmer of understanding. Suddenly it seemed that she was the child, contrite and apologetic, and I was the unforgiving mother. "I don't know," she said softly, girlishly. "I hadn't thought about it really."

"But what does it *mean?"* I cried. "What's happening?"

"What's going on?" Lolly called from the den.

"See you later, alligator," she called to Lolly.

I refused to put on my glasses, and so of course I didn't see what Mr. Sanders looked like. I didn't want to see. Later

Doris told me that he was every bit as good-looking as Butch Dempsey, the star quarterback at our high school. Mr. Sanders was young, too, she said. For an adult. He had a crew cut and he chewed bubblegum. Hadn't I noticed? The whole car smelled like bubblegum. Doris acted shocked that I hadn't developed a keen sense of smell to compensate for my blindness.

Nobody talked much. Mr. Sanders had the radio on low and seemed to be concentrating on the slippery roads. It was pouring down rain. Mother hummed with the radio. Once Mr. Sanders said something about Christmas being right around the corner, and Mother said just wait till she baked him an Open Sesame pie.

She didn't say a word to me. It was as if I weren't in the car. I wanted her to say something. I needed her to say something especially as we passed the Shady Lawn Hotel. I only wanted her to say, "Hey, there's the Shady Lawn." It was the sort of hint she would have dropped if Mr. Sanders hadn't stood a chance. But she ignored it, as if the Shady Lawn didn't have a thing to do with her life. I couldn't bear the way that she was and that I was on my way to a dance.

After we arrived at the high school, I cried so hard in the girls' room that I threw up. "What's wrong with Claire?" everyone asked. They bent over me, blurry, bouquet-colored. "What a beautiful mink cape," they all said.

"It's only squirrel," Doris told them.

"She's going to make him an Open Sesame pie," I sobbed.

"We'll sabotage it," said Doris.

"Poor Father. All along it's been Mr. Sanders making her so happy."

"Stop thinking about it," Doris said. "Here. Give me your dance card. I'm going to sign you up."

"I don't want to dance," I said, wiping my cheeks.

"Not even with you-know-who?" Doris looked horrified. "Claire, get hold of yourself. It's what we came for."

But I no longer knew what I had come for. It wasn't that I didn't know what I wanted. I no longer felt hopeful about what I could actually have. I wanted love in my life, but I wanted it to be definite and clear, not murky with deceit and riddles the way my parents' love for one another seemed to be.

"Let's go get some punch," Doris said. "You don't have to dance. We'll find Mr. Grace and go right up to him and strike up a conversation about poetry or something. It's just what you need. Trust me."

"I look horrible," I said. "I've cried off all my eye shadow."

"You owe me," she said, and it was true. I was the reason we were there.

I let her take me by the arm and guide me into the gymnasium as if I were truly blind. But I saw him right away, even before Doris gasped and tried to turn me back. He stood near the punch bowl. He was wearing the same rumpled suit and crooked tie he'd worn to school that day. He looked tired and bored, and he was holding hands with a thin, plain woman who looked just as tired and bored as he did. I was dumbstruck. For some reason I'd never allowed him such a possibility; I didn't need my glasses to see that she was his girlfriend.

We left after that. We took a taxi to Doris's house first to drop her off. "You'll be okay?" she asked me. "You're sure you want to be alone? I shouldn't listen to you, you're acting crazy. Call me when you get home."

"The Shady Lawn Hotel," I told the taxi driver, startling myself. Then, for some reason, I plucked my glasses from my purse and put them on decisively. My face hardened with purpose. Not until I inhaled the perfumy hopefulness of my mother's past, rising from the little fur cape, did I feel young and sad again.

☆ ♡ ☆

The Shady Lawn seemed more forlorn than sinister. I remember scuffed and buckling linoleum tile in the lobby, a few rusty spittoons, and redwood lounge chairs. I did not see Spike Crawley. There was only a gray-haired woman behind the hotel desk. She was reading some newspaper with gigantic headlines that read: PARENTS EAT CHILDREN. She jumped when I spoke to her. "Oh, you want the *professor*," she said, and hearing my father referred to like that made me truly feel like a visitor.

I knocked on his door and he called out, "Who's there?"

But I couldn't answer. I couldn't say, simply, "Claire." I felt more than just Claire. Standing in the dimly lit corridor outside my father's rented room, wearing my mother's little fur cape, missing my dance with Mr. Grace, I felt more like a girl and a woman at the same time than I have ever felt in my life.

When he opened the door, it was clear that he saw me as different. Maybe it was only the fur cape and glasses, but I remember that he didn't say my name either. Perhaps he, too, thought it might limit or reduce me. He only hugged me very close in a slow, dancing sort of way.

"When did you start wearing glasses?" he asked. And I wondered, since there was so much to say and such an awkwardness about beginning, how we would have managed without my glasses.

"They hide my eyes," I told him.

"They don't hide you," my father said.

In his room a single violin played softly on the radio, a cozy fire burned in the coal grate. He'd arranged his favorite books and pipes on the mantel along with pictures of the family—all of us, including Mother. A small, bright oriental rug lay on the hearth. A lamp with a fringed, pink silk shade cast a soft, ruddy light over the room. A book lay opened on the sofa where he'd probably been reading before I'd knocked. There was no hint of the disorder and loneliness I'd hoped to find. A wonderful contentment seemed to abide with him there. When I saw the room, its atmosphere of self-sufficiency and delight, I knew that my father was never coming home.

"Sit down," he said, "and I'll pour us some tea. You look wonderful."

I was crying by that time. "No I don't, no, I look like . . . the Old Maid card." I looked at him meaningfully. "It would be better to be an old maid, wouldn't it? I *want* to be an old maid."

He held my hands in his own. "You look so wonderful to me," he said, "that I can't quite stop missing you."

I stopped crying and looked at him hard. "What?" I said. "That doesn't make any sense! Say what you mean!"

I'd never yelled so loudly at him before and he looked stricken. I'd forgotten how stoop-shouldered he was. It made him look more humble than most fathers.

"I'm sorry," he said. "I'm not much good at saying what I mean lately. I've been cooped up too long, working. I suppose it's one of the reasons I didn't answer your letter."

"It's all right," I said. "It doesn't matter. It was a juvenile letter."

"Of course it matters," he said. "*Everything* matters. So much so that I couldn't put it all down in a letter."

"Anyway," I told him, "I can guess why you fell in love with Mother. She was the most beautiful girl in your class, right?"

"No," he said, "she was the smartest."

"The smartest? *Mother*?"

"Smart except for her heart," he said, and we both managed small, tentative smiles. "It was unwise of her to fall for an old fossil like me," he added lightly. "When we met, she was only eighteen. She had so much love inside her that she danced everywhere she went. You couldn't keep her still, but she wanted to be still. She wanted to settle. None of it was her fault, you see, it's just the way she was. She imagined our life together as one long, absorbing book that she would sit up reading all night long and be calmed by. She thought I could teach her to be still, and I thought I could. Love never acknowledges impossibilities, Claire.'' He sighed deeply. ''Your mother and I probably began our marriage where we should have ended it: when she was willing to kick off her dancing shoes to be my wife. I mean that figuratively, but she really did have a pair of dancing shoes—red satin ones with little rhinestone bows.'' He shook his head ruefully. ''Listen, Claire,'' he said. ''Never be so willing to please another that you deny something vital about yourself.''

When he saw the look of confusion on my face, he drew me close, and bumped my glasses off.

''I'm trying to understand,'' I said, and as I retrieved my glasses from where they'd fallen I thought how I'd denied myself clear-sightedness just so I might look more attractive to someone who already had a girlfriend.

''I'd rather you tried to forgive,'' my father said gently. Then he poured us two cups of the spicy, orange-smelling Russian tea, and it seemed that we talked about everything else.

It was late when we started for home. As we descended the slippery steps of the hotel, he took my arm to guide me. I waited for the sorrow of my parents' separation to weigh bleakly upon me, but it didn't. Both my mother's fur cape and the tea my father had made me were keeping me warm. I knew that both my parents loved me—separately but enough. The love felt whole. And maybe that was all I had any right to expect. Somewhere in that dreary part of town church bells tolled a Christmas carol.

I knew that Lolly would be waiting up, expecting a tale of romance. But the Christmas dance seemed to belong to another time and place now, and so did Mr. Grace. Instead I yearned to tell Lolly about the Shady Lawn, how it wasn't at all like we'd imagined, how nothing was. Father had spoken of endings the way I'd always thought of beginnings. Perhaps I truly began to enter womanhood the moment I both understood and forgave that paradox.

Before we reached my father's car, the rain changed to snow. I'd not counted on the snow; it happened like a gift. It floated and swirled beautifully across the darkness, making soft shapes out of brittle ones, ornamenting the ordinary. Even the Shady Lawn Hotel looked as if it belonged on a Christmas card.

THE HUMMINGBIRD KIMONO

☆♡☆ ☆♡☆ ☆♡☆

On the very day that Parker Branch discovered his first gray hair, his grandfather died. Parker knew it was no coincidence. It was a double-edged message from Fate. Right before his eyes his own future winked and darkened. Then, after he found out that his grandfather had willed him the gold pocketwatch he'd always admired, Parker went weak in the knees with remorse. The watch clinched it. He would reform himself. It was a real gimcrack of a pocketwatch, which, by God, he was going to *use*. He was going to keep track of time for a change, going to make time count.

Since college he'd been on the road, writing songs, playing his guitar in back-alley cafés—any place they'd pass a hat and feed him dinner. But it was a ragged, disorderly life, seeing the world. Every town, large or small, began to look alike, and that defeated the whole purpose of travel, didn't it? So he'd finally come home to Raleigh, North Carolina, from which he'd set out five years before. Temporarily he moved in with his parents. He shaved his beard and cut off his ponytail and applied for every job in sight. It was a start. Then he went and ruined everything by falling in love with a girl named Lella Fortune.

Why couldn't he have fallen for some responsible, orderly girl like Betty Gail Womble, who lived next door to his parents and taught kindergarten? She positively gleamed with self-restraint and resolve. Her blouses were so crisp that they defied poor posture; her slacks had creases so sharp that he bet they hurt to sit in. You could set your watch by her—even on Saturdays. Saturdays Betty Gail polished and spit-shined all her shoes; she washed and waxed her car—a four-door sedan, basic black, with plastic seat covers.

For a while, before he met Lella Fortune, Parker had fancied himself falling for Betty Gail. What a good influence she was! His mother had introduced them with great hopes, and they'd gone out to eat barbecue every Friday night since. Parker had even got to thinking of her when, on Saturday mornings, he meandered downtown to poke around his favorite old haunts: the salvage and thrift shops. Crumbum stores, his mother called them. But he loved other people's cast-offs; he liked to think of them as wearable adventures.

One Saturday morning Betty Gail Womble was so thoroughly on his mind that without thinking twice he bought her a used Girl Scout uniform. It was so much her style that he got goose bumps just paying for it.

"Why, Parker!" she cried when he presented her with the uniform. "How did you guess that I'd been thinking of becoming a scout leader in my spare time? You must have ESP! This is swell. If it doesn't fit me, I'm sure that one of my troop can use it."

Parker cringed at the perky way she said "one of my troop." Why did it dampen his delight for her to actually *need* the uniform?

On the other hand, Lella Fortune didn't seem to *need* the hummingbird kimono at all. But she wanted it, had to have it. In another thrift store, another Saturday, their hands tangled in a dive for the kimono. It was made of old, yellow Chinese silk. Dozens of tiny green and ruby-colored birds flocked across the shoulders. She crushed one sleeve to her chest while he held tight to the other. They heard the dry putter of tearing silk.

He was struck instantly by her beauty. For a moment his grip on the kimono loosened as he concentrated on her the way you concentrate on a star that is at once bright and elusive. She wore a broad-brimmed straw hat with a crimson ribbon atop hair that couldn't be contained, black and jazzy hair that spewed and tumbled in all directions. She had on green pedal pushers with a flashy pink T-shirt, rainbow-striped socks, and golden sandals with ankle straps. Anybody else would have looked like a crumbum, but she reminded him of . . . well, a hummingbird.

She gazed curiously at him from behind a pair of rose-colored glasses, the lenses of which were heart-shaped. "For your wife?" she asked.

"I don't have a wife," he said. "I don't have a girlfriend either." He felt he should apologize to Betty Gail Womble when he said that.

"What do you want with a woman's silk kimono, then?" she asked. "Or maybe that's too personal."

"I just like it," Parker said, glancing at the price tag. "Good grief!" He let go his sleeve. "It's forty dollars! You can have it."

"Forty dollars," she said. "Oh dear." She dug through a cavernous carpetbag of a purse. Out spilled bubblegum fortunes, barrettes, a yo-yo. He loved watching her agitation. There was an unlabored quality about her beauty that made him think of good, loose music.

She looked up at him from the murky depths of her purse. "Hello," she said suddenly, sticking out one hand. "I'm Lella Fortune. I live on Magnolia Street. I'm not crazy and I'm really rather honest. Could you possibly loan me twenty dollars until Friday?"

☆ ♡ ☆

That Friday he'd expected to find money slipped under the front door in a mauve envelope sealed with wax. Instead, just as he was leaving to eat supper at the Pig and Whistle with Betty Gail, the phone rang.

"May I please speak to Park Bench?" she said.

"Parker Branch," he said.

"Parker Branch? *Really*?" She sounded disappointed. "I could have sworn you told me that your name was Park Bench. I've told everyone I know about that name. I just love it."

"Gee," he heard himself saying, "it really is a wonderful name. But if it *were* my name," he added, "I'd spell Parke with an *e*. Otherwise it would look silly."

"Like your parents had named you after where they first met," she said.

"Or worse," said Parker, and she laughed heartily.

"I don't have the money yet," she said then. "I was behind with my rent. But if you'll give me until next Friday, I'll deliver it in person. We can even meet for lunch. I'll treat."

He felt overwhelmed with opportunity. "Where?" he said. "Shall I be so bold as to suggest . . . a park bench?"

"Parker, who was that on the phone?" his mother asked him after he'd hung up from making the lunch date.

She looked so tired, his mother. Had he done all that to her? Those thousands of gray hairs, the skin of her forehead and cheeks beginning to look barky.

"It was a wrong number," he said. If he'd told her about Lella, wouldn't she have keeled right over? Her heart was absolutely set on Betty Gail.

"You don't fool me, you old honeybun," she said dauntlessly. She shuffled over and gave him a hug. "I'll bet it was somebody calling you for a job interview. You just don't want to get our hopes up yet, right?" She kissed his cheek. "I won't say a word to your dad, cross my heart."

"Thanks, Mom." Let her think it, Parker thought. Give her hope, lighten her heart, even for one measly night.

"Parker," she said happily, "aren't you glad you finally straightened up? People can't say you're a hippie anymore."

"I was never a hippie," Parker said with disdain. He gazed out the window into the hazy summer twilight. "I was more of a . . . hobo," he said nostalgically.

He'd been just about everywhere. Summers he'd traveled to breezier islands like Ocracoke, Nantucket. He'd paint houses, do a gig here, a gig there. He picked apples in the fall and helped run a cider press in Vermont. Winters he dipped southwards—maybe all the way to New Orleans on a train called the Southern Crescent. And he liked prairie towns in the spring when the wildflowers bloomed. If odd jobs failed him, he could always find a diner or café that liked his downhome music.

He was a good musician. But he didn't strive with his singing as much as he simply enjoyed it. He played "Oh! Susanna" and "Dixie" the best and also a song he'd written himself called "The Raleigh, North Carolina Blues." He could sing them all so tenderly that sometimes displaced southerners in the audience would cry. He sang the songs better as he got older. But the day he found his first gray hair, he could hardly sing them at all. He'd felt shocked; it meant something. The hair seemed to zigzag out from his scalp like a lightning bolt headed straight for his heart.

He'd never thought of himself as the homesick type, but that very day in the Tumbleweed Café near Hayes, Kansas, as he was picking out the introduction to "Dixie," tears came sliding down his cheeks. His voice cracked. Whole families of people looked up from their cozy suppers. They gazed at him not just with well-fed, contented faces, but with faces that belonged to one another. That made him cry all the harder.

Somebody called for him to take a coffee break, but he just sat there shaking his head and saying that what he really wanted was a plate of candied yams and snap beans slow-cooked all day with ham hocks, and maybe a half-dozen hush puppies on the side. But the cook at the Tumbleweed Café thought that hush puppies were a kind of meat. Nobody could even tell Parker how far it was to the nearest dogwood tree—maybe a couple of states.

He'd phoned home just as soon as he could, and that's when his parents told him that his grandfather had died that morning. Of course they didn't expect him to come home for the funeral, seeing as how Grandfather had disowned Parker after he grew a ponytail. But Parker went home to the funeral anyway and decided to stay. He'd needed a funeral along with that gray hair to bring him to his senses.

He knew that his grandfather didn't leave him the gold pocketwatch out of pure sentiment. It was more a gift of chastisement. On the back of the watch was engraved the old man's favorite quotation: "I wasted time and now doth time waste me."

He'd agreed to meet Lella Fortune in front of the Magnolia Street Bakery. As he walked along Magnolia Street, inhaling the aroma of baking bread, he put his hands in his pockets and almost skipped. Baking bread was truly the happiest smell he knew.

This was not his first trip to Magnolia Street that week. He'd cruised up and down its shady length five or six times, casing the houses, wondering where Lella Fortune lived. He tried to guess by the style curtains hanging in a window, the tune played by a certain set of wind chimes. She wasn't listed in the phone book, and for a split and sinking second Parker wondered if she existed at all. She'd simply said to meet, Friday, in front of the bakery, which is where he ended up, precisely at noon. He checked his pocketwatch.

"Hello!" cried Lella Fortune, leaping out the bakery door no more than a minute later. She wore the fluttery hummingbird kimono and a long turquoise skirt over which a bibbed apron was tied. What a curvy little waist she had! A tiny paper hat perched atop her gypsy hair. "I've got our lunch," she said, rattling a white paper sack. "Chocolate mousse brownies, Queen of Hearts cherry tarts, and for dessert—meringues shaped like swans." She smacked her lips. "I work here," she said. "It's the only reason I'm punctual. You see, if a stranger owed you money and was even as little as ten minutes late showing up, wouldn't you figure that she'd skipped out on you?"

"Maybe," Parker said, staring deeply into her eyes. It gave him a tumbling sensation.

"Would you have waited for me ten minutes?" she asked.

He felt a fool as soon as the words came out, but he couldn't stop himself. "I would have probably waited for you all day," he said.

If he'd dreamed the afternoon, he couldn't have come up with a better one. They had the park mostly to themselves. They ate all the pastries and drank wine out of paper cups. It seemed to Parker that they talked about everything, and nobody asked what time it was. He even told her the story about feeling homesick at the Tumbleweed Café and crying when he played "Dixie." Tears of sympathy welled in her eyes. She was a tender sort of listener.

"I want to travel, too," she said finally.

"After a while," Parker said, "places start looking all the same." He took her hand. He liked the way she held his hand back, tugging slightly at the fingers as if she were a child impatient to be off. "You get to feeling the way, say, whole towns must feel when you whip past them on a bus or train: expendable. You start hankering for something a little more permanent." He shivered suddenly as if in the presence of a ghost. "That sounded pretty creaky," he said apologetically. "I didn't mean to sound so . . . old."

"I've been saving money for a trip around the world," Lella said. "I decided to postpone college and go right to work. I want to leave on my twentieth birthday."

"You're not yet twenty?" Parker's mouth gaped in astonishment.

"I'm eighteen."

"I thought you were older." He began to feel panicky. "Why, if you're only twenty, you have every right to see the world. It's practically a necessity. I was itching to see it when I was your age." He squeezed her hand. "It's just that I was hoping you'd stick around for a while."

She smiled. "I promise to pay you back the twenty dollars before I go."

"That's not funny," Parker said and pulled her close and kissed her mouth softly. It had a sweet, buttery taste, and she kissed him back.

"I like you a lot, too, Methuselah," she said.

They kissed another long, earnest kiss, the sort of kiss that made Parker forget the world and everything in it. There was no gravity in such a kiss. It was like flinging himself into a warm, dizzying darkness as vast and breathless as outer space.

"Excuse me, do you have the time? Oops! *Sorry!*" A shabby little man had spoken and now scuttled away. He wore dirty overalls and a porkpie hat and carried a little straw suitcase. For a second Parker imagined that the hobo was his grandfather gone to seed. "It's two o'clock!" Parker called after the man, checking his pocketwatch.

"What a beautiful old watch," Lella said. "It looks like pirate loot."

"It was my grandfather's," Parker told her. A sad, homesick feeling came over him. He wished the old bum had been his grandfather. Maybe he could have explained things, undone his grandfather's disappointment in him. They'd been such good friends when Parker was a boy. Age had gotten the better of them both.

"I'm so glad that you don't wear a digital watch," Lella said, and she kissed him on the cheek. "Oh, goodness," she said, "did you really say it was two o'clock? I'll get fired for sure this time." She scrambled around in the leaves looking for her paper hat. Then, she threw a fistful of money at Parker.

"What's this?"

"It's what I owe you, minus three dollars. I had to buy wine."

"But I really don't want it," he said. "Now."

"What's that supposed to mean?"

"I want to pay for half the kimono," he said. "I want us to share it."

She looked amused.

"Whenever I come visit you, I'll wear it. Like a smoking jacket, a leisure suit. I'll wear it tonight."

"I sort of have plans tonight," she said.

"Plans?" he cried. "Not after that kiss you don't. After that kiss we ought to . . . get married. You can't have plans."

"I've had too much wine," she said, laughing. "Okay, I'll get myself free."

He felt dizzy with triumph, but only briefly. He suddenly remembered that he'd asked Betty Gail out to the Pig and Whistle for barbecue.

That evening, all through his dinner, Parker noticed for the first time that Betty Gail had this irritating habit of sectioning off the different foods in her plate so that their juices wouldn't mingle. She patted the food into separate little hillocks and ate one hillock at a time: first the coleslaw, then the barbecue, last the pinto beans. She picked the cheese off her apple pie and ate it separately. She scraped the apples out of the crust and ate the crust last. Her teeth were loud, and she chewed with the soulless, snappy tempo of a high school marching band.

"Pssssst!" his mother called to him from the stairs as he came in. "Any news yet?"

"No news, Mom. Soon, maybe." He'd not looked at a want ad all week. Why was falling in love so debilitating?

"I just hope and pray that it's nothing door-to-door," his mother said. "Promise me it's nothing like selling toilet bowl cleaners door-to-door."

"It's nothing like that, Mom."

"Thank you so much, Parker," she said. "Maybe I can get to sleep now."

On Saturday night Parker went to Lella Fortune's. She lived above the Magnolia Street Bakery in a small, cluttered apartment. The rooms were filled with chocolaty-looking antique furniture, bright paintings in junky, extravagant frames, old broken dolls and toys, fans, hats, shawls, shoes strewn about. The apartment had the aura of a costume party where all the guests had mysteriously vanished right out of their disheveled clothing.

Parker surveyed it happily. "I'll bet when you were a little girl your room was as neat as a pin," he said.

"Neater."

They sat down to a candlelit supper: a casserole of hot dogs and baked beans. There was a platter of bakery macaroons for dessert.

"I'll bet your mom was one of the greatest kitchen slaves that ever lived," he said.

"The greatest."

"Next to mine." He tasted one slightly charred hot dog slice and smiled. "This is my kind of meal," he said.

After supper they tossed their paper plates in the trash. They refilled their jelly glasses with wine and Parker played his guitar. When he played "The Raleigh, North Carolina Blues," Lella harmonized perfectly.

"If I'd found you when *I* was twenty, I'd have never gone away," he told her.

"But I would have only been twelve years old," Lella said.

"It wouldn't have mattered," Parker said. "We would have thought of something. I'd have gotten a steady job and come home to you every night. We would have had kids right away. The oldest would be about five or six now, sitting right here and wanting me to teach her to play some awful punk rock tune on my guitar. A girl, with big brown eyes like yours and ripply, fairy-tale princess hair."

"Oh, I don't know about children," Lella said. "If you have children, you have to join the PTA. I'm really not much of a joiner."

For a moment, the life he might have had seemed more real to Parker than the one he was actually living. "So much time has gotten away from me," he lamented.

"Relax," Lella said, kissing him on the forehead as if he had a fever. She pointed to the hummingbird kimono hanging on a nearby hook. "Why don't you slip into something a little more comfortable?"

Maybe she reminded him of the way he'd been before he started taking life so seriously. When it rained, she still got a kick out of splashing barefooted in puddles. She had wonderful, amusing ideas like eating Hershey bars in the dark to see who could make theirs sound most delicious. Once, when she'd found an injured butterfly, she'd taken it to the vet's. But mostly he loved her because she, too, believed in love at first sight, believed in the pull of the moon, star-crossed lovers, the whole magical bit. For a few weeks, anyway, it seemed to Parker that life was meant to be lived without goals atop the Magnolia Street Bakery. They had love and comfort in abundance there, and wasn't that all you needed?

"I want to get married," he told her one evening. They'd taken big Mason jars to the park to catch lightning bugs (Lella's idea). "I know it's fast and everything, but we could pretend there's a war on. People always marry fast in wartime," he explained.

"But we have everything we want just the way we are," she said, holding up her Mason jar against the sky. Inside the blinking bugs formed a tiny constellation.

"I want to take care of you," Parker said. "I'll find a job."

She squeezed his hand. "I can take care of myself," she said softly.

"I'm no freeloader!" he said almost angrily. "I'm no park bench!"

"What do you mean?"

"All a park bench does is squat," he said forlornly. "I want to *do* something, Lella. And I want you to be there when I do it."

"Don't plan," she said. "Let's just enjoy this. It's a miracle in its own right." She unscrewed the lid of her jar and let the lightning bugs scatter free. "Look!" she said. "They're as bright as stars, and I'll bet they're just as good for wishing on."

He wished.

Then, one morning as Parker was showering, thinking how tough it was to be a man, thinking most men didn't realize how tough it was because they were all too busy *being* men, he heard his mother rapping on the bathroom door and hollering as if the house were on fire. A man from the government had called about a job.

He'd taken the civil service exam in the spring. He'd even had a couple of interviews, but now he couldn't remember which agencies had been most interested. Had he really applied to the Farm Bureau? The FBI? He remembered telling the FBI agent with whom he'd talked that he'd always loved Sherlock Holmes.

His mother had underlined the telephone number three times and made little smiley faces out of the zeros. Come to think of it, being a mother was probably just as tough as being a man.

He had a lump in his throat as he dialed. His palms perspired. He felt moved that somebody was actually interested in hiring him, proud that he measured up to some exacting, standardized system of government evaluation. When the man he spoke with said, "Mr. Branch, we really need you," Parker's heart thrilled with something akin to patriotism. He felt reckless saying yes, the way, he supposed, soldiers felt leaping into battle. You just did it.

"It was the Department of Health and Human Services," he told his mother. "I start training next week in Atlanta." He felt that he ought to salute somebody.

She hugged him, tears rolling down her cheeks. "What will you be doing?"

He almost blurted it right out but blushed at the thought of saying "VD counselor" in front of his mother. What did a VD counselor *do*? He felt panicky with inexperience. Why, he'd never even had VD!

"It's very sensitive work," he told her. "Confidential."

"Top secret?" she whispered excitedly. Her face glowed. She looked ten years younger.

He drove right over to Magnolia Street with his good news. On the way he planned everything. They'd have their wedding in the park, and she would wear the hummingbird kimono. Or maybe he'd wear it. They could decide later.

He took the stairs three at a time. The apartment door was wide open, and he halted abruptly. This wasn't Lella's apartment; it was as neat as a pin! Neater. It was practically empty!

She sat cross-legged on the floor, packing up a box of feathery things: an Indian headdress, a feather boa, a pair of marabou earmuffs. When he sat down beside her, he could tell that she'd been crying.

"I'm not at work today because I lost my job," she sniffled. "I was late to work a million times and nobody said a word. Then, on the millionth and one time, they fired me."

"Congratulations!" Parker cried, hugging her. "That's splendid news! It was a crummy job anyway—all hot and floury and . . . *crumby*, get it?"

She didn't smile.

"Besides, it couldn't be better timing. I just got a job, so you don't have to worry about a thing. I'm going to work with diseases. Nothing contagious, so we can go ahead and get married, and you can come with me to Atlanta." He hugged her again, but she stiffened.

"Parker," she said, blotting her eyes with the marabou earmuffs. "Do you remember telling me how you felt when you gave Betty Gail the Girl Scout uniform?"

He nodded.

"Remember how it dampened your enthusiasm for her to actually *need* the uniform? You felt second-guessed or something. Well, somehow I'm beginning to feel second-guessed, too. All along you've just assumed I'm ready for the same things you are. But I'm scared, Parker. I mean, I still eat baby food now and then!"

"Baby food?"

"It's just so convenient," she said.

"You're trying to tell me I'm too old for you," Parker said sadly.

He felt his throat tightening. "If only you knew what I already know."

"If only you didn't know already," she said, "we could find it out together."

"I wish," he said, his voice quaky. "I wish . . ." But the

wish was too absurd to give voice. Why did he wish that his grandfather were there? To talk some sense into Lella the same as he'd done Parker five years ago? Ha!

He stayed to help her finish packing. They didn't tape shut the last cardboard box until way past midnight. They hadn't talked much.

"How could I have collected so much junk?" Lella said at last.

"I have a theory," Parker said wistfully. "It's because you're basically the homebody sort with tremendous nesting instincts."

She smiled, sort of.

"Which box did you pack the kimono in?" Parker asked. "I'd like to slip into it one last time, if you don't mind."

Lella's face pinkened. "Oh, Parker," she said, "I tossed it."

His jaw dropped.

"I tossed it in the Goodwill bin. It was falling to pieces. It made me sad just to look at it."

"But it was half mine!" he cried. "How could you toss it? It was a symbol of . . . everything! Which Goodwill bin, Lella?"

At one o'clock in the morning, he climbed into the Goodwill bin and began sorting through its rubble. The things people tossed away! He dug past a rubber flipper, a mangy fur coat, a porkpie hat that he almost kept, somebody's wedding dress. But the kimono had vanished; he couldn't find it.

He heard a motor and, peeping over the top of the bin, saw a patrol car headed his way. He lay on his back, hardly breathing as the patrol car circled the bin and glided off into the night. He felt suddenly wanted, sought after, for all the wrong reasons. An ornate smell rose from the dew-damp clothes. It was as if he lay among the tattered patchwork of secret lives that people had lived and cast off, hurrying toward something newer and better, they always thought.

He heard another car, probably the patrol car coming back to check him out for sure this time. He decided he'd put on the porkpie hat and say that he had no home. But the car coming his way sounded all sputtery and broken down. It wasn't a car at all! It was Lella Fortune riding her bike. She liked to clip playing cards in the spokes so that the wheels made a motory sound.

"Parker! Are you in there?" she called. "Did you find the kimono?"

He peered over the edge of the bin. He felt confused, seeing her there in the moonlight. He felt enchanted—as if he, the prince, were about to be rescued by the princess. "It's gone," he said.

"I'm so sorry, Parker. I feel awful."

"Maybe it's for the best," he said. "Maybe it was a souvenir that would have depressed me in later years. Like the clump of grass I still have that the Beatles walked on."

She gave him a blank look.

"*The* Beatles," he said and sighed. "You see, after a while souvenirs get depressing because there's nobody left to remember what they mean."

"Parker," she said, "is Atlanta nice?"

"It's not so much the place," he said, "it's who you're with when you're there."

"Can I join you?" she asked, pointing to the bin. "It's like you're way up on a throne." She held out her arms at the same moment he reached for her, and as she tumbled into the bin beside him, he kissed her. For a while they lay on their backs, looking at the stars.

"I've decided," she said almost sternly. "I'm coming with you to Atlanta. I love you, Mobile Home."

He peered at her quizzically.

"Well, you certainly aren't a park bench *now*."

Acting so decisive made her look older. There was a wrinkle across her brow. Her mouth looked thin and serious. Something about her whole expression seemed ill fitting, tight.

"Don't do that!" he cried.

"Don't do what?"

"Your face. You look like . . . the president of the PTA."

"Well, I'm me," she said, "and I'm going with you to Atlanta. Aren't you happy?"

"No," he said, almost falling backwards from the weight of the word. It felt like the most responsible word he'd ever spoken in his life. "I mean," he said, "yes, I'm happy that you'd agree to come to Atlanta, but no you can't come because if you come, Lella, it won't really be you."

"You're flipping out," she said.

"Already you look older," he told her. "You look full of duty and sacrifice. I can even picture you with a sensible, close-cropped hairdo. You're trying to be the you that you think I want you to be. Admit it, it's a big bore. The beginning of the longest PTA meeting in history."

"Oh, Parker!"

"If you really want to be you, Lella, go out and see the world first. I can't marry a girl who thinks the world's flat."

"You're just saying that," she said, "you're just trying to be brave."

Maybe he was. But bravery was okay, too, wasn't it? He felt downright heroic in a peculiar, lonesome sort of way. He'd always thought of heroes as the ones who went adventuring, not the ones who stayed behind. Bravery felt like a kind of costume, stiff and inert against his heart, full of sparkling bluff like armor. For certain there wasn't one crumbum thing about it.

He remembered the stories Grandfather had told him when he was a boy, stories about world explorers in their tall galleons, threading a course through oceans believed to be teeming with monstrous serpents. If those adventurers had simply sailed forth and never returned, he remembered Grandfather telling him, what enlightenment would have resulted for the world? There was a time for leave-taking, but also a time for returning home. "Discoveries aren't worth a hoot until they're shared," his grandfather had said.

Why did it take so long to learn such simple things?

It was, perhaps, the memory of his grandfather's homey wisdom that caused Parker to dig into his pocket and pull out the watch and press it into Lella Fortune's palm. It was a gift of love, after all.

AURORA ISLAND

☆ ♡ ☆   ☆ ♡ ☆   ☆ ♡ ☆

It was a windswept, raggedy, unfashionable beach. There were no flashy motels, no burger joints, amusement parks, or yacht club. Just worn-down family-owned houses, gaunt-looking on their pilings, hurricane-proud. There was a grocery store, a Pure station, a weathered pier and pavilion, and a couple of boardinghouses. Nothing much to do but swim and daydream.

We stayed at the Carolina Charm, where we rented two rooms with a kitchenette every summer for Mama's vacation. The Carolina Charm was a boardinghouse for women only ("Gulls only," Mrs. Roberts the proprietress liked to joke). From our porch on the third floor, we had a fine beachy view. We could almost hear the Crystal Pier, old and leggy, its wood goitered with barnacles, groaning against each wave. Beside it twinkled the Lumina Pavilion, where every night a band played, brassy accompaniment to the ocean beyond that rolled its dark blue tide like a drum.

Aurora Island was attached to the mainland by a slender drawbridge that whined a twangy nubby music when you crossed it by car. It was a small island, and we could see most of it from our windows. On still, clear evenings the glow of Wilmington tinted the sky like a pale pulsing weather to the west.

Our rooms were large and clean with two floor fans that we didn't really need with our windows raised, because the ocean breathed back a dazzling constant wind. The wind felt soft on our skins like baby powder and just as sweet. Late afternoons, after our baths, Mama and I would stand naked in front of the windows to dry.

Aunt Bunny came with us that summer. She wasn't really an aunt. She and Mama had been girls together, and she had no children of her own, so, out of respect, I was to call her "Aunt."

She was fat: the kind of fat that hangs loose from long-vanished bones like rippling silk, very white. Almost pretty until you remember that it's not upholstery fabric but skin. Just below her nose thrived a little patch of soft hair the color of pussy willow. On the beach she wore her father's cast-off shirts over her bathing suit so that she wouldn't blister. And after supper, if we took a walk to the Lumina to buy ice cream, she put on a thick, textured pair of knee socks so mosquitoes wouldn't bite her.

Mama told me once in private that if she had a month alone with Bunny inside her beauty shop with no refrigerator handy, she could work a miracle. "Anybody with skin like Bunny's has potential," she said. I guess Mama felt guilty, the two of them being best friends but herself with enough good looks to give three-fourths away to Bunny and still come out the better. And if the three of us went walking, even I, not yet thirteen and spider-leggy, felt I'd win *second* place if we all entered a beauty pageant. Aunt Bunny noticed my attitude and called it strutting. "You got to do something about that child's rear end," she said to Mama. "Those shorts are so tight she looks pure raw." She'd stop and yank up her knee socks over pudding-soft calves that sort of bubbled as she walked. I almost believed the socks held them from sliding down into her shoes, and that she made up the business about the mosquitoes.

Some nights Mama went dancing with Marvin Briggs. She'd known him for years and called him her "beach bud." He owned boats and brought us big bags of channel shrimp whenever he visited. When Mama went out, Aunt Bunny and I would go downstairs and uproot old Ophelia Roberts from watching "You Bet Your Life" and the three of us would play Chinese checkers. Ophelia Roberts kept a closet full of board games in case ladies who came to the beach caught nasty weather or too much sunburn or just a bad case of wanting company on a long summer night.

We were playing checkers the night Bud Oleander arrived. Mrs. Roberts had made up so much lime Kool-Aid that I thought we'd never finish that first game for one of us having to run pee. Bunny and Mrs. Roberts were both gone when he came in, kicking a suitcase through the door. "Where's she at?" he said to me as if we'd always known each other. He towered over me, big in his sailor's suit, genielike, and I jumped up. I was not afraid exactly; I just didn't want to seem so small. "Old Ma!" he hollered.

We heard the toilet flush, and he laughed. One front tooth winked silver. "Who's winning?" he asked. He leaned over the table and picked up one of Bunny's marbles. He looked down at the board, flexing his jaw. "Who's yaller?"

"Me," I said.

"You're winning, then," he said, licking his silver tooth and grinning.

"Why, that'll be Buddy," I heard Mrs. Roberts say, shuffling down the hall. "That you, Buddy?"

"Naw, it's Elvis Presley."

"You rascal!" She raced into the parlor, and they hugged. "This is my grandson, Bud Oleander," she said to me. "He's been in the navy two years. Buddy, this is Susie."

"How do," he said. Then he took my hand and kissed it in this sly-devil way.

Aunt Bunny met him, too, but she wasn't impressed. When we returned to our rooms, she arranged us a plate of Ritz crackers spread with jelly. She decorated her own with olives. Then, she sat on the bed I shared with Mama and began unrolling her socks to see if any mosquitoes had sneaked in. "*He's* the one she doesn't keep a picture of," she said huffily. "The no-count. Got a girl pregnant. Married her until things simmered down, then dumped her and joined the navy. Ophelia told me—her daughter's boy. Looks like a pirate, don't he?"

I started undressing for bed.

"Reckon Miss Popularity's going to have any feet left after tonight, dancing and a-prancing, huh? Think her and Marvin Briggs are serious business?"

I pulled my shirt over my head.

"Get away from that window, Susie-Q," she said, twanging the elastic of my underpants. "Honey, there's a man here now." She flicked off the light and I could hear her munching in the dark.

The next morning he was out on the beach when we got there. "Go ask that boy if he's got a cigarette," Mama said. But he had already seen her and came stomping out of the water.

"Introduce me to your pretty sister, Susie," he said, dripping little cold stars of water on me: so cold they made my stomach leap. But I didn't wipe them off.

When he had gone, I said to Mama, "He's a strapping boy, that Bud Oleander."

"He's no boy to you."

"I can't appreciate tattoos much, though," I said. "Why do people go doodling all over themselves?"

"I heard of a man once," Aunt Bunny said, "who had him one on his—"

"Shush, Bunny," Mama said, giggling.

"On his what?" I asked. But I knew.

"It was a skull and crossbones."

"No!" cried Mama, laughing. She was the prettiest lady on the beach when she laughed. Even her fillings were pretty—all gold. Her teeth filled with sun like she was chewing spangles of light. When she laughed, full-faced and openmouthed, hard and sure of the laugh, her throat arched backwards so fine and brown and begging a man's lips to be on it that everybody looked. Bud Oleander looked. Mama waved at him and smiled. She lowered her straps and turned on her stomach. "Do my back for me, will you, punkin?"

Bud Oleander had come to Aurora to fish. He fished deep in the surf without waders, and it was jellyfish season. I'd seen him stung, but he'd pour beer on the sore and heave back into the water that seemed tame and flirty as petticoats, him in the middle. Mama said to me, "Don't you get out that far. There's a current that'll whip you straight away. That boy's crazy. Cray-*zee*!" She shouted so loud that Bud Oleander could hear. "That's no way to fish," Mama called. "If he wants to fish deep, he ought to use the pier."

"What's it to you?" Aunt Bunny said.

"It's just a crazy way to fish," Mama yelled into the sky.

Once he stomped out of the water and straight up to Mama with a crab in his hand. "You're scaring my fish, honey," he said. "You're making them nervous." He had a cigarette on his bottom lip. He was the color of wet brick with eyes pale-bright as shallow water. I tried not to look at his tattoos.

"You can just get that crab away from here, mister," Aunt Bunny said.

Bud Oleander winked at me. He yanked the cigarette from his mouth and held it up to the crab. He let go a pincher and the crab grabbed. He dropped the crab in the sand and laughed. It skittered down the beach, waving the cigarette, as proud as if it had snatched off one of Bud's fingers. "A minute more and he'd have had a nicotine fit."

I felt sorry for that dumb, blustery crab. But Mama opened her treasure box mouth and laughed.

One afternoon, while Mama was rolling her hair, I found the picture in Bunny's magazine. I lay my thumb over the name and showed it to her. "Who's this?"

"Ricky Nelson, silly."

"I mean who *looks* like this?"

Mama studied the picture closely. Then she took her eyebrow pencil and dotted out a tooth. "Ricky Nelson is scrawny. Bud's much bigger."

"Well, he's got Ricky Nelson's face exactly until you drew over that tooth," I said. "Now he looks hillbilly."

The door rattled. "That'll be Bunny with the groceries," Mama hummed through a mouthful of bobby pins.

I carried the magazine to the door with me, reading as I opened it. "Hi, Susie," Bud Oleander said through the crack, and I slammed the door quick as a slap.

"Susie!" he whispered against the door. "You're making me lonesome." And the way he said my name I saw the picture of Ricky Nelson with that handsome curl drooped wetly in one eye and the slight snarl of a song on his lips. I don't know why, but I ran to the bed and flung a pillow over my head.

"If you aren't the craziest thing," Mama said. She didn't even stop to put her robe over her slip. I heard her walk barefoot to the door and open it. "Hi there, Mister Bud."

"You're looking good," he said. "Those doolahlies do a wonder for your hair."

Mama laughed, touching one pin curl. "At the beach I've got to wash it every day."

"What's that ostrich doing yonder?"

I shook the pillow off and sat up.

"I've come to ask you gals up to the Lumina for some ice cream."

"Now that's real sweet of you, Bud," Mama said. "But what time is it? Your grandma lets Susie watch her show every afternoon. What time does your show come on, punkin?"

"She don't have to go with us," he said to Mama in a secretive, sidling-up way.

"Well, she *won't* miss that show, right, punkin? It's the Mouseketeers." Then she said to me, "Hey, you speaking today?"

"*I'm* not going to watch no damn Mouseketeers," I said, leaping from the bed in case she decided to swat my mouth, Bud Oleander or no Bud Oleander.

But she didn't come after me. She just stood staring, looking pale beneath her tan, like she'd seen a ghost. "You go in Bunny's room," she said quietly. "I want a word with you."

Bud Oleander laughed at my trouble, and I felt the laugh buzz all over my skin.

"Well, if you can go now, I'll be downstairs," he said. "Like I told you, she don't have to go with us."

I was crying when she came into Bunny's room and took me in her arms. It wasn't the cuss word. It was both of us putting him first. It made us strangers.

"Why'd you let him see you in your slip, Mama?" I cried.

"Oh, punkin-pie," she said in a voice that seemed fragile and see-through like lace. It enfolded and prettified my mean, ugly heart. There were little seahorse-shaped curls at the nape of her neck. The foamy scent of her sachet swirled like an undertow in the air between us. I felt doomed by her beauty.

He left Friday night, and we didn't see him for two days. Ophelia Roberts said he'd driven to Myrtle Beach for the weekend. There was a quarter-mile Killer Coaster there that he planned to ride a hundred times. He liked amusements, Mrs. Roberts said, shaking her head.

Saturday was so fine and clear that you could see Marvin Briggs's shrimp boats from our windows. Mama made time to dye Bunny's hair a shade called Queen of Hearts Red, only it took the color of canned peaches. But Bunny was proud and wrapped it up in wet handkerchiefs before she went on the beach so that the sun wouldn't fade it.

We painted each other's toenails, and Mama showed me how to use her eyelash curler that made my eyes not my eyes but more like Brenda Starr's in the comics. Mama said give me five or six more years and I might run for Miss America.

"She's got to have a routine first," Aunt Bunny said.

"She knows how to twirl baton, don't you, punkin?"

"I wish I'd brought it," I said. "I could practice."

"She's got to know how to twirl flaming torches and swords, too," Aunt Bunny said. "She's got to be able to make a spectacle."

Nobody talked much about Bud. But lying on the beach, sulky with hot sun and listening to the ocean's sweet talk, I thought of him often. Once it seemed that he came and stood over my blanket, and where the blue shark had been was a valentine with my name in the middle. He touched a finger to my lips and said: *Shhhhh.* He asked me to remember that Jerry Lee Lewis had *married* somebody thirteen.

Once, when Mama went down to the water, I asked Aunt Bunny how old did she think he was.

"Who?" she asked irritably.

"Bud Oleander."

Her mouth sobered and her pussy-willow lip seemed to darken. "Old enough to know better than to mess with a high-class woman like your mama" she said, "but young enough to try."

All Saturday we baked lazy in the sun and listened to Aunt Bunny's transistor radio. It was the sort of living that didn't need words. Nobody asked, Are you having a good time? or, What would you like to do? It seemed too much of an effort to raise a voice above the ocean. A few times I'd catch Mama looking out to sea toward the shrimp boats, her mouth in a small, tender knot. She hadn't gone out with Marvin Briggs in two nights.

After our baths we dried ourselves in front of the windows like before except for Aunt Bunny, who felt shy, I guess, because she was still so white from all the clothes she wore on the beach. "You girls are tempting a peeper," she said.

"He's gone to Myrtle Beach," I said.

She sat on the bed I shared with Mama and fingered her peach-colored curls. "You going out with Marvin tonight?"

"I don't think so," Mama said.

"You two have a little spat?"

"Not really." You'd have thought Bunny would leave her alone.

"I like for you to go out," Bunny said. "I like to imagine you having fun. I like to think *somebody* around here's getting satisfied." Then she started singing "Shrimp Boats."

She'd gotten too much sun and she picked at Mama that way all night.

"Well, if you haven't had a fight, what then? Let's get one thing clear," Bunny said. "You don't have to stay home on *my* account."

"You've got nothing to do with it."

"You're ruining your skin, you know," Aunt Bunny said to Mama. "You're as black as a nigra—maybe that's why Marvin Briggs ain't called, huh?"

Mama laughed wearily. "He's called twice, for your information. Ever think somebody other than Marvin Briggs calls the shots?"

"Well, go out all you like and pay no mind to me," Bunny

said. "I don't need Miss Popularity holding my hand at
night."

During the night their words slurred into the sounds that
finally woke me. I think, in my sleep, I must have heard the
cars cross the drawbridge, a singsong whine of tires whirring
fast on metal links. Or maybe the noise that woke me Sunday
morning was the cry of gulls disturbed from lazy gliding by
the first faint shrill of sirens as the grim squadron of cars left
Wilmington. I turned to Mama and saw she was up and staring out the window. "You can tell it's something terrible,"
she said. "Only I didn't hear a crash."

"Maybe a boat wreck," I said leaping out of bed.

"Something on fire."

We both sniffed, pressing our noses to the window screen.
I shivered despite the warm flickerings of sunlight butterfly-
ing across the floor. "Maybe some fisherman fell off the
pier," I said. "Maybe the whole pier caved in." Then I
realized that, without him here, whoever was in trouble might
just as well be Bud Oleander as anyone else. So I turned
away from the window, because that risked finding out for
sure. As long as there was no proof, I could put him in
Myrtle Beach or on the road home or anywhere I wanted. I
could keep him alive in my head as long as I wanted, even
if he was dead.

Maybe Mama was thinking like me, considering Marvin
Briggs now that I had suggested a boat accident. She left the
window and we crawled back in bed together. Maybe she lay
there dreading the hurt that comes from knowing too much
about a disaster: the telegram from Korea about Daddy,
barely a memory I can claim because I was so young. But
peculiar, aching words to her: noncombat death. She wrote
letters and uncovered a truth she could never talk about, and
the most I knew from listening to Aunt Bunny was that he'd
burned to death in some house.

We heard a knock outside, and I swallowed down my heart: cold it felt and as big as the doorknob. "It's Ophelia Roberts, girls," Mrs. Roberts said.

Mama jumped up, but I stuffed myself lower in the bed, shivering with goose bumps. I couldn't tell my skin from the sand in the bed. "Come in," Mama said to her, opening the door. "What's happened?"

"Glory-oski!" Mrs. Roberts cried, lunging into the room. She had on a frilly pink roller bonnet and black silk pajamas that Bud had bought her in Hong Kong. She wore a thick mask of cold cream. "Don't let me scare you," she laughed, seeing me staring, my mouth open. She turned to Mama and lowered her voice. "A body washed up close to the pier. Female," she said, hugging herself. "Bitten all up by sharks."

"*Sharks?*" Mama said.

"You don't want to know the details."

"Where's Bunny?" Mama said suddenly. She had stopped with three coffee mugs in her hands and turned slowly from the cabinet. "How can she sleep through all this?" She tiptoed to Bunny's room and cracked the door. "Godamighty! Mrs. Roberts, she's *gone*!"

"Don't worry," Mrs. Roberts said. "It was a nigra."

Bunny hadn't been able to sleep; so early, long before sunrise, she'd taken herself walking along the pier where the lights burned all night. A man was hauling in a skate, and everybody on that end of the pier had gathered to watch it gasp through its tiny, bitter-turned slit of mouth. Nothing was biting, nothing, they all said: a rough, tired-looking bunch of men, strange and pale as the creature at their feet. Their fishing rods extended from their torsos like third arms dangling toward the night water, joining them to the sleepless thrash of waves, but not for any profit you could figure. They were a type you never saw in the daylight, Aunt Bunny said.

They huddled over the skate, watching it die, poking it, flipping it over and over as if they suspected it might harbor something they hadn't seen before. After a bit they drifted once more to the railings. Then, when she believed they had forgotten it, Aunt Bunny quietly approached the skate and gently nudged it with the toe of her shoe, inched it toward the pier's splintery edge where she pushed it off, watching as it spun into the dark: a white, flapping kite of skin.

"What the hell you done that for, lady?" yelled a fisherman. "It was already dead. It was my breakfast!" He turned from her and began cussing into the wind. Along the railings men turned to see, and one of them raised his fist at her, his face an eerie blue in the dim pier lights. She'd had the sudden horror that they might throw *her* over, and she'd started backing her way down the boardwalk toward shore.

She reckoned it was his rightful punishment: the very man who'd snarled at her for losing his skate, hooking the body. Only none of them knew it was a body at first. She saw him jerk backwards, something in the water giving him a fit. All the men on his side recast, because something was running—mackerels or blues. He kept calling that his line was sure to break for the bigness of his catch. He yelled to Bunny she could come save this one, too, and everybody laughed. He wrestled it a long time, puffing and sweating, all the others gaping, with envy on their faces. The sea lurched black and curly with wind, and the pier rocked. It wasn't until the sky began to lighten that the man saw what he had on the line. He got sick then, and all the rest of them took turns holding the line until the police came.

"Did you see it?" Mrs. Roberts asked Bunny.

"Just what was left of the arm," Bunny said. "It looked like a beef tongue."

We were changed when Bud Oleander stomped in Sunday night. We sat with Mrs. Roberts in the downstairs parlor watching a family of clowns juggle bananas on "Ed Sullivan." Nobody laughed except the audience far away in New York City.

I felt old when I heard him whistling, fed up. The way he thrust himself into the room, well, it *victimized* you. Nobody nodded to him.

"Well, how are you doing, Bud?" he said to himself.

"Fine," he answered.

"How was Myrtle Beach?" he said.

"You should have been there," he told himself.

"Ain't he funny," Aunt Bunny said sarcastically.

"You got yourself some new hair," he said to her, then he pinched me lightly on the elbow. "Look at them jugglers. They're something."

"They're dumb," I said.

I don't know why we waited to tell him. It was a game, gulls only, making him the outsider of our news, holding back. Holding back felt like a sneaky, rock-bottom magic trick to make him seem smaller and less necessary.

"Need some supper, Buddyroe?" Mrs. Roberts asked, but he said no, he'd eaten in Wilmington.

A cigarette commercial came on the television: a man and a woman lit cigarettes in the snow and suddenly flowers started to bloom all around them and it was springtime. Bud watched the commercial and then he said, "I reckon you know all about that murder."

I felt my eyes zoom up at him then.

"We had *us* a drowning," Aunt Bunny said quickly, as if our surprise wasn't too late. "Right here on this very beach. And sharks."

"That's what I'm talking about," he said. "One in the same." Then he strode out of the room.

"You come right back here, son," Mrs. Roberts called after him. "That's no way to do."

He laughed at us in the kitchen. "I'll be there, Old Ma.

I'm cracking a cold one.'' There came the hiss and sizzle of a punctured beer can.

He'd heard the story when he stopped for supper at the diner in Wilmington. He'd run into a friend of his who worked the body squad. There had been an autopsy.

"Let me get something straight," Aunt Bunny said. She had a crybaby look on her face. "The drowning and the murder."

"One in the same," Bud Oleander said. He sucked beer foam off the top of the can.

"Miss Bunny was an eyewitness," Mrs. Roberts said proudly.

"Is that so?" He glanced at Bunny, who had begun rolling her socks up and down very fast with her palms.

"I saw the body," she said dreamily. "It was all torn to shreds. They *said* sharks."

"Wasn't sharks did the sort of damage I heard about."

"Let's go upstairs now, Susie," Mama said to me.

"It'll be in the paper tomorrow," he said. "They have to identify the body first before they make it public."

"I saw the body," Aunt Bunny said.

"You only saw the arm, now," Mama said. "Don't make it worse than it already is."

As soon as we realized there had been a murder, we started acting weird. Mama said, "We're leaving this place just as soon as I can pack." It was almost 11:00 P.M., but she stalked all over the room, picking up her hairbrush, then laying it down, opening a drawer and then shutting it.

"Wait until we read it for ourselves," Bunny said. "Maybe he's talking trash. I got three damn bites on my ankles tonight. Look at that."

"Maybe it's vampires" I said for no reason.

"Well, you kept rolling your socks down," Mama snapped. "All night long, rolling them up and down, studying yourself."

Mama and I got into bed and listened to Aunt Bunny brush her teeth three times.

"You going to turn out the light any time this year?"

"I got to pee first," Aunt Bunny said, "and then I got to brush my teeth."

Mama had gone downstairs to talk with Mrs. Roberts about a refund for the second week, and when I awoke I felt bruised from her tossing as well as my own. Aunt Bunny was already up, eating a donut and reading the *Wilmington Star*.

"*Was* it a murder?" I asked.

"Oh, *honey*." She looked at me as if she'd gladly trade places in a minute to be spared what she knew from her reading.

Mama came back upstairs and told us Mrs. Roberts had a no-refund policy and had already cashed and spent our check. "But I still think we should go on home," she said. "Everything's ruined now."

"It was a sex fiend," Bunny said. "A white man. There was some of his skin under her fingernails."

"I don't want to hear about it," Mama said.

"She got her picture alongside Ike's," Bunny said. "She was right attractive for a colored girl. Look. Front page news."

"Start packing, Susie."

"Y'all can go on and go," Aunt Bunny said with sudden fierceness. "Waste your money if you likc, but *I'm* staying out the week." Donut sugar littered her pussy-willow lip.

"What's wrong with you? You're acting crazy."

"If you'd seen that body, you'd act crazy, too."

"You got stuff on your mouth," I said, but she just glared and didn't wipe it off.

"I'm needed here," she said. "I'm a witness." She looked perfectly serious, but Mama laughed.

"You saw an arm. Period. That body could have washed in from Waikiki for all you know."

"I imagine the police will be wanting to speak to me," Bunny said. "They took down my name. I had a funny feeling all along that a man had done it. I expect they'd like to know."

"The fisherman who hooked the body—he's the only one they need to talk to," Mama said.

"I knew it was a murder all along," Bunny said. "I felt it and they need to know it."

"Well, while you're making up your mind I'm going to run and call Marvin Briggs and tell him good-bye."

"I've already made up my mind—don't you listen?" She plucked another donut from the box.

"Aren't you scared?" I asked her.

She shoved a big hunk of orange-colored bangs off her big blank forehead and sighed. "Susie," she said. "You just get to a certain age."

Marvin Briggs came over that afternoon while Bunny was grocery shopping, and he and Mama had a long, serious talk. Everything about him matched. He wore a pink-striped seersucker suit and a straw hat with a peppermint-colored ribbon circling the brim. It was his dandy's outfit, he said. He was on his way to sing barbershop quartet. Still, for a man, he seemed awfully partial to pink. His face was sunburnt and shaped like a beet; he rummaged in his trouser pockets and fished out a pink package of Teaberry gum.

"Have a stick," he said to me, grinning. "I'm sure glad you didn't go home." A police car cruised by and he waved at the officer.

"There's not much choice with Bunny behaving so strange," Mama said. "I guess we're safe enough. What do you think, Marvin?"

He peeled a stick of gum for himself. He rolled it up into

a neat little carpet and poked it under his tongue. "Police are everywhere. You're safe as the president." Gently he patted her hand.

"She's called the police station three times today. She's called the newspaper, too. It's all she wants to talk about."

"She's just upset. It was a shock."

"She just sits and stares and talks about it all the time."

"You need to get out, sugar," Marvin said. "We could go see a movie."

"I better stay close."

"You'd make this boy awful happy."

Mama smiled. "No, Marvin, I just can't."

"What can you do that the police aren't doing?"

"Me and Mrs. Roberts can look after Bunny, Mama," I said. "That Chinese checkers game is getting dusty."

Mama leaned over and kissed the top of my head. "Punkin-pie," she said. "Think it's safe to send her on an errand?" she asked Marvin Briggs. Another police car rolled by and this time I waved. "Run down to the Lumina then, baby doll, and get me a pack of Chesterfields."

The Lumina Pavilion was vast as a barn and cool, with salty-smelling dark plank floors, oily and gummy beneath bare feet. Upstairs was the ballroom where a band played every night. Downstairs you could play pinball or Midget Bowl while a rack of pink-and-blue teddy bear prizes gazed on. If you scored high enough, you won one of them.

There was a concessions stand at the Lumina where you could buy Sno-Cones, fried pies, ten flavors of ice cream, and foot-long hot dogs with sauerkraut. You could sit at the counter and sip a soda if you didn't mind watching a jug of pigs' feet close up. I liked to drink suicides. A suicide was a mixture of cola and grape and ginger ale and orange poured over crushed ice. I liked to listen to the jukebox, too: five hits for a quarter. There was usually some sailor hunched over the jukebox, hogging it, punching something like Slim Harpo's "Baby Scratch My Back."

I could stroll around the Lumina for hours, soaking up its twinkly, beachy spaciousness. But what I liked best of all, what I was drawn to most, were the LAFF-A-MINUTE mirrors. You could pose in front of them all day, watching your shape change for free. Because the reflections weren't really me, I suppose, I acted crazy in front of those mirrors. I contorted myself and flipped this way and that, crossed my eyes, made a snout face, did horse lips, did a log tongue, rolled my eyelids inside out.

I bought Mama a pack of Chesterfields and stopped by the mirrors. I'd been dancing in front of the Noodle Leg mirror for so long that I'd forgotten there was anything in the world left but silliness. I hardly noticed the other blurred pair of noodle legs wading behind me in the watery light. Then, suddenly, two hands clapped over my eyes and Bud Oleander said, "Guess who?"

It wasn't that I knew him simply by voice. I knew him so fast it was as if I'd been waiting for him. My skin lurched beneath his touch. I heard myself laugh like tooting through a straw. A whining, gay voice came out of me then, full of twirling and gush. "You cut that out," it said.

"Why, Susie-Q, I didn't know you smoked," he said, letting my eyes go.

I turned to face him, but I couldn't look him in the eyes. I stared at my toenails peeping out the lattice of my sandals: the Satin Doll polish had about all chipped off. "Now and then I do," I told him. "When I feel like it." I waited to feel guilty, but the lie felt absolutely right.

"Lemme bum one then."

I handed him the Chesterfields, believing it was a miracle, my meeting him alone. If I'd planned it, it would have never happened.

He offered me a cigarette. "Here, help yourself. Where's your mama?"

I took the cigarette and my eyes found a new resting place. I twiddled it in my fingers like a teeny baton.

"To my mind you favor your mama some," he said, striking a kitchen match on the leg of his jeans. "Here you go, gal. Grab a light."

"No thanks," I said. "I think I'll wait."

He laughed. "Okeydokey."

I kept thinking: Susie Higgins, you have got to look him straight in the face so that there will have been one close-up moment to remember forever no matter what.

"Why you reckon your pretty mama is so hot for Marvin Briggs?" he said right out of the blue. "She could sure do a whole lot better."

"She was going to be a movie star, before she had me," I said. "She sent Julius La Rosa her picture and he wrote her a letter once."

"What's this Marvin Briggs got up his sleeve?" Bud Oleander asked. Then he laughed and said, "Shrimp?"

"Oh," I said. "I expect she's in love with Marvin Briggs. He's rich."

He got quiet for a second and I could hear him sucking the cigarette smoke deep into his lungs. I felt glad I'd told him, whether it was true or not. I darted my eyes at his shoulder. "Marvin Briggs is most near her age," I said.

I snatched a quick glance at his face, but he was gazing at the rack of teddy bears. "I'll walk you back to the Charm," he said, and the tease was gone from his voice.

We left the Lumina not saying a word; he kicked a beer can all the way down the alley. I walked fast, feeling proud, feeling the coolness of his shadow on my skin. I knew that if Aunt Bunny could see me from her window, she'd tell Mama I was strutting.

When we stepped up on the porch, that's when it happened: quick like a cut, so that when he did it I hardly knew it or felt it because I hadn't had time to imagine it yet. He jerked me to his chest and kissed me so hard and fierce on the mouth that I forgot I could breathe through my nose and was panting when he pulled away. His lips looked red and wet as jelly.

"I'll bet you niggerlip your cigarettes," he said, wiping his mouth. Then a slow smile wriggled across his face. "You tell your mama that Bud Oleander don't kiss like no shrimp." He trotted up the steps of the Charm and went inside, banging the screen door behind him. For a long time it was all I could do to just sit still on the porch steps, feeling the kiss, second by second, dry on my lips. I wanted to lick over the kiss, retaste it with my tongue, but that would erase it. It was going by too fast as it was. I began to think that it hadn't really happened; there are some things that if they happen fast enough, *don't*. I tried to remember how it had gotten done. Where had our hands gone? Mine had simply disappeared. His felt like warm blurs: a pressure at my elbows, near my waist where my blouse bloomed loose from my shorts. It hadn't *really* happened.

Marvin Briggs said, "*There* she is. We were worried, Susie." He popped out the screen door and squatted down beside me. "What took so long?"

"I got a sand burr in my foot," I said.

I talked Mama into going out with Marvin that night; she needed calming. "For your own good," I told her in this worrywart voice, like I was the mother. So I didn't tell her that midway through the checker game, Aunt Bunny left and I couldn't stop her.

"I got to see about some things," she said.

"What things?"

"I need some sea breeze."

"You can't go waltzing out there by yourself," I said. "It's pitch black."

"No-siree-bobtail," Mrs. Roberts said. "Not if you value your life."

"I ain't some nobody nigger," Bunny said.

"But we're still playing," I said.

She heaved herself out of the armchair and the cushions wheezed and gasped.

"Why don't we *all* go?" I said.

Mrs. Roberts shuddered. "*I'm* not going out there."

"Let's ask Bud if he'll walk us down to the Lumina for some ice cream," I suggested. What a cheerful solution it seemed.

"Just what is this?" Aunt Bunny cried. "You don't tell me what to do. I can strip myself naked and run down the beach if I like." Then she clomped out of the room and the whole house trembled with her leaving.

"There's nothing you can do," Mrs. Roberts told me. "Let her go, she's a growed-up woman. It's your move, honey."

"Well, I'm going to get Bud," I said. Only I didn't get very far.

I might have told Mama about Aunt Bunny, but I knew she would ask why I didn't fetch Bud Oleander for help. I couldn't tell her about *that*. Down the hallway I saw that his light was on, and I might have knocked and entered easily except for the kiss. It was as if in those few close moments he had absorbed me in a blushing, private way, and I felt shy knowing that the next time we spoke there would be between us his knowledge of how easy I'd been, how wispy and small with too-wet lips.

Quietly I tiptoed past his room and out the screen door, creeping along the porch until I stood beneath his window. I felt crazy with power. The shade was drawn, but there was a tattery gap on one side. With my cheek pressed flat against the window screen I could see in. I would be able to watch him as long as I wanted, until my eyes turned to stars.

He was in there all right, sitting on the edge of his bed, touching the muscles of his arms and thighs, flexing himself. When he stood up, I saw that he wore only a pair of underwear. But I couldn't turn away. I felt a heat inside myself, both dangerous and exquisite. I was setting myself on fire on purpose. I watched as he swaggered across the room and stopped before a tall mirror hung on the back of the door. He traced the tattoo on his stomach with one blunt thumb. He turned around and around, studying his calves, his shoulders, jutting and observing every angle of his body, a sideshow muscleman.

His face was slack and distant. I should have been warned. I watched it, though, like I would probably watch the face of a ghost if one came toward me. Maybe he wasn't there. Maybe *he* was the ghost. It was as if he were feeling himself to make sure he was really there, to make sure he had what he needed to keep fooling other people that he was alive.

When he pulled his underpants down and revealed himself then, I knew I'd been waiting to see if he would. I felt rippled, like I was nothing but water. He was small and white there like something you'd thread on a hook, but as he filled his hands with himself, it looked as if he held a club.

He turned to face the window, and I ducked and jumped over the porch railing, smashing into the sand, flattening myself to its coldness. The night was so quiet that I could hear the fiddler crabs crackling in the sea oats. I started to cry because I'd seen so much, because there was no taking it back and what did it mean? I saw his room go dark. Then I heard a rustling in the dune grass and from a clump of moonlit sea oats Aunt Bunny said, "I saw you."

Finally my own craziness rose up to be recognized. It slid from me as if summoned, gliding across the sand to meet an ally. A feeling of losing myself passed over me then. It was not unlike Bud Oleander's kiss.

Aunt Bunny walked on the beach every night after that, and I said nothing. She dressed up. She left her knee socks curled in a drawer, and she wore charm bracelets and so much rouge that she finally looked sunburnt. She'd wait until Mama and Marvin Briggs had gone out, then she'd roll up her hair and sip on a beer. Sometimes she'd ask me to zip her up or hook her bra for her. Most nights, before she went out, she'd call the police station to hear if they'd caught the murderer yet.

I ached to go home, where I hoped my old self waited, where perhaps all our old selves waited: our smells haunting clothes left in closets, the old innocent shapes of our fingertips pressed into what would be bone-dry soap. I almost believed the letters we would find in our mailboxes would bear unfamiliar-looking names on the envelopes.

I wanted Mama to guess of my trouble, and I begged her with my sullenness. I hoped for some silent code that would flutter between us, swoop past my brooding and shame. But I couldn't tell her. The words cowered in my throat and she went out every night. She laughed too loud and her bright teeth made me blink. She woke me when she came in late and I could see her red lips in the dark. I could hear her humming some dance tune, the rustle of a crinoline as she dropped her clothes in a chair. Her perfume seemed to grow all over the room like a jungle. When I finally fell asleep, I had nightmares. Once I dreamed of myself as Bud Oleander kissed by Bud Oleander.

On our last afternoon at Aurora Beach, he asked Mama for a date. He swaggered noisily up to our rooms without a shirt, drinking a Blue Ribbon beer. "I've been too damn patient," he said.

"Too late, that's all," Mama said coolly. She was ironing a pair of turquoise pedal pushers that Marvin Briggs had bought her.

"I sent you a message, honey," he said. "Ask Susie what it was."

Mama rubbed her eyes as if to be rid of him. She unplugged the iron and wound up the cord and hummed "The Tennessee Waltz."

"Hey, you want to go dancing with me tonight, Susie?" he said directly to Mama.

"She's too old for you," Mama said.

I thought he would laugh, but he didn't. He slammed his empty beer can on the table and left.

"Don't have anything to do with that boy," Mama said to me. "He's a loser. And crazy, too."

"Everybody's crazy," I said. "I can't stand it."

But it was her last night to go out with Marvin Briggs, and she stepped happily into the blue, freshly ironed pedal pushers, grabbing my shoulder for balance. All she cared to know right then was if they fit.

Aunt Bunny was still in the tub when Marvin came. "You wait on her to finish," Mama told me, her voice full of a light, whispery ignorance that I hated. She called good-bye to Bunny, and Marvin made a little joke about not getting sucked down the drain. He left two sticks of Teaberry on the table for us, but I chewed them both.

I just sat down at the table and chewed the gum, lost in the sugary juice of it. After a while I concentrated on the sounds of Bunny's bath, the squeak of her slippery fat skin against porcelain. It was as if she were so heavy that the water grunted under her weight. I heard the prickly sound of a razor going up and down her legs, then a rush and swirl of water as she climbed out. She tiptoed to the doorway, a towel wrapped around only her waist. Her breasts were enormous, the nipples brown and hairy as macaroons. "Susie-Q," she said. "Run ask Mrs. Roberts for some fresh towels. These in here are as soggy as wet bread."

I stood up slowly, stretching like I had all day. "I ain't no slave," I mumbled low-down, and I walked to the window and looked out. "I think it's going to rain," I said. "There's no moon and no stars."

"You deaf or something, Susie-Q?"

"I'm going," I said, but instead I sat down on the bed and ruffled the pages of a magazine.

"You're going, all right," she said irritably. "Going crazy."

"I'm on my way," I said, but somebody knocked on the door. Bunny jumped back inside the bathroom, maybe the tub.

"Who is it?" she called as I opened the door.

There stood Bud Oleander. He grinned, his tooth winking. "Who's going to be my woman tonight?" he said.

"Who's that?" Bunny called again.

"It's Jack the Ripper," he laughed, stumbling against the door. I smelled the sweet-and-sour smell of his drunkenness. But he'd dolled himself up some, had on clean blue jeans and a long-sleeved white stepping-out sort of shirt. You could smell the laundry detergent in the shirt where he sweated. He had on an ID bracelet around his left wrist. "So where's my woman?" he whispered close up in my ear. "Where's my woman?" he shouted at Bunny. The words left breath-steam on my skin, drying up quick like the kiss.

"You just hold your horses now," Bunny said, giggling.

"Susie-Q! Take a dollar out of my billfold and run out and amuse yourself awhile."

"You don't have to go," Bud whispered. "Wake up, Little Susie," he said, touching my shoulder.

"Not me." I shoved past him then, and I ran.

I ran hard toward the Lumina, and only the wind felt real, slapping my skin, tangling my hair. It was the wind and not my legs that took me along. In one terrible moment I wondered if I had risked Bunny's life, because a murderer hadn't been caught and certainly Bud Oleander carried a fish scaler in his pocket. Finally, I thought I understood the kind of death Bunny had sought, walking the beach alone at night. It was my easiness and her readiness that I had confused.

I did not stop in front of the LAFF-A-MINUTE mirrors. I went right up to the snack counter and bought a pack of Chesterfields that I never opened. I simply held the Chesterfields, rubbing the squealy cellophane with my fingers, staring at the jar of pigs' feet like I could stare at it all night. I wondered if the toenails on the pigs' feet were soft from their long soak in the vinegar. The evening went right along; I could hear the band upstairs playing a polka. I bought a Sno-Cone and two Nutty Buddy ice creams. I spent the whole dollar. I amused myself.

When I returned to the Charm, Aunt Bunny was washing out two coffee mugs and the seashell ashtray. Her hair looked wild and lopsided. She was wearing a bathrobe you could see her nipples through. "Lord, it's almost eleven o'clock," she said. "I was getting real worried about you, Susie-Q." But she spoke so strangely soft I could hardly hear her. She did not go back out on the beach that night, and she was the first one of us packed the next morning. I was watching her from our window as she loaded her suitcase into the car trunk. I saw Bud Oleander walk past her and blow her a kiss.

☆ ♡ ☆

Driving across the singsong bridge, Mama mentioned that the night before a gang of boys had thrown a manikin off the Crystal Pier. Marvin had heard about it before he picked her up. It was a terrible joke and they ought to have been arrested, Marvin had said.

I felt a chill when Bunny laughed. She threw her head back against the seat, and her entire body went sloppy with the laugh. She blushed a porky red and continued laughing until she had to wipe tears from her eyes. I thought I'd missed something on the road—a Burma Shave sign maybe, and I glanced over my shoulder to see. "Boys do like their amusements," Aunt Bunny said.

Mama laughed, too, then. Not a fake, emptily agreeable laugh, but one that swelled and burst all over the car. There they both were, laughing together, pals. The laughter made me feel I should have expected it, wanted it. But in the backseat I drew myself into a ball: the only one of us scowling, with what seemed a deep truth creeping over me, deep as drowning. Together they sailed away from me, safe and intimate and so easily rescued by the laughter that I wished I felt jealous.

"Think they'll ever catch the murderer?" my mama asked.

Aunt Bunny giggled. "Poor thing if they do."

And I was sure that I felt him: smuggled into the backseat with me, his head on my lap, his mouth making a moistness on my knees where he breathed. I scooted across the seat and rolled down a window. I leaned as far out as I could, gulping air, feeling its pale, heavy lash. Aunt Bunny grabbed my arm and jerked me back inside the window and told me once she had read of a girl who lost her head that way, riding into a tunnel.

I pulled away from her. I moved across the seat to the

other window and hung myself out where nobody could reach me. Where I could just be myself for whatever gloomy truthful time I had left.

CAMOUFLAGE

☆ ♡ ☆   ☆ ♡ ☆   ☆ ♡ ☆

She was only sixteen, and hers was a difficult labor with complications. Earlier that afternoon, when the contractions had started, Mary sat on the divan, calmly timing them by the mantel clock, waiting for her mother to emerge from her bedroom, perhaps take charge. Her mother was drunk. Finally Mary called Alexia, her older sister, and it was Alexia who drove her to the hospital and held her hand off and on all night until the doctor ordered a Caesarean. Alexia kept taking cigarette breaks for which she apologized, but Mary was secretly glad whenever Alexia slipped away. She relished the chance to die—for surely she was dying—without frightening anybody who knew her. Whenever Alexia left the labor room, Mary screamed. She was sick and tired of bravery.

The baby was normal—that's all the doctor told her. A girl with reddish hair. The doctor lay the child casually on Mary's chest as if Mary were a shelf. Instinctively she touched the top of the baby's sticky head and felt life beating furiously: the eager, steamy warmth of it, the warmth dissipating into the cool, stoic air of the delivery room. She longed to cradle the child against herself but felt too shy. She wanted to press it against the cavelike void of who she'd been once. Who was she now? She wanted the child to make some sort of difference, to heal her from her vague, repentant self. What did she have to repent now that it was over? The baby lay upon her, soft and pink like gathered flowers. When she began to cry, a nurse scooped her up and swaddled her in towels. Mary never saw her again.

She slept a sleep like falling: there was pain when she hit bottom. She awoke, crying from the pain of her incision, but also crying from some darkly unimpeachable center of herself where she knew her suffering was for nothing. A nurse brought her medication and she slept until late morning. She dreamed that Jim Davenport stood over her bed with a paper cone of flowers. In her dream he was as old as her father. He combed his thinning hair backwards, and you could see the furrows left by the comb. He talked of bank loans and car repairs and where you could still get a good shoeshine cheaply. He talked as if she were on his list of things to do.

Yet, when she awoke, she half-expected him to be there. She'd known he wouldn't be, known he never would be again. Still, she kept wishing for him—it was the only thing that made her heart feel alive. If only the doctor had been able to deliver her from foolishness, too. You got rid of your innocence, but that was nothing, really, in the great foolish scheme of your life.

She couldn't eat breakfast. Looking at the tray nauseated her. She drank a few tentative sips of hot tea. The epidural hadn't worn off, and she wasn't allowed to sit up. A nurse helped her with a sponge bath.

Around eleven o'clock Alexia appeared with their mother. Mrs. Spencer was wearing dark glasses that she didn't take off. Her smile wobbled, but she bent and kissed Mary lightly on the cheek and handed her a heart-shaped package with a glamorous pink bow.

"How are you feeling today, hon?" Alexia asked, brushing her hand across Mary's brow in a motherly, fever-testing way. She'd bought a *People* magazine in the lobby and placed it on top of Mary's bedside table. One of the buttons on her car coat was missing and so she'd fastened the coat together with a diaper pin. She looked tired, ragged. She was nearly thirty, with three young children and a husband who traveled during the week. She patted Mary's hand. "Life will get back to normal now. You'll see."

It was what Mary wished her mother would say. But her mother only walked to the window, parted the shade and looked out, silent. Her mother didn't act like a mother anymore. It was like she'd given up: there had been one disappointment too many. She walked haltingly, like an invalid.

Most days her mother slept until noon. She hardly cooked anymore. For her supper she ate ice cream out of a paper carton and drank a glass of sweet sherry. She never argued. If something disturbed or angered her, she'd retreat to her bedroom and cry. She'd hardly said a word about Mary's pregnancy. She'd neither condemned nor consoled. When Mary had tried to talk with her, she'd stared out the nearest window as if she were dreaming up a plan, as if advice were on the tip of her tongue if she could only order her thoughts. She'd acted aloof, and, considering her circumstances, it had been easy to mistake her aloofness for courage.

But Mary had looked out windows, too, into the bleak, resourceless night of her decision, enduring Alexia's heartless wisdom. "It's a family tradition," Alexia had said. "Husband *then* baby."

The nurse came in and gave Mary two pills: one for discomfort and one to dry up her breast milk. "What a pretty package!" the nurse exclaimed. "Now that should cheer you up."

Mary's mother turned from the window and smiled. But the smile had no energy source. It came from nowhere and went nowhere like a statue's.

"Open it, Mary," Alexia said.

She drew the heart-shaped package into her lap and loosened the ribbon. It was candy: expensive-looking chocolates wrapped in golden foil. The sort of gift that reminded her that her mother didn't know how to go about knowing her, the sort of gift that unleashed unexpected sadness. She'd already opened Pandora's box, hadn't she? Last April in the backseat of Jim Davenport's car. The awful surprise of how easily it had happened. She'd thought of sex as some sort of complicated contraption that she could never fathom: too many nuts and bolts to unloosen, too many opportunities to be clumsy, to wreck the mission, snared zippers, tangled straps. She'd believed that passion required dexterity. But passion had grown its own quick fingers, appendages that bloomed magically in exquisitely empowered places.

Nobody felt like talking, but Alexia tried. She tried to avoid talking about her children, but Alexia wasn't very good at talking about other things. She brought out a piece of quilting from her handbag and talked about that. In a little while, she excused herself to the lobby, where she could smoke.

"Well," Mary's mother said, sitting down in a chair, folding her hands together. "Why do you suppose Alexia smokes? *I* never smoked."

There seemed nothing to talk about because everything was known. Mary tried to guess the weather, thinking that her mother's dark glasses were a clue. "Is it sunny out?" she asked, feeling stupid and inadequate.

Her mother started to cry. "How can you forget all this?" she said. "You'll have that awful scar."

After Alexia and her mother left, two girlfriends, Bev and Lisa, dropped by. They were the only friends she'd kept up with since she dropped out of school that fall. They brought flowers and ate the chocolate candy and turned on the television to watch a tennis match. They'd gone to the Homecoming Dance on Saturday night, the night Mary was having the baby. They said the dance was "pathetic." Mr. Houston, the machine shop teacher, and Miss Keck, the art teacher, had gone out to dinner before the dance and gotten wasted. Then, they'd fallen all over each other, dancing at the gym. They'd done the Dirty Dog and the assistant principal had made them leave. They'd probably get fired.

A lot of the students had come to the dance drunk or stoned. Some sophomore boys got arrested in the bathroom for fighting, ripping toilet seats off their hinges and using them for weapons. Everybody said that David Cannon and Jim Davenport were so stoned that they traversed the entire school parking lot by jumping from car hood to car hood. "Oh, *sorry*," Bev said, casting Mary a guilty look. "I guess it's pretty tacky of us to mention Jim Davenport."

"He didn't bring a date," Lisa said in a conciliatory way. "And he looked totally miserable." She popped a piece of chocolate candy in her mouth and leaned toward the television. "What a bod," she said to the tennis player.

"Who got crowned Homecoming Queen?" Mary asked.

They made similar faces of disgust. "Candace Yardley," they said in mincing, jeerful voices. "The dream whore."

Whore. The word seemed to darken the room like the curse of an uninvited witch. But Mary saw by their bland, unremorseful expressions that Bev and Lisa hadn't heard what they'd said. How pure and changeless they were. Mary laughed, but not for the reason they thought. She felt *relieved* that all of it was lost to her. It had been lost to her while she was pregnant, but in a different way: the kind of losing in which what's gone is gone but you still yearn for it. Now, hearing about the Homecoming Dance, she felt absolved. Her baby seemed a living, breathing talisman against all trivia. Even Jim Davenport. Especially Jim Davenport.

"Jim Davenport," she said stonily, and her friends looked

at her. "Jim Davenport. Krispy Kreme. Mello-Yello. Disneyland. King Kong."

Her father had been out of town on business, and since his divorce from her mother his contact was infrequent at best. He said he wouldn't have even known about the delivery if he hadn't bumped into Mary's mother in the grocery store. "So she told me," he said, shaking his head. "Right there in the grocery store while she examined apples for bruises. 'Oh, by the way, Fred,' she says, 'it's over.' " He sighed ruefully. " 'A head of lettuce, a dozen eggs, a baby.' "

Mary squirmed beneath her sheet.

"She didn't really say it like that," he said.

"Please, Daddy," Mary said, but she was glad to have him there and didn't give her request the force of a protest. It was a cajoling voice she used, so wry it made him smile.

He kissed her on the forehead.

He was only forty-eight, but he had a sober, grandfatherly air, sitting on the edge of her bed, his shoulders stooped, his hair silver and wispily receding from his forehead. The gold-rimmed glasses he wore gave him a fragile look. When he leaned forward to kiss her, she smelled the professionally starched aroma of his shirt. He always carried a handkerchief in his pocket. When she missed him most, she missed the way he smelled, smells that evoked sensations of ritual and order: shoe polish and aftershave and cinnamon-flavored toothpicks.

He held her hands for a moment, rubbing them, and then in an odd, congratulatory voice he said, "At least you didn't marry your mistake."

That night she thought a lot about her mistake. She supposed she should hate the baby now, hate how it had changed her life. But she didn't hate it, had never hated it. The truth was that having the baby had made her feel bolder and expansive. She was not just herself anymore. From now on she was herself *and* a baby, filling up two places in the world, not one. They would be absent from each other but never alone. Invisible threads of love would always connect them.

The counselor from the Crisis Pregnancy Center had come by the hospital to talk with her, encourage her to express her anger and sorrow forthrightly. When Mary could only talk about the invisible threads of love, the counselor looked concerned. When had she decided to give the baby up? Whose decision had it finally been? Alexia's? Her father's? Mr. and Mrs. Davenport's? Her own? All she remembered was that the decision had been made long before she ever held the baby. There was every reason in the world to give the baby up except one: its quickening luster as it lay upon her at delivery, its power to make her feel necessary.

Nights in the hospital when she couldn't sleep, Mary imagined that her body was telling her that somewhere her baby was wakeful, too. She envisioned its adoptive mother slipping on a bathrobe to warm milk for a late-night feeding. The mother held the baby in a room silvered with moonlight and the milk had a sweet, flowerlike scent. The woman who held the baby was learning to love it. She'd been wanting a child for many years and Mary had granted her a miracle.

In this way, thinking about what the pregnancy counselor had said, Mary calmed herself and didn't feel expendable. Sometimes she even pitied the adoptive mother whom she imagined feared the baby in the dead of night, feared its insatiable needs and eventual understanding, perhaps wondering if she could ever love it enough. For it seemed to Mary that the baby would almost expect to be loved more by a woman who was not its natural mother and yet had so fiercely chosen to rear it. That a child would be infinitely comforted by the knowledge that it was no accident in the life of such a person.

Then, on the last day of her hospital stay, when no visitors came to distract her, Mary began to believe that she'd made a terrible mistake, giving the baby away. That it was the baby she needed more than anything else to help her distinguish what truly mattered from what did not.

She was released from the hospital on Thanksgiving Day. Bruce, Alexia's husband, came to get her and drove her straight to their house where Alexia was making Thanksgiving dinner. Mary's mother was already there, sitting in the den, watching a Snoopy cartoon special with the children. She waved at Mary from the sofa and smiled her distant smile.

Alexia threw her arms around Mary and made a big deal of her arrival. "Look how skinny you already are!" Alexia cried. "It's always taken me six months to get my figure back." She was drinking a glass of wine and she poured one for Mary. "Cheers!" she said.

They'd never been particularly close, Alexia and Mary. They were thirteen years apart. But Mary sensed a new bond now, the sort of bond in which Alexia acknowledged Mary's adulthood in the generous-spirited way of friends rather than with the investigatory rivalry of sisters. They were actually drinking wine together; it felt peculiar and cozy.

Mary sat on a kitchen stool and chopped up celery for the salad. Bruce carved the turkey so attentively that it looked as if he were repairing something. Each slice was paper-thin, and Alexia was so pleased that she threw her arms around his waist. "Hey, you'll mess me up," he said.

"I'd love to mess you up," Alexia said with a low, throaty laugh, and they exchanged an intimate look.

Bruce laughed at her. "Better watch the wine," he cautioned.

Alexia reached for the bottle defiantly and sloshed out another rosy glassful. She held it up and stared at it intently until Bruce noticed. "What are you doing *now*?"

"I'm *watching* the wine," she said.

Bruce put down the carving knife, grabbed her wrist and pulled her against him. They kissed a long time until finally Mary left the kitchen. She felt light-headed, squirmy with embarrassment. It was too warm in the kitchen, too suddenly sentimental. It felt like Bruce and Alexia were cooking valentines for dinner. They seemed on display to her, their behavior, like Alexia's sterling flatware, reserved for special occasions only.

Most of the time Bruce was gone, traveling. And so often she'd heard Alexia say that he had a short fuse, sounded off at her and the kids for the least infraction. Nothing very passionate or romantic ever came to mind when she thought of Alexia's marriage. They had money enough, but Alexia didn't seem to care. She spent the money on furniture and forgot about the way she looked. She dressed like a slob and her hair was a mess. She ran around in a shabby, unstylish coat fastened with a diaper pin, taking care of kids with chicken pox, coping alone. With Bruce away, Alexia slept alone five nights a week. What had she been after in the first place and where had it gotten to?

Mary slipped on her coat and walked out into the backyard to the swing set. She slumped down on the sliding board and her hips just fit within the narrow borders. She began to think about her baby. But her sense of the baby was different now than it had been at the hospital. What would she have named it? ''Christabel,'' she said aloud, as if to make the baby more real. Already she could feel the whole experience slipping beyond her, the invisible threads of love thinning. She could almost imagine that it had never happened, and it seemed that the rest of them were eager for her to forget. Chopping celery in the kitchen, talking about getting her figure back, hearing the comforting hum of the Snoopy show in the background, giving birth had begun to seem like just another kind of domestic event. First you are in one place, then another, misfortune simply part of the landscape of travel. That simple. Having a baby had been like stopping off for a minute in a ghost town. You certainly couldn't get off the bus and stay. There was nothing for you there, so you just rode on and you didn't ask where.

"Christabel," she said again. Why had she thought of such a name? It came from something she'd read at school. Some poem. It sounded antique and breakable. Sweep up the pieces and throw them away.

Alexia opened the back door. "You feeling okay, Mary?" She could tell by the casualness of Alexia's tone that they expected her to act weird. "Eke's coming out to join you," Alexia called cheerfully.

That's right, Mary thought, pretend to the crazy person that you think she's normal as pie.

Eke hopped down the back stoop wearing the roller skates she practically slept in and her Walkman. She was ten years old, Alexia's only daughter. Her real name was Ethyl, the same as Bruce's mother. Eke liked to say that when she first heard her name, after she'd quit gagging, she'd screamed "Eeek!" She skated expertly across the wintry grass and flopped, belly first, into a swing beside Mary.

"Want some gum?" she asked, digging into a pocket of her skintight jeans. She had long, brittle-looking, coltish legs. She gouged out a piece of Bazooka.

"Thanks." Mary opened the gum and read the fortune aloud: " 'Love conquers all.' "

Eke sneered. "I hate fortunes like that. It's like the pamphlets they give you at Sunday school. It's like the damn Care Bears."

"Please," Mary said. "My stitches. It still hurts when I laugh."

"Mom sent me out to tell you dinner's almost ready," Eke said. "You want to listen to the Pre-Minstrels first?" She took off her headphones and offered them to Mary. "This group is monumentally sick," she said fondly.

Mary put the headphones on and listened for a while.

"Bet you think they're called the Pre-Minstrels because of PMS, right?" Eke said, grinning. "Wrong. They're called the Pre-Minstrels because none of them have started their periods yet. These chicks are all eleven years old. And foxy."

"They sound a little like Madonna," Mary said, thinking she was being complimentary, but Eke made a face and looked insulted.

When Mary took the headphones off, Eke said more softly, "I'm sorry you couldn't keep the baby. Mom said it was a girl." Eke shook her head and gestured toward the house where her younger brothers were still watching cartoons. "Boys are such a pain," she said. "Damn," she said, "a girl sure would have been nice."

They ate Thanksgiving dinner on Alexia's new dining room table with Queen Anne legs. Alexia acted nervous. She made the two boys eat with their fingers rather than utensils they might use to bang on the new table. One spilled his milk, and after she'd mopped up the spot with a damp cloth, she brought out furniture polish, too. The bitter smell of the polish sickened Mary and she excused herself.

"Go lie down in Eke's room," Alexia said kindly. "I know you must feel worn out, hon."

Eke's room was painted black. Neon-colored posters of rock stars papered the ceiling. A mishmash of bumper stickers plastered the wall above her bed: ARMS ARE FOR HUGGING. IF YOU CAN READ THIS GET OFF MY ASS. LIFE SUCKS AND THEN YOU DIE. On the bed lay a worn-out Raggedy Ann doll, her hair restyled in a Mohawk, her skirt trimmed to mini length. She had diaper pins for earrings.

Mary stretched across the bed, closing her eyes, but she couldn't fall asleep. Downstairs voices praised the meal. She could hear the twinkling babble of china and silverware, ice rattling in glasses, sounds so reassuring and homey that she felt gathered-in. For the first time in a long while her heart felt quiet; she was back in Little Girl Land. She would go to the private Catholic school across town like her father wanted. He would pay the tuition, and she would make new friends. Her past wouldn't follow her. She'd forget the invisible threads of love. She'd stop wearing makeup, let all the blond grow out of her hair. Cut her hair short. Cut her fingernails and resume piano lessons. Make good grades. She'd be a better friend to Eke, help Alexia more with the kids. She'd invite her mother to go to the movies. They'd take old-fashioned dancing lessons together at Fred Astaire. They'd dance *together*, no men.

It exhausted her to think about all the possibilities, the choices. Pick a card, any card: the magic trick of life. She felt dizzy the way shopping for pantyhose always made her feel dizzy. There seemed an overwhelming amount to decide: not just color and size but seamed or seamless, textured or nontextured, control top, sandal-foot, reinforced toe, cotton crotch. Why should variety blow your circuits? Why should choice feel like punishment? Maybe she was crazy. Maybe you couldn't go through what she'd been through without going crazy. Her hands felt for the spot on her chest where the baby's weight had rested. She couldn't remember, not the color or the size. She pressed her chest until it hurt.

The door cracked open suddenly and Eke poked her head into the room.

"I'm not asleep, it's okay," Mary said.

"I caught a fly for the Lord," Eke said, skating over to the window ledge.

Mary thought she'd heard wrong and sat up.

"I-doo-widdy-caught-a-fly-she-bop-she-bop. I-doo-widdy-caught-a-fly-for-the-Lord," Eke sang.

"Did I die?" Mary said. "Is this heaven or hell?"

Eke laughed. "He's my lizard," she said. "Actually my *anole*, if you want to get technical." She opened a small plastic cage and released the fly she'd caught. "Lord *Alien*," she said softly, unabashedly tender the way children are around animals they love. Her broad goofy smile, with its missing teeth, gentled her, made her spiked, carrot-colored hair and earrings seem an illusion, a special effect.

She set the plastic box on the bed and they watched Lord Alien stalk and devour the fly. "He likes you, Mary," Eke said knowingly, pressing her lips on the cage as if to kiss the lizard. "He's putting on his happy suit."

Obligingly the lizard turned from a mottled brown color to the luminous green of a blade of grass. Eke laughed and said, "He's a dude. Work out with him, Mary." She put the cage in Mary's lap.

"What do I do?"

"Just be his friend. Sing him a song. He likes reptile music."

Mary giggled. "Such as?"

"Try 'Glow Little Glow Worm'—Grandmother Spencer sings that to him. Or 'Puff the Magic Dragon.' Now *that* one inspires him."

Mary tried to imagine her mother singing to the anole and wondered if she'd been drunk. She sang one verse of "Puff the Magic Dragon" but felt silly.

"Look at him eyeballing you," Eke said. "He acts like he's in complete control."

"He's got no choice," Mary said, leaning closer to study him. She felt a swooning sensation. His beauty seemed remote and powerful. He knew absolutely who he was. She was astonished by his feet, so fragile and digital, the long toes—if that was what they were really called—almost transparent, splayed, his little haunches resting on a leaf, positioned the way puppies cooled themselves on the floor in hot weather. His color was that livid green of the objects she had always imagined were most alive: big gracious summer trees, ferns that thickened early in the woods. His scales were as tiny and metallic as dots of dime store glitter. All the while she gazed at him, his own eyes swiveled at odd angles to detect and diminish surprise. "He has *ribs*," Mary said reverently. "I want to hold him."

Eke scooped him quickly from the leaf and drew her hand slowly from the cage. "He's really freaking," she said.

Mary slipped her hands around Eke's and felt the cool, sticky flesh of the anole fluttering against her palms. Carefully Eke withdrew her hand and Mary clasped her palms together, upright, prayerful. The lizard's head poked out between her thumbs. "Hello there," she said. "You're a dude."

"One good squeeze and he'd be lizard soup," Eke said.

"I'll put him back now," Mary said. She felt unaccountably sad. The lizard made her feel bigger than she had a right to be.

Eke fed him a couple of mealworms, in honor of Thanksgiving, then Lord Alien crept under a slab of bark and turned gray. He looked exhausted, or maybe Mary was. She flopped across the bed, and Eke went outside to rollerskate.

Mary wondered what it felt like to be cold-blooded. It seemed to her a terrible fate, a cosmic shunning. A kind of stark and absolute apartness, like floating in outer space. Not to be able to warm oneself or another. Touch made no difference in such a life. No-frills survival, Mary thought, drifting to sleep. No one expects a thing from him and he expects nothing in return, his existence singular and detached. There was true but abominable peace in such a thought. She imagined that she felt the dark weight of sleep settle on her, encase her protectively like a strange new skin.

The days prior to Christmas were long and shrill with cold. She'd dropped out of school fall semester and wouldn't begin at Catholic Academy until mid-January. Occasionally her friends Lisa and Bev dropped by to visit, but she refused to go out with them to places like McDonald's or down to the Rexall for a smoke—they were still sneaking *cigarettes*!

Once her dad invited her to lunch and she went. She wouldn't be seen by old high school acquaintances midday at the Steak & Ale. With her father she felt safe and, in an embarrassed way, womanly. She'd had a baby, after all, and he was her father who knew it. There seemed so many silences to fill that sometimes she dropped her fork on purpose, just to make a sound, just to have something to do. Three mornings a week she baby-sat so that Alexia could go to aerobics classes at the Y. Eke and her older brother, Brucie, attended school, so her only charge was Spencer, the baby.

Spencer was two and into everything, but Mary enjoyed his busyness. She made clay for him out of salt and dough, and they built simple things: totem poles and rainbow-colored snakes. On sunny days they trooped down to the barren winter park and collected sycamore balls, acorn crowns, rocks with mica, bottle caps. Once in a while they baked cookies. Sometimes she'd turn on "Sesame Street" and leave Spencer to his own devices. Then she'd go upstairs and feed Lord Alien mealworms, talk to him the way she might have written in a diary. Sometimes, and she knew this was crazy, she felt they understood one another. But then, just thinking of him that way, like a confidante, made her shake her head and laugh. Had she really gone backwards to this: such girlish safety and goodness?

Bev and Lisa bored her. They wanted to be friends with her, she could tell, and they tried hard. But she suspected that they only tried out of pity or out of an obligation to protect her from being a total outcast. They thought that she'd have nobody were it not for them.

Their sympathy, vast and ready, was ultimately self-serving. They tried to be her friends because they were curious. *Who was she now?* She was different and remote and her knowledge was forbidding.

Once, while Spencer was watching television, she imagined she was his mother, home alone with him all day while Jim Davenport worked. She planned to make spaghetti for supper and a chocolate pie. She planned to dress up, to bathe the baby and dress him in a fresh outfit before Jim came home. They'd be waiting at the door for him. All of them would eat dinner by candlelight and listen to soft music on the radio, and she and Jim would lean across the table, while the baby smiled at them, and kiss this glorious victory kiss. She held up her skirt in front of Eke's dresser mirror and gazed at the scar that spanned her pelvis. Then, she called Jim Davenport's number, but when his mother answered she hung up.

She tried to befriend her mother. Near Christmas they went shopping together. Her mother drank three cocktails at lunch and started crying in the lingerie department of Thalhimer's when Mary suggested that they buy a gift for the pregnancy counselor.

She tried to discuss their mother with Alexia, but Alexia defended her. "Look," she said, "it all makes perfect sense. Mom's miserable towards Daddy because he left. She's miserable towards me because I was their big mistake. She's miserable about you because you remind her of everything she threw away when she was seventeen. No wonder she sulks and tries to anesthetize herself. Look what a price she's had to pay for a few seconds of pleasure back in 1957. Except it's not really pleasure when you're so young," Alexia said grimly. "It's something else, but I sure wouldn't call it pleasure." She lit a cigarette and blew the smoke out through her nose.

"You think if Bruce left me, I'd act any different from Mother? Be any less miserable? Hell, I'd be *more* miserable, honey, because I'd be in jail. I'd have shot the bum."

When Eke got home from school, she begged Mary to take her to the Natural Science Center to see a special exhibition of reptiles. They took Alexia's Honda, and Eke played a tape by her latest favorite band, a British punk group called Edible Body Parts. Listening to the lyrics made Mary feel old: the arbitrariness of meaning, the aimless, chaotic rhythm. The music sounded goading and hostile, victimizing music like *na-nana-na-na* chanted cruelly out school bus windows. Mary imagined the band members spitting on an audience of cowering, tattered orphans. When she glanced at Eke, Eke was snapping her fingers to the beat, glassy-eyed.

It occurred to her that Eke might be experimenting with drugs. Mary had watched Alexia and Bruce roll a joint now and then, but they were always discreet. She wondered if Eke were happy. She wondered why every little girl she'd ever known, herself included, tried to rush life. She wanted to say: Don't do it, and her hand shot involuntarily from the steering wheel and closed over Eke's, squeezing it. Eke's hand was small and warm and dry, the stubby fingernails painted tomato red. It was difficult to imagine such a hand holding pills, a joint, an anole all in the same day. But Mary knew anything could happen nowadays and usually did.

"I knew you'd dig this group," Eke said, squeezing Mary's hand back. She closed her eyes and miraculously mouthed the nonsensical lyrics.

At the Natural Science Center they watched the feeding of the boa constrictors. A handsome young man offered the boas live mice. He talked a kind of lullabye talk to the snakes as he handled them. He called them names like Adam and Eve, and the audience laughed. He had strong, brown, sinewy arms. He wore a Hawaiian-style shirt printed with tigers and palm trees; the shirt made him seem exotic. Mary watched the young man entangle his arms with snakes until she felt she couldn't breathe, it was all so beautifully ghastly.

Once the young man smiled directly at Mary. He had a brown beard and kind brown eyes, and the smile should not have mattered, should have seemed the throwaway sort. Except that the young man's gaze lingered and appraised with an eagerness she hadn't earned. She left the room and went to the ladies' lounge and, inexplicably, washed her hands. She tried to summon a memory of her child. She took a brown paper towel and wrote "Christabel" in lipstick, folded it, and stuck it down inside her brassiere. Just let him try something funny, she thought. Just let him try.

Outside the bathroom, near the rocks and minerals display, she saw Eke, talking to a boy, holding hands. The boy was taller than Eke with longer hair and a bracelet. If she'd had a bad dream she could not have dreamed up worse. "I'm going," she said curtly. *"Now."*

Eke dropped her friend's hand and scurried after her. "Where'd you go? I looked everywhere."

But Mary didn't answer. "Who was that boy, Eke?" she cried as they buckled their seat belts. "Level with me. What in the hell are you up to?"

Eke looked at her as if she were crazy. "What are you talking about?" she said, incredulous. "That's my friend Angelica."

"Yeah, tell me another one," Mary said. "I know them all."

"What is this, the Inquisition?"

"Yes!" Mary shouted, slamming on brakes. "At the rate you're going, you'll be pregnant at eleven." She laughed bitterly. "Pregnant and foxy."

"You're weird and you're freaking me," Eke said, unbuckling her belt. "I'm getting out."

Mary lay her cheek against the steering wheel and began to cry. "Please don't get out, Eke," she said over and over. "Don't leave me."

"Okay," Eke said, touching her shoulder. "Just please stop acting like Mother for a while."

They drove on for several blocks in silence. "Maybe I

need glasses," Mary said. "I mean if I thought Angelica was a boy."

"She's no boy," Eke sneered. "What an insult. Can we stop talking about her now, please?"

"I'm sorry, Eke," Mary said. "Sometimes I just forget."

"Forget?"

"Forget that you hate boys," Mary said.

"I hate the veritable guts of all boys," Eke said.

Mary smiled. She began to understand just how far she had traveled from innocence. When was the last time she had held a girlfriend's hand in public, swinging it, believing that touch was the most honest language of friendship?

The day before Christmas Eve she saw Jim Davenport. She was in the park with Spencer, playing hide-and-seek among the beech trees. Up the hill, on the opposite side of the park, she saw Jim Davenport walking with a girl. Most likely it was one of his sisters, but she couldn't tell. All the Davenports were tall, and this girl was as tall and slim and dark-haired as Jim. They wore shirts of similar plaid and they weren't holding hands. Mary's heart began to pound, but she was certain nobody could recognize her from such a distance. To them she was just some little tot's mother, out for a morning baby walk.

It was the way Jim Davenport walked that disquieted her; his kicking a can or a rock up the hill with each pace, a walk with a kind of disengaged energy. He hadn't been changed by any of it, had he? Still performing that glib, wasteful stride of energy without purpose that everybody young performed. The walk reminded her of the way he'd moved against her, planting her flesh with the hard sapling force of himself. In his hands she'd parted easily like soft earth.

Back at Alexia's she tried not to think of the way he'd kicked the can up the hill, his lean, tight, vigorous thigh. Alexia called and asked if she might go out to lunch with a friend, so Mary made sandwiches for herself and Spencer, then she put him down for a nap. She leafed through a *Good Housekeeping* filled with Christmas recipes, crafts, and fashions. She wanted Christmas to be over and January to arrive with piles of snow and people so bundled up that you couldn't recognize them, couldn't determine the shape of their bodies, male or female. Maybe she'd cut her hair short like Eke's and wear no lipstick like Angelica.

She went to the refrigerator and took out a couple of mealworms. She felt sorry for them in a way. Taken from their limbo of cold storage, they came alive gradually, seduced into activity by the heat of her hand. Awakened only to be devoured.

But the anole wouldn't eat. From beneath the slab of bark his eyes glinted dully. She put his cage under Eke's study lamp to warm him, but he flattened his head and closed his eyes. She dropped in a worm anyway, but he ignored it and slept. She watched him sleep. She imagined herself shrunken to his size, sleeping beside him. She wondered if it would matter, if her presence would be more comfort or burden. If only his lips were not so set. If only his face moved in recognition of her or his eyes lightened. It was his sameness that seemed merciless.

When Alexia got home, Mary was crying. She couldn't tell her why she was crying because Alexia would think she'd flipped out. A pathetic incommunicado lizard was dying, that's all. He was dying absolutely alone, lost in the outer space of himself. Why did she want him to feel otherwise?

Alexia held her for a while and rubbed her back. "It's probably just now hitting you, like a death," Alexia said. And Mary cried all the harder for Alexia's incomprehension. What was wrong with her that she'd never cried so hard about losing her baby? Somewhere deep within her she was dead to it all. She pretended otherwise to the adults in her life, but it had never been very real to her, the baby. She struggled from Alexia's embrace because she didn't deserve it. Alexia smelled of another life—restaurant spices, perfume. She was wearing little silver wishbone earrings.

"What nobody ever tells you, growing up, is that it's going to be one damn thing after another, plus MasterCard debt up to your eyebrows," she said. "A baby you didn't plan, a man you shouldn't have married, an unhappy love affair." She looked away quickly and lit a cigarette. "I ought to write a song," she said. She drew deeply on the cigarette. "Don't ever tell."

Mary felt confused, uncertain what her sister meant. She felt a heaviness in her chest, truth seeming to beat her from within like something trapped against its will. She wanted to touch the truth like she'd wanted to touch her baby, but she felt shy and out of place. The truth felt too soon for who she was. It had an aura like a flower picked from someone else's garden.

"Don't ever tell what?" she asked.

Alexia laughed, but without humor. "About *life*. It can be your revenge on the innocent. They have it too easy."

"Too easy?"

"Never mind," Alexia said briskly. "I keep forgetting you're just sixteen. *Sixteen*." She said "just sixteen" with a gift-giving exuberance. But when she repeated the word, she lingered over it as if trying to figure out how she could keep the gift for herself.

Eke and Brucie had gone to visit their Grandmother Ethyl in the mountains and wouldn't be back until tomorrow, Christmas Eve. Mary missed Eke. If Eke were there, she'd know what to do about Lord Alien, and Mary thought of calling her long-distance.

"He's been acting that way for days," Alexia said tiredly, flipping through her *60 Minute Gourmet* cookbook. "Frankly, I wish he'd go ahead and die. I hate keeping live worms in the refrigerator.'' She slammed the cookbook shut and said, ''Let's all go to McDonald's tonight for supper.''

Mary winced. ''I don't want to go to McDonald's. It's so . . . public.''

''So's life,'' Alexia said, ''if you're to be any good at it.''

On Christmas Eve afternoon Mary called the Natural Science Center to inquire about anoles.

''You'll have to speak with Mr. Morrison, our naturalist,'' the secretary said. ''Hold, please.'' Mary listened for a while to a simpering recording of ''Love Me Do.'' At last the secretary returned to say that Mr. Morrison had gone home early. After all, it was Christmas Eve. ''But we'll be open December twenty-sixth,'' the secretary added brightly. ''Happy holidays.''

''Excuse me,'' Mary said, her voice resonant and forthright. ''This may be a matter of . . . life and death.''

There was a pause. ''May I ask who's calling, please?''

''Oh, I don't know Mr. Morrison, if that's what you mean,'' Mary said. ''I'm calling about a very sick animal.''

''What kind of animal?'' She sounded relieved. ''Maybe someone else could help you.''

When Mary told her it was an anole, the secretary admitted that anoles were Mr. Morrison's specialty. She took down Mary's name and number and promised to contact Mr. Morrison. ''I'll have him call you just as soon as he can.''

All afternoon, even through dinner, Mary crouched by the telephone biting her fingernails the way she used to while she waited for Jim Davenport to call. Eke came home and told her she was acting insane, but Eke had been grandmothered to death by Ethyl and was in a bad mood. ''Let him die if he wants to,'' she said sullenly. ''He knows what he's doing. Next time I'm getting a hermit crab, and I'm naming her Ethyl.''

Alexia called everybody to come string popcorn for the

Christmas tree, but Mary sat solemnly by the phone. She wasn't thinking about the anole anymore—this was the curious part. She'd begun to think wholeheartedly of Mr. Morrison.

Which one was he? She'd visited the Natural Science Center many times, strolling through the glittering displays of rocks and minerals, saltwater fish in shallow tanks, dinosaur bones, space technology. There were several friendly young men who worked there, eager to be asked questions, eager to show off their knowledge, their bravado. They could hold tarantulas without flinching, pressure an alligator's jaws into opening. They gathered up the snakes like jump ropes.

Was Mr. Morrison the man with the coiled brown muscles ready to spring from his tropical jungle shirt? The man with the soft-looking brown beard and eyes that had sorted through the crowd to smile at Mary?

Downstairs she could hear Alexia and her family singing carols, pulling it off: love and dissatisfaction co-existing. Love and grief. Love and loss. Even her mother was downstairs singing—what a miracle!

She imagined the phone ringing and Mr. Morrison speaking to her. She would describe the Lord in great detail, only certainly she would have to call him something else. She would posit theories: Was he depressed? Would he be happier with a mate? She heard herself laughing into the phone, yet telling Mr. Morrison: *"Don't laugh."*

And what if something should come of it? What if they continued talking, she and Mr. Morrison, and he was only a little older and they liked each other? What if she followed his expert advice and the anole got well? What if he called her back to check and she said yes, happy and grateful, and he was flattered and asked her out? Would she wear lipstick? What if he invited her to become his assistant at the Natural Science Center? What if her job was to hand him the mice to feed to the boa constrictors? Well, she would just have to be brave, wouldn't she? That was part of the deal.

Waiting for the phone to ring, a kind of greed rose up in her and she acknowledged it, indulged it, her hand poised over the telephone, poised to receive. Wouldn't she feel the ringing first in her bones, her skin humming with its summons as if touched? Listening, she could feel herself brightening into the hopeful girl she could not for the life of her resist.

TOY PARIS

☆♡☆ ☆♡☆ ☆♡☆

And to think that I thought Doug Reilly would last! What was I supposed to think and how long was I supposed to think it? Just yesterday Doug Reilly and I went Christmas shopping together and kissed snowflakes off each other's eyelashes. We exchanged gifts: I bought him a watch; he bought me a sweater. Of course he probably only bought me the sweater out of pity. So that I wouldn't freeze to death when he asked for his varsity jacket back.

Well, the timing couldn't be worse. Just check out your new watch, Doug Reilly. Only three more days until Bernadette Spivey's Christmas Eve party. It's going to be a mistletoe jungle at Bernadette's, and what's Christmas Eve without romance?

So I'm thinking this way, gruesome, glowering, slamming my empty locker shut like it's my dead heart, when Robert Redford saunters down the hall. Not *the* Robert Redford, silly. Just that plain, skinny sarcastic kid whose mother probably star-struck out on movie mags during her pregnancy. Like why would *the* Robert Redford be cruising around our wormy high school? Checking out the competition? Ha!

Anyway, as he passes me, Robert "Grade B" Redford says jeerfully, "Gee, you're pretty when you smile."

I curl my lip at him. "Hello, Grade B," I say. "Created any horror flicks lately?"

"Ah" he says, "the girl of my screams."

"So why should we wait to get married?" I say.

Ask anybody. I'm a beast when I don't have a boyfriend. Although leave it to my older brother Harrison to remind me that I'm a beast when I've got a boyfriend, too. Then I start worrying about losing the boyfriend. I get into perfecting things, according to Harrison. I act lofty and serious and doomed. Harrison says that when I've got a boyfriend I've got too much time that's not filled up with *want*. I'm best at want. Failure and suffering become me. But then Harrison is this dreamy philosopher type, and he does ramble on and on.

All the way home from school I try to imagine things worse than they really are. It calms me down. For example, I'm picturing myself not at Bernadette's without a date but in the most forlorn places I can think of: the dentist's office for an emergency root canal or seated in a carved-up school desk at the echoey center of a deserted gymnasium—the only beet-head who signed up to take SATs on Christmas Eve. But it feels good, this mental torture, like the dreamy controllable pain you feel when you press on a mouthful of new braces.

Then I get home and everything goes haywire plus. First off I see that Mom's not perched in front of "General Hospital," as usual, eating her Milk Duds. I don't smell anything remotely resembling supper, and Wednesday nights we always have spaghetti with a special sauce that Mom simmers all day. The house looks bleak; the television is cold to the touch. I holler, Is anybody home?

"Upstairs," Mom answers dimly.

She looks like *she's* just broken up with Doug Reilly. She's lying facedown across her bed, cradling a box of pink

Kleenex. She's wearing her ratty chenille bathrobe that she puts on whenever she's sick and her tennis socks with pompons and her green beach flip-flops. I know. It sounds crazy— tennis socks with flip-flops in the dead of winter—but that's just Mom. She even cuts slits in the socks to accommodate the rubber thongs. She says flip-flops are the answer to her prayers—whatever *that* means. It's like other things she says, for instance her expression, "Well, I'll be a ring-tailed tooter," whatever *that* is. It's certainly nothing you'd ever sit down and analyze. Ordinarily she's kind of overly happy and sort of a goofball, so when I see her distraught like this, it gives me pause.

I pat her shoulder and take a guess: "Mr. Rogers got killed." I mean Mr. Rogers our tomcat, of course, a cat with no humility. A cat who chases cars and bullies the German shepherd next door.

"I wish," Mom says rather heartlessly, snapping a Kleenex from the box. "It's your brother Harrison."

"*Harrison's* dead?"

"Of course he's not dead!" she wails. "Sometimes, Sunny, you act like you're from outer space. Do you think I'd be sitting here like this if Harrison were dead?"

"I *am* from outer space," I say defensively. "And what would you be doing?"

She looks absolutely shocked. She stops crying. "I don't really know," she says. "I'd be out of my mind." She gestures disparagingly at the wads of spent Kleenex littering her bed. Her face turns quirky and luminous. "Oh, Sunny!" she exclaims. "Maybe this is nothing to cry about after all." She sits up and says bravely, "The dean called this morning. There's been an incident. If it was drugs, they'll kick Harrison out of school. He'll lose his *scholarship*!"

Now I haven't seen Harrison since he went off to college in September, but the last time I checked he was this bookworm poet type, and the biggest drug-related trouble he'd ever gotten into was for chewing Aspergum during Sunday school. Of course, people change.

The story went that Harrison and three of his buddies, all of them good boys, scholarship students, student council types, had *volunteered* to shovel snow from their dormitory walkways. Harrison was the one who went over to Maintenance and got the shovels. It was still snowing. Everybody was feeling good: Christmas spirit, youth. Exams were over. Then, somebody tossed the first snowball and, one by one, they laid down their shovels and started pitching.

When a campus police patrol car cruised by, the officers only smiled and waved. And when the students aimed a few mischievous shots at the police, the police got out of their car and returned the volley. It was a friendly, kidding exchange. But in no time the pace of the throwing quickened; the snowballs began to *thwack*. Then, a headlight in the patrol car shattered, and the policemen waved for the boys to stop. But they didn't. It was as if they couldn't. It was as if they weren't who they were supposed to be anymore, the dean had said in a spooky, sinister way.

Instead of stopping and apologizing, the boys let loose a last barrage of snowballs, then turned and ran. All of the boys eventually turned themselves in, bedraggled, frozen, bewildered—except Harrison. Much later, when it was dark, he'd slipped into his dormitory and gone to bed like nothing had happened.

"The dean's at a loss," Mom says. "It seems a bit much to blame on high spirits."

"Harrison's coming home tonight, isn't he?" I say, patting her shoulder. "We'll just *ask* him why it happened."

Mom gives me this look like what a dunderhead! Then her face seems to crumple in her hands like a pushed-in paper bag, and she starts crying. "It's drugs," she says, "I just know it."

I go downstairs and start the spaghetti sauce. I use purple

onions instead of the yellow ones. It's a bet I make with myself that Dad will ask what those purple things are in the spaghetti sauce. Dad's a detail man. He used to be a troubleshooter for this huge tobacco company. Then he struck up a pen-pal relationship with the surgeon general somehow—they even exchanged birthday cards—and eventually Dad made an appointment with Dr. Seigfrid Zweigenhaft, the hypnotist, and completely gave up smoking. He didn't get fired from the tobacco company because *he* quit smoking; he got fired for appealing to his co-workers to do the same. The surgeon general wrote him a letter of commendation that he had framed. Now he works at the local newspaper, where he writes a consumers' complaint column called "Outrage."

Everything changed after Dad lost his tobacco company job. He joked about his "downfall," but the truth is that he and Mom acted goofy with happiness—a couple of ex-flower children who, having strayed from the faith, were finally getting back to basics. Dad sold his fancy foreign car and Mom took a part-time job as weekend projectionist down at the Rialto Theatre. Mom said all she'd ever wanted anyway was for Dad to stop smoking cigarettes, no matter what the consequences. Dad said, Well, here's the consequences, driving up in this heap of a station wagon that was to tide us over until we could afford something better. It was a '69 model. At one time somebody had painted marijuana plants on the hood in psychedelic colors that you could still see through its cheap new paint job. Oh well. It was a deal, wasn't it? It ran, didn't it? It got us where we wanted to go. Dad and Mom sang the car's praises like they were tickled to death over *what*, I'd like to know. I named it the A-Bomb, short for abomination.

But that's just the tip of the iceberg. You want to know what's wrong with my family? Everybody's always talking cheer around the awful truth, so that when the truth hits, they don't recognize it; they're not prepared; they're knocked winding. You want to know why I'm so cynical? Well, *some-body* in this family's got to be.

So anyway, while I'm making the spaghetti sauce, I'm *not* dreaming of a white Christmas, no sir. Here's my forecast: smog, chemical spills, volcanic ash. Things are about as pre-deep tragedy as they can get: even Mom's flip-flops look depressed. Harrison's flipped out and he's the *stable* one in the family, Mr. Scholarship. Now Dad's due to rumble up any moment in the A-Bomb, his eyes fiery with rage over things like goofed-up roller balls on deodorant roll-ons. Suddenly, when the phone rings, I jump for it like it's some kind of lifeline out of this quicksand we call family.

"Boohoo," Bernadette Spivey says, "I'm so sorry to hear you and Doug Reilly broke up."

"I wasn't good for him," I say. "He needs a cheerleader type."

"How did you guess? He's bringing Trixie Sprinkle to my party. I just hate her prissy cartwheels, don't you? Anyway, I hope you're still planning to come."

"I don't think so," I say forlornly.

"You don't have time to sulk. Get cracking, Sunny. Only three more shopping days left."

"Don't worry," I tell her, "I've already bought your present."

"Don't be such a beethead. You *know* what I'm talking about. Hohoho!" Then she lowers her voice and whispers, "I hear Robert Redford's on special."

"The brand's familiar," I say, "but aren't sales always for stuff you don't need?"

Bernadette clucks her tongue at me. "You know," she says in a fed-up way, "he's the only person I can think of who's smirkier than you."

After we hang up, this Robert Redford Horror Show plays in my mind. Robert Redford, the Brain that wouldn't die. Robert Redford, the Talking Head. I close my eyes but I can't get shut of his clever, smirky face, those lips just percolating with wiseguy remarks. Hey, Bernadette! We're talking about a date for Christmas Eve, not Halloween!

I cover the spaghetti sauce and turn the stove dial to SIM-MER. I slip on my Red Riding Hood–style cape and walk toward the park. It's snowing hard, but I need out, and Toy Paris is waiting. She could care less about the weather. She could care less about just about anything except me.

Yes, already I see her. She sits on the little stone bridge that spans a creek. She waves. She's wearing her plastic, leopard-skin mini-skirt and red high-top sneakers with purple shoelaces. In spite of the snowy twilight, she's got on dark glasses. She's bundled up in the black leather jacket with a skull-and-crossbones embroidered on the back. Heavy, her boyfriend, gave her the jacket. He's the lead singer in this famous band called Conqueror Worm. They're madly in love and I think they're secretly married, only Toy Paris won't say. Anyhow, they do incredibly romantic things like taking candlelit bubble baths together.

Toy Paris is very beautiful in a tough and scraggly way. Her wild red hair seems to leap like flames away from her heart-shaped face. A little diamond tiara rests tipsily on her forehead. Today her lipstick and fingernail polish are black and give her a spooky, graveyard look.

"Yoohoo, Sunny, where you been?" She offers me an opened pack of cigarettes, but when I shake my head she laughs and says, "They're only bubblegum."

Maybe I should laugh, too, but I don't. It irks me for her to clown around. I like Toy Paris to act hard.

"So, long time no see," she says.

"I've been trying to give you up."

"Everybody needs a fairy godmother, Sunny," she says, dauntless.

"It's such a crutch, though," I tell her. "I'm fifteen. I

should be able to cope. What's wrong with me that I can't? That I start feeling pitiful and lackluster?"

"Did you and Doug Reilly break up?"

"Let's just say your spell wore off. One of us turned back into a toad."

"Whoa!" Toy Paris shouts at me. "You aren't losing your *sang-froid*, are you?"

"Worse than that," I tell her gravely. "I'm losing a sense of what I *want*. Listen," I say, cautiously. "I thought I wanted Doug Reilly to take me to Bernadette Spivey's Christmas party. Yesterday it seemed real important to me, and now it just seems trivial."

"Hey! Trivial! I can really dance to that, babe!" Toy Paris swivels her hips. "Your wish is my command."

"Other things are happening," I whisper. "Harrison's in trouble. Drugs, maybe."

Toy Paris hoots in my face. "You know what Harrison's notion of a drug is?"

"Aspergum," we say together.

"So, hey! Let's worry about *you*, toad," Toy Paris says. "Think only of Bernadette Spivey's Christmas party. Forget Doug Reilly. I can arrange something better. Who'd you like to go with?"

"Who do you think would be good for me? Who might last?"

"Whoa, Sunny." She puts up one palm in protest. "I don't do philosophy. If you want me to deliver the goods, you got to say what you want."

"Happiness."

"The blue bird of? Come *on*, sunshine."

"Love."

"Too general."

"Okay, okay," I say wearily. "How about a ring-tailed tooter?"

"Now that's what I call growing up!" Toy Paris sneers.

"Thanks anyway," I tell her hastily. "I guess I don't feel much like playing anymore. Happy Christmas, Toy."

"You wouldn't recognize happiness if it sat on you," Toy Paris says.

"I know that it's too much to ask for," I say grandly. "That it's murky. It blinks off and on and makes you think that you're getting somewhere and you *are*, but then suddenly you aren't. A date with Doug Reilly solves nothing, really."

"Bingo!"

"So I wish you'd stop pretending otherwise."

"Wish granted!" Toy Paris says huffily, and when I blink, she's vanished. The spicy aroma of her perfume drags at the dark, snowy air.

Now I'm sitting on the bridge crying, feeling really stupid and cold. If I don't know any better what it is that I want, then how can I assume that it's lost to me forever? But I'm crying as if I expect this lonesome moment to last forever, to ice me out like some dagger-shaped snowball slammed into my heart.

Then, two real, warm arms encircle me from behind and Harrison says, "Found you! I followed your tracks. Mom guessed you'd come down here to talk with Toy Paris. Hey," he says, lifting my chin in his hand and studying my face. "Tears?"

I shrug. "You look great, Harrison," I say. "You don't look crazy at all." I can't believe I say this, but it's such a relief to see him. He looks like an elf, his cheeks and nose rosy from the cold. He's not wearing a hat and the snow melting in his dark hair, which he's let grow longer, is making his cowlicks stampede. There's something older, something proven-looking about his face, too.

"You've grown a mustache!" I exclaim.

He grins, but his look of concern quickly returns. "You all right, Sunny?"

"Heard of the Stone Age?" I ask.

He nods.

"The Dark Age? The Nuclear Age?"

He nods.

"Well, I'm living in the Endless Age," I say.

"It gets better," he says, pulling me close. "I'm living proof."

"*You're* living proof?" I say bitterly. "Poet turned maniac?"

He laughs and hugs me. Then slowly, arm in arm, we walk home through the glamorous, lacy weather and he tells me everything.

During dinner Dad says *always* read the ingredients on candy bar labels to see if the list includes real chocolate. Mom mentions the blitz of trashy movies down at the Rialto lately—all about teenage hostility and waste. Dad asks what the purple things in the spaghetti sauce are. I talk vaguely about the demise of Toy Paris, how she and I sort of duked it out in the park, how lately she's gotten kind of mean and uncertain and how, really, what a baby thing it is to have a punked-out imaginary friend.

"Not really," Harrison says, helping himself to more spaghetti. He gives me a conspiratorial wink. "Not if it helps you talk about your problems."

Of course nobody has brought up the problem of the snowball incident, and this is just so typical. Everybody's chitchatting away, pleasant, loaded with holiday spirit, a family you can really live with. If everything can *seem* normal, then the snowball incident isn't even an issue anymore. And maybe it never even existed. Merry Christmas and pass the garlic bread! Happy parents! Happy teenagers! Mom's wearing her gold hoop earrings and party caftan. Would you believe that she's dressed up her flip-flops with festive little sleigh bells? Am I the only one of us who remembers her stretched across the bed all afternoon, sobbing? Did I *dream* it? Which is my dream and which is my life? Did I dream the time I caught Dad trying to summon Toy Paris for advice? It was right after he'd left the tobacco company and everybody thought he was so happy.

"About Harrison's snowball fight," I say, puncturing all their cheerful little balloon faces. Well, *somebody* has to do it, right?

Mom and Dad look up, startled, forks of spaghetti held mid-mouth.

"You can relax," I tell them, my voice resonant with authority. "It wasn't drugs." Then I say, matter-of-factly, a diagnostician, "It was simply high spirits. Mom and Dad, Harrison's *in love*."

Harrison blushes deeply when I say this, but he's glad I've told.

"It's a weird story, right, Harrison? But he can explain everything." When I look at Harrison, though, I'm not so sure he *can* explain everything. His whole expression has turned daffy at the mention of "love."

But Mom and Dad aren't listening for explanations. They exchange quick, blissful glances, and it's as if they never doubted things wouldn't turn out okay. They do this silly routine of tapping their spaghetti-filled forks together like toasting champagne glasses. Then they kiss. Right there at dinner: SMACKO. Proof all around me that love is all that matters.

"What's her name?" they ask eagerly. "What's she like? Oh, Harrison!"

Harrison gives me a shy look, then he takes his plate and holds it up for them to see. The spaghetti's all gone. He's picked out chips of the purple onion and arranged the chips to spell out ROSEMARY.

Now I ask you: do I belong in this family? Why, it's such a heart-melting little scene that I'm not sure I can live through it in solid form. I'm thinking that after supper we should just all pile into the A-Bomb and go Christmas caroling. Everybody around this table really cares about something, really cares about someone. Maybe they're really happy after all and not trying to fool anybody. Maybe *I'm* really happy, too, but don't quite recognize my luck.

When Harrison ran from the campus police, he'd ended up hiding in a graveyard behind the college chapel. He'd hunkered down among the tombstones until dark, listening to police call his name through a megaphone.

"Weren't you scared?" I'd asked him when he told me the story as we walked home from the park.

"I felt *invincible*," he'd said dramatically.

"But there you were in a graveyard!" I cried. "A fugitive from justice."

"I know," he said. "I'd done something *really* crazy." He didn't mean the snowball fighting; he meant the running. "I'd acted wild and stupid. Then I kept on acting wild and stupid. That was the mysterious part. It felt so *good*, this craziness. How long could I make it last, knowing as much as I do about smart and stupid?"

Then Harrison explained that the colder he'd gotten the more he'd thought of the people he loved: Mom and Dad, me, Rosemary. And the more he'd thought of the people he loved, the more he'd sensed that love and protection and forgiveness were always waiting at the end of the craziest craziness he could devise, so why rush it? The craziness was teaching him something. A new perspective. Appreciation, maybe. It was as if he suddenly knew that all the shelter and privilege in his life were worthless if he couldn't hold himself back from it. He needed to lose it for a while in order to believe it. "It was a chance to see the wonder of my life from a distance, Sunny," Harrison had told me.

I think about all he said in the park while I wash the supper dishes. I'm trying hard to make his sense of appreciation fit my own life. But Harrison's in love, and I only feel wishful. He'd said holding himself back from the wonder was part of the wonder. But it seems that I've come to a kind of bursting point in my life, and I just can't hold back serenely anymore. Maybe I scare the wonder away. And when I do put on the brakes and try to wait, it seems I'm only waiting for the worst to happen.

Outside the snow has stopped. In the honey-colored glow cast by our porch light, the lawn looks as ornate as a wedding cake. I think of Toy Paris and how she used to be. In the old days, when I first invented her, she seemed much older than me. She had all the answers, the admonishments, the rules for success. She wore twinkling, fairy tale dresses, and wild birds perched on her shoulders. She preached patience. She talked about the future, not now. *When you grow up* was how she began her advice. And the sense of postponement had felt delicious to me rather than agonizing.

Why is it that people always talk about the fabulous advantages of youth? The word itself has a spirited, uplifting sound: youth. Like *zoom*. So why do I feel immobilized by it?

The phone rings, and Harrison leaps to answer it, expecting a call from Rosemary. "Long distance," he says quizzically. "For Sunny."

"For me?" I say. "But I don't know anybody long-distance."

I take the receiver and say, "Hello?" and an operator's flat, unexcitable voice says, "Miss Sunny Gillespie?"

"Yes?"

"Go ahead, sir," the operator says to the caller.

"Is this *the* Sunny Gillespie?" a man's voice asks. It's a warm, dreamy, important-sounding voice. "Hello? Sunny? This is Robert Redford calling you from California. Your friends have told me all about you, and let's just say I'd like very much to meet you. What say we shake up the town and I take you to Bernadette Spivey's Christmas Eve party?''

I'm stunned, breathless. I don't even think that I'm waiting for a joke to be declared. I'm simply waiting for my wits to assemble so that I can *speak.*

"Hello, Sunny?" says *the* Robert Redford. His voice makes me think of poured caramel. "Sunny Gillespie?" The way he says my name—it's like a roll call from heaven! And still I can't speak. What would I say if I could? Finally it's as if I'm caught up in some horror movie gimmick: desirous woman trapped in body of awkward, ineffectual girl.

Harrison notices the stricken look on my face. "Who is it, Sunny? What's happening?"

Then, in place of that handsome silkified voice, Grade B says in his normal, sarcastic, and freckly honk, "Good impersonation, huh? I faked the operator, too. I have range."

But the weird part is how relieved I feel. A clearing in the muddle of my heart presents itself. What would I have done if this dream of Robert Redford had come true? Now really think about it. Which is my dream and which is my life and which do I want it to be? What should I wish for? *Don't say a boyfriend, Sunny! If you say a boyfriend then the world will shrink so small that only toads will be satisfied to live and dream here.*

"Range," I say suddenly. But am I talking to Grade B Redford? A funny thing happens when I say the word. It's as if the restlessness and fakery and yearning and mockery of my Endless Age is filling up my heart a whole new way. Becoming a kind of heart's fuel, necessarily volatile to zoom me in directions I haven't yet dreamed.

"Fooled you, didn't I?" Grade B says smirkily.

"You're good," I say, "but you're not *that* good." See,

I know my lines by heart. But let me try one wobbly ad lib here: "Grade B," I say, "hey, Merry Christmas anyway."

NO NEWS

☆ ♡ ☆   ☆ ♡ ☆   ☆ ♡ ☆

Bobby Rex didn't get famous overnight. I knowed all along he'd get a name for hisself, but he wasn't no overnight star. He was picking guitar, Pa says, when he was eight. Bobby Rex would say, "No, Pa. You forget. I was six. For Christmas you and Ma gave me that plastic crank-a-tune job. But I started using the strings. Remember, Pa?" But Pa always argued that Bobby Rex was eight and that no six-year-old knothead could play no guitar. And now Pa got away with it cause Bobby Rex wasn't around to defend hisself. I would've been on Bobby Rex's side, only I wasn't born yet when Bobby Rex was six. Pa even told the man from the newspaper who come by for an interview that Bobby Rex was eight when he first played guitar. I wrote that to Bobby Rex in a letter once, but he never said nothing about it when he wrote back. So I guess he didn't worry what Pa said anymore.

The first time I knowed Bobby Rex was going to be famous was the night I went with Ma to the homecoming dance over at the high school. There wasn't anybody to stay with me at home cause Pa was at the tobacco auction in Zanzibar and Paddy was going to the dance herself. Ma was going to pour punch, and I had to sit in one of them cold slick folding chairs that circled the shiny gym floor. Bobby Rex was the main attraction, and I felt real proud when he come out on stage and all the girls cooed and crinkled their faces at him. His brown hair swooped back from his fine wide forehead, and his big eyes were like two bright holes in his face. He pronounced the words in his songs real careful so that his dimples showed up good. He looked straight into the lights as he sung, and his body jacked the rhythm like a pump. He was proud of hisself, but it was the kind of pride that showed itself open-faced and honest, and nobody hated him or was jealous. When he done "Lonesome Town" everybody in the audience was so quiet I was afraid his voice would crack. But they was swaying and dreamy-eyed, and I got a little shiver in me like he was somebody I didn't know. I felt I was important just for being his brother and having all the girls know I'd seen him in his pajamas before. He told me once that his new girlfriend Phoebe had asked him what he slept in and that girls liked to know things like that about men they was sweet on.

Bobby Rex told me a lot about girls, mostly cause he had plenty of them to talk about. We shared a room then, and he'd keep me wide-eyed till midnight with his stories. Like the one about him and Denise Rutledge going skinny-dipping in Sawyer's Creek only cause Denise thought that with no moon out Bobby Rex couldn't see nothing. But he said he seen plenty of what counts. He told me the water was so cold that Denise's tits stuck out like huge red goose bumps, and he started calling her Pompon Queen after that even though she wasn't. I felt real shameful the next time Denise Rutledge come to the house. My ears burned like somebody's boxed them good, and I couldn't look her in the face when she patted the top of my head and poured out her sugary voice on me, "How you doing, little brother Leon?" I felt bad cause my mind had done a lot of wrong to Denise Rutledge.

I knowed for certain that Bobby Rex was going to be a star

after I seen him sing at the dance. It was different seeing him in them bright red lights than at home where he sung kind of soft and let his voice swing free and careless. He'd stop and cuss if he made a mistake and tighten a string and then go on, throwing in words that didn't belong if he was tired. But there at the dance he was smooth and slick as a tomcat. He knowed it, and so did everybody else.

After it was over he walked with me and Ma out to the car. His face was real sweaty and little brown crisps of hair was falling on his brow and he was happy and talking a lot. People waved and hollered at him, "Bobby Rex, Bobby Rex, that was a fine show." He'd shrug and grin like he'd done it a million times and backwards before. But on the inside he knowed it was something and he was proud.

That summer after graduation Bobby Rex worked at Hogan Royal's Esso station and saved his money in a bank account. He only allowed hisself one night out a week, and he called it his weekly splurge. That's when him and Phoebe Jenkins was thick, and he'd take her out to Woody's Danceland where everybody went in the summertime on Saturday nights. You couldn't miss Woody's even if you was a stranger just riding through. For ten miles on either side of it there was signs saying THIS WAY TO WOODY'S . . . NINE MILES TO WOODY'S . . . EIGHT MILES TO WOODY'S . . . TRY OUR CIDER. The signs was shaped like a foot cause everybody danced barefoot at Woody's in the summertime. There was a big sawdust floor and a jukebox and long pine benches that bled sap in hot weather so you had to be careful where you sat. They sold cool hard cider and snowball cones and watermelon and fried apple pies, and sometimes Bobby Rex would slip me home some cider in a paper cup and maybe one of them pies. I'd lay in bed propped up on one elbow and sip the cider slow so I could feel it sting me all the way down. And Bobby Rex would tell me about Blimpy Miller getting beat up in the parking lot or how Shilda Hawk was making eyes at him all night or about Willard MacIntosh getting so drunk that he started spitting watermelon seeds on everybody and laughing and dancing around so hard that his pants split and they had to carry him home. Bobby Rex made me feel I'd been there myself, and pretty soon I'd be laughing at everything he said and feeling fuzzy. Bobby Rex would talk while he undressed, and after the lights was out and we was in bed, he'd start telling me about Phoebe and how she wanted to get married and rode in the car with her hand on his leg and talked about having babies and wondered if it really hurt as much as people said. Bobby Rex said he didn't know if it hurt all that bad but that he'd seen our cow drop a calf and it seemed to him there wasn't much to it. He asked Ma one night right out of the blue at supper if it hurt to have babies. Ma got pink in the face and her mouth pinched up like a little white wire and she told him that the supper table was no place to talk about womanly things but that all good things hurt a little.

Bobby Rex stayed home a lot that summer he was working at Royal's. If he wasn't at the station, he'd be home with his guitar practicing his picking mostly, cause he said he'd done all of what he could ever do with his voice. He'd sit out on the porch swing after supper and thumb out all the songs he knowed. Midway through the evening, Ma would come out with some buttermilk and a piece of pie for us both. Me and Bobby Rex, we'd sit there eating our pie and watching the moths catch fire in the porch light, and the crickets would chirp so loud it was like they was trying to make up for not being heard when Bobby Rex was playing. We'd finish our pie at almost the same time and wipe our mouths with our arms and then without saying nothing Bobby Rex would take up his guitar and start his playing all over again.

One night when we was eating our pie, he told me what he was going to do with the money. I knowed it was his big

secret cause him and Pa was always having words about it.
Pa was sore cause Bobby Rex wasn't in the fields that summer. Pa said Hogan Royal was a swindler and besides he
needed help with the crop and it was Bobby Rex's duty as
oldest son to help his family out. But Bobby Rex said he
made eighty-five an hour at the pumps and that was thirty-
five better than he could do in tobacco. Pa's face would go
red as liver and he'd ball up his fists till the knuckles popped
out big and yellow as corn. "Well, if you're making that
much, boy, you'd maybe just better move on out and git
yourself your own house and buy your own food. You and
that Phoebe Jenkins ain't planning to run off, are you, boy?"
The blood veins in Bobby Rex's temples would bulge dark
and his jaw would scrape back and forth and he'd look at Pa
so mean and hard that I'd think he was going to belt Pa's
nose flat. But when he was really mad, he just couldn't get
it out with words. It was all inside him, kicking around,
mashing up his thoughts so bad that he'd finally just walk out
on Pa. And I think that got Pa worse than if Bobby Rex had
punched him good like he ought.

Nobody could get Bobby Rex to tell why he needed the
extra money. He'd never been much of a saver before and
Ma and Pa thought it was awful strange for him to be stashing
his money away in a bank. But I never asked him what it was
for. I guessed he was most likely saving up for a new guitar,
as his was just about wore out. And even if he wasn't saving
for no guitar, I figured he needed the money real bad for
something just as important. Anyhow, I felt special the night
we was sitting on the porch just after eating our pie, and he
struck up talking about the money of his own notion. He told
me the secret was beating on his insides and had to get free
and that I was the person he had picked to tell cause he
knowed I wouldn't tell. I felt real proud Bobby Rex trusted
me like he did. He said he reckoned I was just about the only

one in the family that understood him any. He said him and Paddy weren't all that close on account of her being a girl and him being three years older. I said there was seven years between him and me and he said, yeah, but you're a fella and that makes a lot of difference. Besides, he said, Paddy was a bigmouth and was bent on telling Ma everything she got wind of. And Ma, she didn't keep much from Pa, even though for her own good sometimes she ought. Anyhow, he said the time was right to tell somebody who would listen and understand what he aimed to do with the money, cause pretty soon the whole town would know about it.

There's a big talent show in Nashville the last week in September, Bobby Rex told me. And that's where I'm going. It's put on by all the local TV stations, and there's a five-hundred-dollar top prize. Hogan Royal says I need plenty of spending cash for Nashville. Some in my wallet and some in my shoe in case I get rolled. Then, Bobby Rex told me what it was like to get rolled, according to Hogan Royal's cousin Merve, who had it done to him one time when he went to Nashville. Course he was dead drunk, Bobby Rex told me, when two fellas put him down, and I don't aim on getting drunk. I've got nearly two hundred and fifty dollars saved, Leon, and that's enough for my bus ticket and food and a room for a week and enough money left over for any emergency matter and shopping for a new guitar. Nashville's the only place to get a guitar, Bobby Rex said. I asked him how come he knowed about the contest, and he told me that Merve Royal brought him a poster about it from his last trip to Nashville. He said he'd heard about the contest in the spring and that's when Hogan Royal had offered him work at the station, cause Hogan knowed how bad he needed the cash. He said Pa would blast him if he thought he was aiming to blow all that money taking a trip. Pa never did fancy anybody spending a lot in one place. And Ma would say that entering a contest was like gambling. Ma always said that Bobby Rex's voice was a gift from heaven and that he should give of it freely and expect nothing in return but the satisfaction of pleasing the ears of those less fortunate in their talents.

I watched Bobby Rex's face bobbing gray and white in the shadows with its calm, proud look, and I felt a great chill run over me like I always done when a secret cracked open and I was on the inside. I grinned up at him through the dark, but his eyes was far away and he was reaching for his guitar again.

2

The morning Bobby Rex left, I was awake before he was. The alarm clock he put under his pillow hadn't buzzed off yet, but something told me I'd had all the sleep I was going to get and my eyes popped open fresh like they always done on Christmas morning. I laid in bed staring at the ceiling and waiting to hear the clock go off. I waited a long time, and then I started thinking that there was too much light in the room for it to be just past five. Bobby Rex had a bus to catch at 6:07 in front of the Esso. I kept still long as I could, then I whispered across the room to Bobby Rex. He was all knotted up in his covers, breathing hard and steady. But when he caught my voice he jerked straight up and said, "Is it time, Leon?" I told him I'd been listening for the alarm a good while, so he fished around under his pillow until he found the clock, and it read quarter to six. "I must of forgot to crank the goddurn thing!" he grumbled. I knowed he'd have to run most of the way to Hogan's to make that bus now.

He slid into his shirt and pants faster than I'd ever seen him move. He spat on his hands and slicked them backwards through his hair. Then he counted his money out of his wallet and slipped out ten sawbucks that he rolled real careful and stuffed down inside one of the new boots he had bought special for the trip. They was fine boots, black cowhide with some red and yellow curlicues running up the sides. When he took them out of the box, I smelt them all over the room. He looked real fine in them boots with his guitar strapped over one shoulder, and I got the feeling looking at him that he wasn't no part of me. That here was a stranger standing in the middle of my bedroom. I didn't know what to say to him, seeing him all dressed up and the time running out so quick. But Bobby Rex, he took care of all that. He come over to my bed and hugged me hard against him and said, "Thanks, Leon." Then, quick, he drawed away and shook my hand hard and asked me if I could handle things and I said I guessed I knew what to do and he told me he'd send me a postcard and then he was gone. He walked out of the room on his toes so his new boots wouldn't talk out, and he didn't turn around at the door to say good-bye like I thought he would. Ma always says folks who say good-bye ain't aiming on coming back.

I guess I went back to sleep after Bobby Rex left, cause next thing I knowed Ma was calling through the door that I'd be late for school if I didn't get up. I yelled back that I wasn't going to school that day, I was sick, and Ma said let her come in and feel me for a fever. But I said no, it was the stomachache and that I didn't have no fever, it was just my stomach. She said come down and eat something and let Pa have a look at me. So I put on one of Bobby Rex's long-tail flannel shirts over my underpants and went downstairs.

Pa was eating oatmeal and flipping through a tractor catalog, and Paddy was laying the rest of our places. "You don't look sick to me, Leon Moseley," Paddy said, but I pretended I didn't hear her.

"Bobby Rex up yet?" Ma asked, setting a platter of steamy eggs in front of me that made me near gag just looking.

"He's *been* up," I said.

"What the matter with you this morning, boy?" Pa grumbled, not looking up from the page with the yellow tractor on it.

"My stomach feels like I'm going to upchuck."

"Sit down and eat some eggs, Leon. You need something in you," Ma said, testing me for fever with a damp hand she laid cross my forehead. "Why, you're cool as I am."

"I said it ain't no fever, Ma. I said it was something wrong with my stomach."

"Bobby Rex been bringing you sweets from the station?"

"No he ain't."

"I seen you up there yesterday drinking a Coke," Paddy butted in.

"No you ain't either," I said.

"Did too. You just want to lay out of school today cause you ain't got your lessons. Right, Leon?"

"Didn't have none 'cept spelling, and Bobby Rex called my words out to me."

"Where *is* Bobby Rex?" Ma asked all of a sudden.

"I'll just bet he called them words out to you," Paddy huffed.

"Bobby Rex is gone," I said, looking down at the tablecloth, feeling like I was going to bust out smiling any minute. I planned to let the secret come out slow. It was like chumming little hungry fishes, tossing out bait a tidbit at a time.

"Hogan Royal sure does have that boy under his thumb," Pa mumbled, oatmeal running down his jaw. "Since when did they start taking cars before eight?"

"Oh, they still don't take nobody before eight." I said it slow and careful.

"Leon, you better get dressed for school. Strother'll be by soon," Paddy nudged me.

"I said I ain't going."

"Eat your eggs, Leon, and then we'll see how you're feeling." Ma spooned a big mushy hunk of them on to my plate and poured me some coffee.

"Hogan Royal's a swindler," Pa said, flipping to another page of the catalog. "Them recaps he sold me ain't been worth two cents. I should've knowed not to trust him."

"Bobby Rex don't think Hogan Royal's a swindler," I said.

"Your eggs is getting cold, Leon," Ma said, touching my shoulder.

"Hogan's been good to Bobby Rex, Pa."

"Hogan Royal's making something off Bobby Rex, boy, and don't think he don't know it. He didn't have half the customers he's got now before Bobby Rex started working the pumps for him. All Bobby Rex's friends come around now and things is picked up for Hogan. That's what the fellas down at the Texaco say. They say Bobby Rex has got a way with customers Hogan ain't."

"Did Bobby Rex get breakfast?" Ma asked.

"No. Didn't have time."

"You see? You hear that, Wilma? Rushing off to the station with an empty gut. Hogan Royal's got his thumb on the boy and he's squeezing hard."

"I didn't say Bobby Rex went to the station, Pa." I waited what seemed a long time for somebody to say something, but it was like they didn't hear me. Pa bit into his toast and chewed with his mouth open.

"Pass me the butter, boy," was what he said. I watched him spread the butter thick on the end of his toast. Some got on his big red fingers, and he licked them off clean so he could turn the pages of the catalog.

"Bet you're feeling better now, ain't you?" Paddy said sweetly, knocking my leg with her foot under the table.

"I can't eat no eggs," I said. And then, cause I couldn't stand it no longer, I said, "Well, don't nobody care where Bobby Rex is?"

"If Bobby Rex wants to pump gas for Hogan Royal the

rest of his life, it's his bad luck and I ain't meddling in it no more," Pa growled through his chewed-up toast.

"He ain't pumping gas today, Pa. Don't nobody hear around here?"

"Where is he, then?" Ma asked. She said it in her wore-out voice, in the same easy way she might ask how much is potatoes a pound. She didn't even crunch up her eyebrows or come close at me in my face like she always done when she knowed I was holding a secret. She moved away from the table with the coffeepot in her hand, not even waiting on hearing the important thing I was ready to say.

"Bobby Rex is gone to Nashville." The voice I said it in was a new one. Each word come out clear and fine by itself and hung in the air between me and them with the kind of long-drawed-out hum Bobby Rex's guitar strings made when he plucked them hard one at the time. I listened to the sound of them roll away, but nobody said a word. I seen Pa raise his eyes up slow from the catalog. His head was still bent over the page he was on, but his eyes was up so the whites drooped like meal sacks and the rims underneath showed bloody red. Them eyes was on me hard like they was trying to poke a hole clean through my skin. I looked over to Paddy, who had let her jaw drop down like she had the palsy. I couldn't see Ma behind me with the coffeepot going to the sink, but I knowed she stopped solid when she heard what I let out. I couldn't hear no sound at all but the drip of water from the faucet spitting out the time I was going to have to wait till somebody said something. I felt all prickly inside like the wind had blowed out of me, but I felt good, too, and I knowed Bobby Rex would've been proud to see how I handled things. I thought about him sitting on the Greyhound in them new cowhide boots with his guitar in one seat and him beside it in the other, riding along without a care in the world, and how he'd said he'd send me a postcard.

"What did you say, boy?" Pa's voice was quiet and kind

of bubbly like he needed to clear it. But his eyes looked mean and bloody.

"I said Bobby Rex is gone to Nashville, Tennessee. He left on the Greyhound bus this morning and he's gone to be in a singing contest."

"You ain't lying, are you, boy?"

"Bobby Rex is gone to Nashville," I said again. I looked Pa straight on in the eyes, not blinking or letting my mouth twitch, which was the signs he looked for when he knowed I was making something up on him.

"No sir, you ain't lying, goddammit!" And Pa's fist come down like thunder on the table till the dishes rattled and the coffee sloshed out of the cups. "I knowed it would come to this. I knowed it but nobody would listen. Goddam him! Hogan Royal's put the notion in his mind. He's done it to the fool boy. That man's a swindler and a big talker. He blowed up Bobby Rex's head with hot air, same as he would a tire. How much money did he take, Leon?"

"I reckon he took it all, Pa."

"Bobby Rex is a crazy fool! How come a man don't know what's coming in his own house? I tell you, it's the devil working his will. The devil is into Bobby Rex now, and Hogan Royal put him there." Pa slammed the catalog shut. He was sitting tall in his chair with his chest heaved out. His face was hot and dark as boiled beets and his jaw jutted out, grinding back and forth like a mule's lip cribbing corn.

I twisted around in my chair and looked at Ma. Her long bony hands was knotted up in little balls at her sides, and her face was white as soda. "Why didn't he say nothing, Leon?" she said soft, like everything had been pumped out of her and it was her last breath she was asking with.

"I'll tell you why!" Pa bellowed. "Cause he knowed it was the notion of a crazy man what had got into his brain, and deep on the inside he was ashamed of hisself. Breaking his back over them pumps all summer long, stashing his money away for something he made us think was of high and mighty importance. Wouldn't talk about it none. Just kept stashing away that cash. Wouldn't work with the crop. Not enough pay, he said. Now, what's he going to have when he comes back, if he comes back? I ask you, what's he going to have solid in his hands to show he worked a whole summer getting it?''

"He aims to get a guitar, Pa.''

"Now ain't that something! Wilma, did you hear that? Bobby Rex is aiming to buy hisself a guitar. Dammit, boy, he's *got* hisself a guitar. What's a fool going to do with two guitars less he has four hands?''

"His is just about wore out, Pa.''

"So, he has to ride to Nashville on a Greyhound bus to buy hisself a new guitar? They got a passel of guitars over at Wilbur Rice's Variety Store. But no, Bobby Rex got to ride three hundred miles to Nashville to do hisself some shopping. Now, ain't that a hooting laugh!''

"He says they make them good in Nashville, Pa. Real good guitars.''

"Bobby Rex ain't got a lick of sense.''

"He knowed you be sore, Pa, but he done what he thought was right.''

"Right? *Right*, you say? Blowing money like it comes natural? Sneaking round my back like a pea-eyed rat, slipping off at the crack of dawn not telling nobody nothing, not caring about nobody but hisself? Comes a sad day in a man's life when he finds out his son don't know right from wrong.'' Pa ripped his fingers through his hair while he talked.

"You ain't said nothing about the contest, Pa,'' I said.

"Don't matter. Bobby Rex has his head puffed out. It's stuffed full of sugar talk by Hogan Royal and his likes. Bobby Rex ain't even been in a big city before. He won't know no contest when he seen it.''

"Tell me about the contest, Leon," Paddy said, leaning forward on her elbows.

"It's a singing contest in Nashville," I said. "There's a five-hundred-dollars top money prize that Bobby Rex is going to try for."

"It'll be fixed, too, you can bet on it," Pa said. "I seen them things before at the State Fair. Like beauty contests. Them judges is already been tipped off and them clapping machines is always rigged. Any fool knows that."

I turned around to Ma. She was sitting on the counter stool with her hands over her eyes, and her shoulders was trembling. I felt sorry for her cause I knowed it was hard on her. Pa just blowed it out of hisself and that was it. But Ma kept it all twisted up inside herself. Her and Bobby Rex was like that the same way. I got up and went over beside her and patted her real friendly.

"Why didn't he tell nobody, Leon? Why didn't he say?" she asked.

"I done said why, woman," Pa busted out again. "He knowed we take him for the fool he is, and that boy's got pride. He's got pride you can smell a mile off. The boy don't know his place no more. Folks telling him all the time, why, Bobby Rex, what a fine voice you got. Bobby Rex, you sure do pick guitar good."

"He could of told somebody," Ma sniffed.

"He told me, Ma," I said.

"I know, Leon," and she squeezed my hand.

"You know what people's going to say now, don't you?" Pa grumbled. "They're going to say Bo Moseley can't keep control in his own house. You can bet on it. The blame'll be on me. They'll be saying Bobby Rex broke loose on account of his old man being easy. First he don't work the crop no more. Gets hisself a job down at Royal's Esso. Farming ain't good enough for him. Then he slips off to Nashville without a word like he don't owe nobody nothing."

"How'd he know about the contest?" Paddy asked.

"He just did," I said. I figured Hogan Royal'd been reamed enough already without bringing it up about his cousin Merve giving Bobby Rex the contest poster.

"And to think I had the idea he was saving up for him and Phoebe Jenkins to run off on." A mean, hard laugh sawed its way out of Pa's throat.

"Him and Phoebe ain't nothin' no more, Pa. I knowed that," Paddy said. "They was picking at each other all summer."

"Bobby Rex don't know a good thing when he seen it!"

"Phoebe Jenkins has got a big head," Paddy snapped.

"Well, the two of them would make a damn good pair, then. A woman like that might be just what could settle Bobby Rex down. When I was his age I wasn't running off to Nashville to buy no guitars. No sir! I was breaking my back in them fields and buying food for my own table and fixing to be a daddy soon. And them things sober a man. Them things is what *makes* a man. Bobby Rex ain't never going to grow up." Pa rubbed his chin with his napkin till it was pink and shiny and then scraped his chair back from the table and stood up. "I've a good mind to just take myself a little ride up to Nashville and hunt that boy down," he roared. Then, he flung his napkin on the table, like it was a rock he was aiming at somebody, and stomped out of the kitchen. The screen door blasted shut behind him, and a creepy quiet took over the room like it does on the insides of a church. I stared at my face rocking back and forth in the cold coffee. It gave me a big swelled-up nose when I leant in close.

"He ain't really going to Nashville, is he, Ma?" Paddy asked.

Ma didn't answer. She was still drooped over the counter with her chin in her long white hands. Her eyes was gray as rain and stared wide out the window. She wasn't no little woman, but she looked small then, all crumpled up on the stool. The veins in her arms and hands stuck out bright blue, and she had sad little flowers on her apron. "Pa ain't going after Bobby Rex, is he?"

"Your Pa'll do what he thinks is right," Ma said, never turning her face from the window.

"You going to school, Leon?" Paddy whispered to me.

"No."

"Me neither," she said.

3

Bobby Rex told me he'd most likely stay in Nashville a full week. The day he left was a Monday, and the contest wasn't till Saturday night, but he said he needed time to check out the city and to look for a good guitar. He told me it took time to break in a new guitar and that by going early he'd have time without rushing hisself into a quick deal. If he won the contest he might come back early, he said. But if he lost, he'd need some private time to hisself to get over his blues. Anyhow, he told me not to count on seeing him for a week.

It was lonesome having a room all to myself. That first night I couldn't get to sleep. I laid in bed on my back, and my eyes pushed at the ceiling like they was waiting for the roof to open up. The wind crackled in the curtains and swung them out from the windowsill so that the moon come in strong and poured itself all over the room like melted money. It was too bright to sleep, so I did some thinking, and mostly it was about Bobby Rex and how I knowed that he was going to win that top prize money. I tried to think what he was doing right then, and I decided he was pulling off them new cowhide boots and dropping into the sack hisself. I wondered what it would be like to go to Nashville on my own, but I knowed I'd never have the nerve like Bobby Rex. And then I seen Bobby Rex. He was on a big wide stage with purple lights in his face so that I hardly recognized him. And he was wearing them new boots and a silver shirt and silver jeans and singing so hard that tears was running down his face. Phoebe Jenkins was there, too, trying to climb up on stage. But a big fat man in a checkered coat kept poking his cane in her face and saying, "Shh! Shh!" Then, Phoebe Jenkins's head started blowing up, and it got bigger and bigger until she was rising off the ground, waving her arms, frantic to keep her balance. All the time Bobby Rex was singing like his throat was going to bust, and the sound boiled in my ears so bad that I had to put my hands to my head. That was at the moment when Phoebe Jenkins's giant face split right down the middle, and shiny gold powder spilled out of her mouth. It must of been the prize money cause everybody in the audience cheered and screamed that Bobby Rex had won. But he kept on singing and wouldn't look. He kept singing so that the veins in his neck bulged out like thick green rope, and his eyes popped big as eggs, and he couldn't stop for nothing. I woke up sweaty and beat the alarm clock with my fist, but the sound kept drilling at my ears till I had to burrow under my pillow and wait for things to be quiet and my heart to stop knocking so fierce. I was still breathing hard when Ma tapped at my door and told me I was going to school this morning, like it or not, and had better not be late.

I went down to breakfast and Pa wasn't there. His place was cleared off clean, and Ma was washing his dishes in the sink. "Morning, Ma."

"Your eggs is in the oven, Leon."

"Where's Pa?" I opened the oven door and took out the warm plate.

"Your Pa's gone off on business," Ma said, wiping her hands on her apron, handing me a fresh-washed fork.

"Where'd he go?"

"Sit down and eat or you'll make yourself late."

"Where'd he go, Ma?"

"Tell him where Pa's off to," Paddy said, strutting into the kitchen with a smug, smart look on her face.

Ma sighed. "He's gone to see Hogan Royal down at the station."

"What he done that for?"

"Your Pa says he aims to get at the bottom of this thing."

"What thing?"

"Leon Moseley, you know good and well what thing," Paddy snipped.

"And I reckon I don't neither. What thing, Ma?"

"It's your Pa's affair. His and Hogan Royal's. Now, eat up, Leon."

"Don't nobody tell me nothing."

"Bobby Rex told you plenty," Paddy snapped. I stuffed my food down and didn't say nothing else.

It was a mile walk to school. Paddy rode with Strother Mottsinger in his old rebuilt Dodge he'd painted nigger pink. Most mornings they gave me a lift, too, but I felt like walking and being to myself this morning, so I was gone before Strother come by.

Narrow Gauge Road run right by our house and took you into town if you wanted to go that way. I knowed a short cut, though, by cutting across the road and down a cow path on the other side. The path run into some woods that edged Sawyer's Creek where us kids swam in the summer and Bobby Rex had took Denise Rutledge skinny-dipping. The path crossed the creek in a spot that was dry this time of year, and then petered out at the start of a cornfield that was behind the school. It was a fine walk this time of day. The path was powdery with dust cause we ain't had rain for a while, but the grass and leaves was dewy wet and smelt like bugs and animals. The smell was thick in my nose, sweet and damp like a cool rinsed washcloth pressing on my face. There was some of them brown puffballs growing off to one side of the path. The kind you can kick and they explode. I knocked a few with my foot and little chocolate-colored clouds of smoke puffed out the split-open tops. Bobby Rex always said them things was spitting their seeds out when they got ripped open, but I didn't see no seeds.

I felt happy about the day except when I thought about Pa storming in on Hogan Royal. But I didn't let myself think about it long. I felt full with a kind of lightness and strong like running, and I knowed I'd be important at school when I gived out the news about Bobby Rex.

Sawyer's Creek wasn't wide where I crossed to get to the cornfield. It was a good spot for getting fish bait cause it was shallow there. In summer we'd wade there and trap the crawdads and minnows that got theirselves washed down. Me and Elmo Rice had set up a fish bait stand last summer on Narrow Gauge. We catched ourselves a pailful of creatures, and Elmo made us a sign with flashy red paint his daddy gave him, and we sold five dollars' worth in a single day. Some fella in a big white Caddy convertible pulled over and snapped a camera picture of me and Elmo before we knowed it was us he wanted the picture of. The lady in the seat beside him wore a bright scarf and had great big purple lips that smiled so wide I said to Elmo they must be made of rubber. She made the man buy a can of crawdads even though he said he wasn't aiming on doing no fishing. She laughed and smacked them giant lips and said we was something off a picture postcard and she just had to have a can of our crawdads. When they drove off she turned around and grinned wide at us with them lips as fat as two squished grapes. Elmo said he'd like to buy a set of them wax lips for Halloween and go as that lady, and I reckon we laughed all afternoon about that.

This morning there was just mud in the hole where we waded in hot weather. It was that kind of black spongy mud that has a good rotten smell to it like fish drying in the sun. I seen a toad there, hidden under a little cape of leaves in the

creek bottom. He was still as a twig when I bent my face
close down. His back was bumpy as the mud and just the
same color. I watched his goosefleshed throat glob and his
eyes never blinked at all. And I could have stomped him flat
with my foot and them eyes would have never blinked at all.

I hurried on down the middle of the cornfield. The stalks
was dried and stiff as wheel spokes and picked at my shirt
like fingers. The wind rattled through the papery leaves and
made a chatter like teeth burring a chill. I seen the rags of a
scarecrow hung loose on a pole near the edge of the field.
They blowed limp in the wind like dead men's clothes, and
I wondered what good they was doing now or if they ever
did any good anytime. Looking straight ahead I could see
the brown fuzz of the ball field and the school rising tall and
somber above. I thought I'd hear the first bell ring on my
way across the field, but then I didn't see nobody and I
knowed I was late. I broke into a run and didn't let up till I
was at the door.

When I seen Elmo in the hall, it come into my mind that
he was the one I wanted to tell first. It was good to be back
in school when I knowed I'd be important that day. Elmo
seen me and flapped his hand.

"Bell done rung, Leon. You walk to school this morning?" Elmo said when I got close.

"Yeah."

"I seen Paddy and Strother come in. Thought you was
sick again."

"I wasn't sick, Elmo."

"Figured you was laying out." Elmo grinned. He had
little brown nubby teeth like a possum's. He banged his locker
shut and we moved off down the hall. I was busting to tell
him. "I heard about Bobby Rex," Elmo said.

Everybody knowed about Bobby Rex. It was like I'd come
to school yesterday and spilt it all. Paddy had blabbed or
maybe it was Pa down at the Texaco, but everybody knowed.

I felt like I was getting in on the tail end of things cause the surprise had wore off and everybody was pretty much happy with what they'd been told already and didn't need no more details. Elmo wanted to hear what Pa'd done about it, but that wasn't what I'd come to say.

After school Elmo said let's go to Hogan's for a root beer, but I said no cause I figured it was best I stayed away from there after what Pa had done that morning. I didn't know what he'd done, but I figured Hogan Royal would be remembered of it if I showed up. Elmo even said he'd treat me to a drink if I'd come with him, and that was hard to say no to. But I done it, and Elmo said I'd blowed my marbles and grinned with them teeth brown as a mouthful of pennies. We walked up to where Narrow Gauge Road run by the school, and Elmo took off walking toward Hogan's in the direction of town. I turned the other way for home.

I walked slow all the way. The sun burned hot on my shoulders and I wondered why I'd come this way since there wasn't no shade along the road. I thought about the wet fizz of a machine-cool root beer washing down my throat and almost turned around to start for Hogan's. Then I heard a horn that sounded like hit duck, and it was Paddy and Strother Mottsinger pulling over for me. Strother mashed the brakes real quick so that the car left squealing smoky tracks as it slid up to where I had stopped. "Want a lift, Leon?" Strother asked.

"Reckon so." I jumped into the backseat, and Strother jerked off before I had the door closed tight. I banged back hard against the seat. Paddy was sitting close up to Strother with her arm looped casual round his shoulder. Between them I watched one of them rubber shrunk heads jiggling from the rearview. Paddy was sipping a Cheerwine and passed the bottle to Strother, who swilled a big gulp down and wiped his stained mouth on the top of his sleeve. "You been to Hogan's?" I asked.

"Yea. Wanna sip?" Paddy asked, twisting round toward me.

"No thanks." She turned back in her seat and snugged up to Strother, tossing her head real prissy.

"Did he say anything to you?" I asked.

"Nope."

"Nothing at all?"

"What's he got to say to me?"

"Did he say Pa come this morning?"

"Hogan Royal didn't say nothing, Leon," Paddy said sharp. Then she laid her head on Strother's shoulder and sucked on the empty bottle with her tongue down inside.

Strother swung into our drive and bumped us right up to the front porch. "Thanks for the lift," I said and got out. Paddy was still sitting close up to Strother, sucking on the bottle. Strother spit out the window and drawed a toothpick out of his shirt pocket and screwed it between his front teeth.

"It's all right, Leon," he nodded. I liked Strother, but he wasn't much for talking. Bobby Rex said it was cause he was shy and that was the reason he painted his car nigger pink. Cause he wasn't noticed just for hisself. I went on up the front steps and inside.

Ma was scraping carrots in the kitchen. She looked up from the bowl when I come in. "Hi." I gave her a peck on the cheek and she smiled. "I get any mail, Ma?"

"No, Leon." She bent back over the carrots.

"Bobby Rex said he'd write me from Nashville."

She didn't say nothing. Her head hung low over the bowl and there was just the whipping sound of peels flopping to the side of her knife. Her face was gray in the dim kitchen light.

"Did I get a postcard or something, Ma?"

"He ain't had time to write yet, Leon."

"Guess so." I hadn't really hoped to get word so soon. "Paddy home?"

"Yeah. Her and Strother give me a ride. They're outside."

"It's just as well," Ma said, putting her knife down. "I got some things need saying to you, Leon." Her face was long as an empty sack. "Sit down, Leon," she said. And then she told me how important it was that I listen to her cause she was right and she was afraid that lately a lot of wrong things had been put in my head. She said she knowed I loved Bobby Rex and there was nothing wrong with that, but then she said how Bobby Rex wasn't no hero and it would be wrong for me to think of him that way cause he'd let his family down. She said Bobby Rex had his head rattled with dreams that would only bring him hurt cause they wouldn't come real, and it was wrong for him to fill my head with his private fancies. She said in her heart she knowed the Lord was frowning down on Bobby Rex this very minute and would more than likely punish him for running off by not letting him win the contest. "The Lord shows no mercy when a person flaunts theirself," she told me. Her face got pink as she talked and her voice growed firm till it was very loud, and I couldn't remember her ever being this way before. I figured it was the Lord giving her the strength to get it all out. "Do you understand, Leon? Do you?" She pushed her face close to mine, boring in with her eyes which had turned cold hard gray as BBs. Looking down I said I did, careful not to meet them eyes of hers. But it seemed to me she and Pa had everything wrong. Seemed they was making a mountain out of a molehill. But I said I understood to her so she could go back scraping carrots, feeling calm and happy in her heart that she'd put the truth before me and I'd swallowed it. I saw a little smile crack the two tight lines of her mouth as she picked up her knife. "Tell Paddy to get in and set the dinner table, Leon."

I went back outside where Paddy and Strother was sitting in his car. Paddy was doctoring her mouth up with lipstick, and it made a greasy orange gash in her long white face.

Strother was slumped against his side of the car, still poking his gums with the pick he'd pulled out earlier. Paddy heard me coming on the gravel and twisted her neck out the window. "What you want, Leon?" Her mouth crinkled up in a little *o* and hung bright in my eyes.

"Ma wants you in to set supper."

"I'm comin'. Tell her I'll be there soon as I tell Strother bye."

"Okay." I wondered how long it took somebody to say good-bye.

4

I didn't get brave enough to go up to the Esso till Thursday. Pa hadn't said nothing about seeing Hogan Royal, and I didn't ask. Pa hadn't said nothing about Bobby Rex since that first morning when he blared off, but it was brooding in him and showed itself in his eyes. I guessed he had got a lot of it out of hisself by telling Hogan off.

Truth is I wouldn't of went up to the Esso at all except Elmo Rice kept badgering me and I was curious. I wanted to get home and read the postcard I knowed Bobby Rex had sent. All the way to Hogan's I kept wondering what it said. I figured Ma would've read it and Paddy, too, but it wouldn't matter cause it'd be mine. It'd have my name on the front cause Bobby Rex had said so.

Lots of kids dropped by Hogan's on the way home from school to buy a soda. It was closer than walking on into town to the drugstore, and Hogan had a machine with three choices. Sometimes they'd be so cold there'd be a long lump of yellow ice all the way down to suck on while the cold stream of sweet fizz flowed by on either side. Since Bobby Rex had come to work there, more kids came by. Pa said this, and it was true. Mostly kids Paddy's age and older. They all thought Bobby Rex was something and liked to hang around him. I reckon Bobby Rex had always been popular, even before he started singing in public. And he wasn't envied for it neither. He had a small handsome face like the Cisco Kid's I seen on Elmo Rice's TV and dimples and eyes dark as plums. The girls all said he had movie star looks. It didn't go to his head though. He took it natural and didn't make nothing big out of it. Some people with good looks liked to watch theirselves in mirrors, or passing by a big pane of window glass they might sneak a gander at theirselves kind of sly out of one eye. But Bobby Rex didn't do none of this. He was real private about hisself. I reckon he was popular for lots of reasons, the least of them being his face. But the thing that stood out clean as if it was tattooed all over him was his friendliness. It was honest, too, and not put on. He could get along with anybody. Doodle Esquire Washington, the colored boy that worked up at Hogan's, said Bobby Rex had a special kind of *style*, and I guess that's what it was. Doodle said some people had style running in them like blood, and it was magic. Doodle said it was the style that gave Bobby Rex his pretty face. He said a pretty face was like a Christmas tree light waiting to be turned on. The bulb by itself was okay, but when the light come on inside it, that made all the difference. That was style.

All the way to Hogan's I kept wondering what Hogan might say when I saw him. I knowed he'd be sore after what Pa had said, and I guessed he'd act unfriendly. Hogan Royal wasn't no bad man like some of the fellas down at the Texaco liked to say. He'd lived in Orfax all his life, same as Pa. Fact, they'd growed up together. Then Hogan'd done a year off at some college in Georgia and Pa said that made a change for the worst in him. He'd always been a little queer with his ideas, Pa said, but after that year at college he wasn't never the same.

Pa said Hogan had come back to Orfax with some high-hat ideas of starting his own business with money he'd got when his old man died. But them was war years and cash was tight. So Hogan joined up with the army and nobody saw him again until the war was over. Pa said he'd come home from the war bragging and boasting about some award they gave him for being a hero and getting hisself shot. And he still walked with a limp so I reckon he got hurt pretty bad. I seen the souvenir the army had give him for his trouble. He had it hung from a chain near the cash box at the station, and Bobby Rex said it was his good-luck charm. The purple ribbon it dangled from was nasty with grease spots from all the times Hogan's big oily black hands would finger it while he stood behind the counter. There was a little gold picture of General George Washington in the center of the medal, and every now and then Hogan would grin wide at Doodle and say, "Here's your daddy, now what do you think?" Doodle would rare back and show his fish-slick gums, and them chunky teeth white as ice cubes would rattle down on his laugh.

Hogan had been to college and the war, and them things, Pa said, turned on him to make him different from most folks in Orfax. Made him think he was better and knowed it all. Pa said Hogan Royal'd learnt one thing in life and learnt it good, and it was how to swindle people. Pa said it mainly cause Hogan's prices was always a penny or so above the Texaco's. And since his station was on the main road to town and the Texaco was on a side road, strangers driving through who didn't know the difference would pull up at Hogan's and pay extra without batting an eye. Pa said Hogan probably needed the extra pennies to make up for the change Doodle Esquire was most likely pocketing on the sly. You sure couldn't trust a nigger round money, Pa said. But even if Hogan was getting hisself robbed, it was no reason to make folks who didn't know better pay extra.

Even though Hogan's prices was higher, it didn't stop local folks from buying from him. His station was big and new

with two pumps he always kept fresh painted and little blue
and red flags strung up all around. Plus he sold all kinds of
tires, even for tractors, which is something the Texaco didn't.
Pa said Hogan had took him on those recaps for the pickup
cause they blowed out the first week. But Bobby Rex said it
was just Pa talking cause the fellas at the Texaco was giving
him a hard time about trading with Hogan. Anyhow, Hogan
Royal had always been fine to me. And he usually offered
me a Chiclet when I went by.

It was just three long blocks to the station from school, and
it was a nice day for walking. On the way Elmo asked me if
I'd heard from Bobby Rex, and I said no, but that I was looking
for a postcard to come that day. I told him I couldn't stay long
at the station cause I wanted to get home and find out what
Bobby Rex had to say. We was almost there, in fact we could
see the little flags jerking in the wind like tied-up birds, when
I heard a horn blast behind us and I seen Ma in the pickup.
She pulled over to our side, and I ran around to her door.

"Where you going, Leon Moseley?" She had her head
wound up in a dull wrinkled scarf and her face looked lumpy
and dusty in the clean sharp light. She squinted at me with
them saggy eyes like the daylight was too bright for her.

"Me and Elmo is going up to Hogan's."

"It's too near supper for a soda, Leon."

"I ain't going to buy no soda. I'm just going with Elmo
to keep him company. I ain't been all week, Ma."

She sighed and looked beyond me down the road. Her
face was stiff and crusty with powder.

"Please, Ma?" I begged, and I kissed her quick. Her
cheek tasted like clay.

"Get in. I'll let you out there. I'm going to the Variety for
some thread and I'll get you when I'm done." She looked
straight ahead, her lips set white and dry as a scar.

"Hop in, Elmo. Ma, did I get a postcard?"

"No. You ain't got no postcard." She said it so fast something caught at my gut and ran clean through me. I looked at Ma's hard drab face as she steered the truck back on the road again.

"You sure, Ma?"

"I been home all day, Leon."

"Postcards is little, Ma. Sometimes they get laid down flat in the box so you can't see them unless you're looking for them. Are you sure you looked real good?"

"I'm sure." She pulled into the station and we got out.

I didn't feel like no Coke or seeing Hogan Royal, and I wished I'd rode on with Ma. I wished I hadn't counted on hearing from Bobby Rex so soon. After all, it was only Thursday. I shouldn't have got my hopes hung out so high. I knowed he was probably real busy and I'd hear the next day for sure. "Come on, Leon." Elmo was ahead of me, skipping toward the drink machine.

"I'm coming." I seen Hogan Royal just then. He was striding out the station door to meet a customer who'd driven up. He seen me, too, and we waved at the same time. He was a short fat man with a pile of curly hair the color of cedar shavings and a kind of orange fur on his arms and hands. It was strange how I felt when I seen him finally. I'd been scared of coming eye to eye with him after what Pa done cause I was afraid he'd be sore. But when I seen him, I felt good. I felt a part of Bobby Rex. It was like with Hogan there Bobby Rex couldn't be all that far away. I knowed Hogan was all for what Bobby Rex had done, and I was tired of being around folks who weren't.

"Whatcha want, Leon?"

"Huh?" Elmo already had hisself a drink and was blowing across the bottle top and making a hollow wind sound. "Nothing."

"Aw, come on, Leon. Your Ma ain't going to find out."

"I don't have time to drink a whole one."

"Then have a sip of mine." I took the bottle and gulped a swallow down hard.

"Thanks."

"I'm going to get some Goobers, too," Elmo said, and I followed him into the station house. It was bright inside and shiny clean. Green and gold oil cans was stacked like a metal Christmas tree in the wide front window. All over the wall there was shelves loaded with waxes and pastes and engine cleaners and juice to keep cars going when it got cold. There was a pinball machine in one corner of the room, and I seen two guys I knowed was old friends of Bobby Rex's hunched over it. They turned and grinned at me when I come in like they knowed me but couldn't remember how. Elmo went over to the glass case where the cashbox was and peered in at the candy. "Can't decide 'tween Goobers or a Reese's cup," Elmo said. Just then Doodle Esquire Washington come in the side door from the garage, wiping the grit off his black fingers with a rag.

"How you doing, Leon?" He gave me an easy pat on the back and grinned with them chunky bright teeth. His sweaty face was shiny dark as an eggplant.

"Okay, Doodle."

"You ain't been here in a while, boy." Doodle went behind the case, still rubbing his fingers with the rag. "What you need, Elmo?"

"I'll take a box of Goobers."

"What you know, Leon?" Doodle slid the box of candy across the countertop and took the nickel Elmo handed him and rung it up on the cashbox. "Say what, Leon?"

"Nothing much." I shrugged.

"You heard from the man?" Doodle smiled and his gums flashed like a quick pink light.

"Who?"

"Bobby Rex. He something. That Bobby Rex is a tomcat man."

"I ain't heard nothing," I said. The front door swung open and Hogan Royal came in.

" 'Lo, Elmo, Leon." He nodded and slapped a bill in Doodle's hand. "Make change for the lady in the white car, Doodle, and check her oil." He said it all in one breath, and Doodle went out. "Missed seeing you, Leon," he said, pulling a cigarette from his chest pocket. "You been okay?"

"I reckon so." I thought to myself I'd been silly to be scared of Hogan Royal.

"Good . . . good." He drawed in the smoke and rolled the cigarette around in his fingers. "I seen your Pa this week. He come up, ah . . . I believe it was Tuesday. Yeah, it was Tuesday. Day after Bobby Rex left."

"I know." I looked at the floor.

"He don't take much to Bobby Rex's plan, does he?" Hogan Royal laughed sudden. It was a wheezie laugh like a choked engine.

"No, he don't. Ma neither." I felt my cheeks burn hot when I said it.

"What do you think about it, Leon?"

"I reckon I'm glad he done it," I said. The words come off my mouth real easy.

"Think he'll win the contest?"

"I hope so."

"I think he'll win," Hogan said in a proud voice.

I tried to swallow down the dryness in my throat. My hands was dripping sweat, but I got my nerves up and looked Hogan square in the eyes. "Did Pa act mad or anything when he come up Tuesday?" A smile shucked open Hogan's face.

"He was friendly enough, Leon. Why you ask?"

"Oh, I don't know." I looked down again. "Seems he's been mad at everything and everybody since Bobby Rex took off."

"Nope. He come to look at tractor tires. Didn't find what he wanted, though. Didn't say nothing about Bobby Rex, except—'' Hogan paused and dragged hard on his cigarette, his eyes squinty from the sting of the smoke—"except as he was leaving, he asked me if I thought Bobby Rex was going to win the contest. I told him, yes, I thought Bobby Rex was a born winner.''

"Then what'd he say?'' I was looking Hogan square on now.

"Nothing. He said he had to go and would check back later about the tires.''

I felt something crawling up and down my insides like a big laugh that wanted to push out. It wasn't no glad feeling though. I felt sad and guilty for Pa, and the laugh was on myself and Ma and Paddy cause we believed him. When I thought about Pa now, I seen the ragged dummy in the corn-field near school, and it scared me. I wished it was Hogan Royal who scared me. But it wasn't. It was Pa.

"By the way, I heard from Bobby Rex yesterday,'' Hogan said.

"You did?''

"Sure. Got the card right here.'' He fumbled under a pile of magazines on the countertop and pulled up a picture post-card and handed it to me. I looked at the picture of Davy Crockett on the front and the big yellow letters that splashed out HELLO FROM TENNESSEE; GREENEST STATE IN THE LAND OF THE FREE. I held the card in my hands, rubbing the glossy front with my thumb. I couldn't turn it over. I didn't want to turn it over. It was like holding a part of somebody I didn't know no more, somebody that belonged to other things and other folks than I did. Yet I didn't know who *I* belonged to anymore. It didn't really matter what was written on the other side. It wasn't meant to be said to me.

"What does he say?'' Elmo asked, straining for a look at the card.

"Go on and read it, Leon,'' Hogan said in a kind voice.

"Naw, it's okay. I'll be getting my own card in a day or so," I said.

"Go on and read it, boy," Hogan said. "It's for you, too." I turned it over slow. It was Bobby Rex's handwriting all right. Black and stringy. It said:

Made it. This sure is a big city. Hope things is fine at the station. Tell Doodle Hi. Thanks for all you done. Bobby Rex
P.S. Tell Leon Hi if you see him.

I smiled and handed the card back to Hogan. He slid it under the magazines.

"There's your ma, Leon." Hogan pointed to the pickup as it swung into the station.

"Come on, Elmo. We can drop you off," I said. I told Hogan good-bye, and Elmo and me went out. Doodle was washing the windshield of a big white car and waved to us as we passed. I kept thinking about the postcard and Pa coming up to buy tractor tires and I wished I weren't no part of it. The whole business made me sick and ashamed of myself.

"Hey, did you see her?" Elmo whispered all of a sudden, cupping his hands to his mouth.

"See who?" I said with a tired, old voice.

"The lady in the white car. It's *her*."

"Who, Elmo?" I turned but I didn't see nobody I knowed.

"The lady who bought our crawdads. Remember? Last summer. The lady with them giant purple lips. I seen her in the car Doodle's with now. Look, Leon!"

"So what?" I said and climbed in the truck side of Ma.

5

Things ain't been the same since Bobby Rex left. Not that they've got any worse or better. It's just that things is different, that's all. I guess if I had to say the reason it'd be that things slowed down some and voices got softer in the house.

Pa's softer. He ain't interested in nothing lately except that big new colored TV set that he bought with the last money Bobby Rex sent. He says it gets a bunch of channels, and I reckon it's so cause after a half hour he can tell you whether or not the Yanks is going to win the Series or how Muscles Mooney put the scissors on Weasel Roach or what the day's price on tobacco is. Ain't no one picture going to bring you all that. Pa don't let nobody mess with that big set. Ma comes in to dust, but he won't let her lay a finger on it. Says he'll do it hisself. Says he'll take *pride* in doing it hisself, but I ain't seen him dust it yet. I ain't ever seen the top cleared off since the day it come. He keeps it stacked with his TV guides and cartons of Luckies, and there's a picture of Dinah Shore he cut out of a magazine after he seen her on the set once. Pa eats his supper on a tray now so he can snatch the news, he says. He says TV brings the world to your front door so that the only reason to go anywhere anymore is to get food. He tells Ma they even got religion on TV Sunday mornings, right during church, so he don't have to get into his Sunday suit no more. Ma tells him the Lord is no television star and that Pa is just making excuses and being contrary to her wishes. Pa lets her say it, though, while a little smile peeps out of his lips. He's softer now, Pa is. Or maybe it's the way I seen him. Paddy's fixing to hitch up with Strother Mottsinger in June, but Pa don't say nothing. And I started work at the Esso after Hogan finally said I was old enough. Pa don't say much about that either. I reckon I should be glad.

A man from New York City come out to the house the other day to do some writing about Bobby Rex. He asked me could I pick guitar like Bobby Rex. I said, no, I couldn't sing neither. About the only thing like Bobby Rex I could do was pump gas at the Esso. It was funny how the man pinched in his face when I said it and his mossy eyebrows mashed down on his eyes. He wrote it down and left. I always hoped to see it in print but I ain't yet.

MY MOTHER'S CONFESSION

☆ ♡ ☆   ☆ ♡ ☆   ☆ ♡ ☆

One morning in March, she arrived at my door, and as if grief were dismantling her, collapsed in the hallway, hugging herself and sobbing. She lay on the little linty rug in the foyer, facedown, beating the floor with her fists. "Don't let me do this," she said, and "I have no right," and "Oh, Josie! I'm so ashamed." When I bent to touch her, she rolled away.

"It's all right, Mama. It's good for you." I didn't know what went wrong, and I'm not sure I meant any of what I said. Since Sam had left me, I didn't know what was good for anybody anymore, unable to distinguish tears you cried out of habit from the ones you cried out of need. Tears that clarified, tears that muddled—was there a difference?

It was not yet nine o'clock. I could tell that my mother had left her own home in a hurry. Her hair, uncombed, was bunched under a rain hat. She wore a mismatched running suit and old sneakers with frayed laces. Everything about her seemed in uncharacteristic disarray. It was March, but a cold brutal smell like January rose from her clothes. Outside a freezing rain glassed over everything, dooming the camellia buds. The bird feeder was empty. The newspaper lay ruined on the sidewalk.

During my growing-up years and even as an adult I'd rarely seen my mother sad, and with a daughter's sheltered knowledge of such things thought of her as a uniquely brave and satisfied woman. She was the sort of person who dramatized happiness, who laughed heartily in public places, who twirled before dressing-room mirrors in swank shops. You felt encouraged when she was around. People respected her opinion; it was the choice, concentrated opinion of a sanguine disposition, a comfortable untroubled life. She'd had, after all, a strong marriage, healthy children. At fifty-eight she was still handsome, blond, upright. My mother was one of those people about whom it was often said, "She has everything."

Not that she had no reason to cry. My father had recently begun a grumbling retirement from his beloved university teaching. My brother's young wife had just learned that she was unable to bear children, and Sam's leaving me for someone else was another story. As if the litany of family turbulence wasn't bad enough, in February her old friend and neighbor, Jean Blake, had died of cancer.

For a long time we said nothing more. She abandoned herself to the mission of her crying. She seemed oblivious, weeping open-mouthed and loud, sometimes angrily. Then, when my phone rang, she stopped abruptly and said, "Don't answer it."

"Why not?"

"Because it's him, your father. I can tell by the ring."

"Does all this have to do with Daddy?"

Tears ran unchecked down her cheeks. "It's just that all my life he's been able to track me down," she said.

I went into the kitchen and made some hot tea and sat down at the breakfast table to drink it. I stared out the back window at the little fenced-in rectangle of winter-drab condominium grass. The yard was about as spacious as a grave plot. I felt a rush of failure. It wasn't so much for where I was, right at that moment in my life, but for the realization that I could only look backwards rather than forwards in times of trouble. All I could think about, staring out the window, were the broad, grassy summer lawns of my youth, the dawdling sunlight, my brother and me racing for the two rope swings that hung from monstrous shade trees. Our knees and shins and elbows were bruised from a summer's worth of fearless play, of carefree failures. We were daredevils; nothing stopped us because nothing seemed to hurt for very long back then.

And if I allowed memory the panorama toward which it sprawled, my young, beautiful mother appeared toting cold glasses of lemonade—what she then called "pick-me-ups." As if we needed picking up, a loftier view than the one we already had. As if life could be made to glisten more than it already did.

I got up from the table and went to check on her. "Want some tea?" I called softly.

She sat up and took off her rain hat. "I'm making you late for work, darling."

I took her hands and guided her from the floor to the sofa. When the phone rang again, I turned to answer it, but she said, emphatically, "Don't. *Please*, Josie. I'm *not* talking."

I let the phone go a second time, and after it stopped ringing, called the Browsery Bookstore, where I work. "Did you just phone mc?" I asked Helen when she answered.

"What for?"

"Check out the clock, I'm late," I said.

Helen laughed. "How shocking."

"I may not come in at all this morning," I said. "Something's happened."

I heard the ringing of the cash register. "Hey," Helen said. "I'm still on." I could hear her making change. "Thank you,'' she said to a customer. ''Josie,'' she said with sudden excitement. ''Is Sam back?''

She couldn't help herself. Ever since Sam had left, she'd been counting on some fairy tale ending to my grief. We'd grown up together, Helen and I. We'd been best friends since grade school and we had no secrets. I often wondered how I could have managed without her. I hung up feeling light-hearted despite my mother's strange sadness, despite the dreary weather. I thought: *That's* what love is, Helen.

My mother was pouring herself a cup of tea in the kitchen. She'd combed her hair and put on lipstick. ''So?'' I said. ''Feel like talking now?''

''Oh, I'm all right, darling,'' she said apologetically. ''I feel much better now. I just needed a place where I could go and cry, no questions asked.''

But already her frail little smile was fading. Her face seemed to buckle as she put her head on the table. ''My God, I miss Jean Blake,'' she said.

There are many things that I could say about my mother's friend, Jean Blake. At one time I felt nobody loved her any better than my mother did. I suppose her husband, Leonard, might have, yet as a child, playing with their daughters, I never saw Leonard and Jean exchange the sort of searching, misty looks my parents did. They never kissed or caressed each other publicly. They seemed old that way. My mother explained their lack of demonstrative love as a facet of Yankeeism, Leonard having been born and reared in Vermont. Vermonters, my mother said, were more circumspect, more taciturn than we gushy folks in North Carolina. Jean Blake was from North Carolina, however, and so her inability to conquer Leonard's reserve somewhat mystified me. I suppose I grew up thinking that women had the great joyous power of being not only able to rescue men from their own incommunicable personalities but also to inspire huge changes for the better in them. All my life I'd watched my mother rescue my father: jumping in to smooth feathers he'd ruffled, calming his rage by a swift, gentle touch of her hand, a chirpy compliment. As a child I'd had no doubts that women were the superior psychological wizards of the world.

Jean Blake was the sort of woman that people who lived on suburban Sunrise Drive in Raleigh, North Carolina, during the late fifties called a "character." She didn't work, although she'd once been an editor's assistant at *Time* magazine in New York. In our little town, where most working women we knew were secretaries or schoolteachers, this gave her a matchless aura of grandeur.

But there was nothing haughty or superior-acting about Jean Blake. Plain as any old shoe, people said of her, referring to her local upbringing. My mother, however, never viewed Jean as plain, and therein lay the spark that ignited their brief but splendid friendship. "Plain!" My mother fumed at the word. She and Jean Blake made war together against plain.

Her daughters rode the school bus in the morning like I did, and there stood Jean on the front porch stoop, waving to them gaily, wearing her Chinese silk bathrobe, red with a green dragon embroidered on the back, usually wearing her prescription sunglasses because she could never find her regular glasses. They were always crumpled under a sofa cushion where she'd last curled up to read. Or squashed in some book, serving as a marker. She read constantly.

It was all she did the whole day long: read and smoked Camel cigarettes, curled up in her Chinese bathrobe. Near four o'clock, when the school bus disgorged her daughters, she'd close her book for the day, bathe, dress, and wash up the egg-enameled breakfast plates before starting supper. By six o'clock order reigned at Jean Blake's house. There was usually even a pan of brownies or a pie baking in the oven for Leonard to sniff as he came through the door. He was always, despite his aloofness, a satisfied-looking man.

I wouldn't want to suggest that Jean lazed away her time. It was my understanding that she had, at some earlier point in her life, decided to withdraw from the world at large and sink herself into a single, pure activity that did not require the involvement of others to make her happy. Some neighbors said she was shy or snobbish. My father once called her "unmotivated." Her worst detractors called her an "egghead," but the same was said of Adlai Stevenson, so it didn't seem too shameful. I remember thinking of her as being distinct and queenly and, because of the red silk robe and dark glasses, maybe a spy.

Few women in our neighborhood had full-time jobs. One taught piano in her home; another was a nurse. Mostly the women on Sunrise Drive were homemakers and mothers and did their socializing over the heads of small children, cups of sugar borrowed. They engrossed themselves with PTA and shepherded scout troops.

Jean Blake was the exception. The only time the other women in our neighborhood glimpsed her was occasionally at noon, darting out of the house in her flame-colored robe to check the mail or chase the postman down the sidewalk waving one of her lavender envelopes that needed mailing. It was after one such sighting that word got out she was reading *Lady Chatterley's Lover.* Someone had seen her drop it in the driveway, the first unexpurgated edition to hit Raleigh. It was her New York connections, everybody said.

I used to think that it was Jean Blake's flair that first attracted and enthralled my mother: the spectacular red kimono, her lavender envelopes, the ubiquitous sunglasses, the ropy black braid of hair that hung Rapunzel-like below her waist. But mostly I think it was her fierce hermitage, her self-imposed exile from mainstream expectations that my mother deeply admired. It was Jean Blake's bold dismissal of the world's ordinary strivings that convinced my mother Jean Blake would make a difference in her life.

Not that my mother ever acted unhappy about her own choices. She often said she was a joiner by nature. It wasn't individuality that she lacked so much as the courage to be self-indulgent or she might have been able to say "No" more often when women devoted to volunteerism deluged her. My mother was counted upon as a staple of community effort, a doer, a go-getter, an organizer. I suppose that she was all of these things, but such involvement left her little time for herself, for rumination.

The first time they met, in fact, my mother was calling on Jean Blake to ask for a contribution to some charity. The door opened slowly and Jean Blake peered out, wearing her kimono, of course, her hair in a disheveled braid that had been slept on. She pressed a book to her chest with one hand and held a cigarette holder in the other. Her expression was deadly blank, but tears streamed down her face.

"Oh dear," my mother said. "I've come at a bad time."

"Not at all," Jean Blake said. She even grabbed my mother's hand, surprisingly eager for company. "Oh, don't mind these," she said, brushing at her tears. "It's that damn Madame Bovary. Just why she couldn't be happy with her husband and let well enough alone I'll never know. There are just so many ways she could have *made* herself happy, don't you think? I mean you can practically *will* your own happiness, can't you? Conjure it out of the thinnest old junk if you've a mind to."

"Madame who?" my mother said.

Jean held up the book she was reading. "What I need right now is a strong cup of tea and a dose of the real world. You are the *real* world, aren't you?" she asked, removing her dark glasses and squinting at my mother. "All you'd have to do would be to say, 'My name is Emma Bovary,' and I'd keél right over with a heart attack.''

My mother quickly introduced herself, and Jean pulled her inside and shut the door. They drank tea out of two Pyrex measuring cups because that was all Jean Blake had clean.

That evening at supper my mother claimed that she'd not had such an adventure since my father had taken her to Niagara Falls on their honeymoon and they'd ridden under the falls in one of those *Maid of the Mist* boats. She'd left her first encounter with Jean Blake feeling a similar vertigo, for their talk had not been without dizzying moments of danger. Most everything she counted on as solid and serene, Jean Blake had roiled up with a question. Yet they hadn't talked about real life at all. Mostly they'd talked about Emma Bovary.

"I didn't know you'd ever read *Madame Bovary*," my father said to my mother.

"I haven't," she said. "But I'm certainly going to now." And eventually she did.

It seemed to me that the longer their friendship developed, the looser my mother became. She wore short shorts despite her remorse over her varicose veins. When another neighbor, Mrs. McGehee, alluding to the red kimono, referred to Jean as Tokyo Rose, my mother resigned from the neighborhood dance club. She sat in a lawn chair in her bathing suit and did watercolors of surrounding plant life, and she read books. Sometimes I'd catch her staring into space just contemplating.

I was eleven or twelve about this time, old enough to sense the most minor interruptions in the rhythm of my life. Although my mother's interior life had grown immensely, or so she claimed, I could not detect any detrimental effects, any dropped stitches in the tightly woven fabric of our family. And I was at an age when I searched for such defects.

I do recall fleet bouts of jealousy over the time she spent

in Jean's company when I thought she might be serving my interests better. I remember some irritation over their phone conversations which seemed to drawl on for hours. But I also felt that something slightly magical had happened to my mother since Jean Blake had entered her life—something risky and enlivening. She did not seem at all like the other mothers. She stood out as if spotlighted. She had an air of display.

"What on earth do you two talk about for so long?" my father asked after one of Mother's and Jean's longer conversations.

"The truth," my mother replied with an imperious gladness that delighted me in a way I didn't fully comprehend.

"It takes that long to tell the truth?"

"If you tell *all* of it," my mother said.

My father laughed at her. He was a mathematician, and I suppose he thought he had her number. He had a way of speaking to her sometimes that made me think of her as a pet, the leashlike tone of his voice attempting to gentle her down.

"So what *is* the truth?" he'd say. "Tell all."

"About what?"

"Oh, any old thing."

"And bore you to death?"

So I came to understand, as my mother eschewed discussion with my father, that truth had a quantitative aspect to it, a cumulative effect that my mother was willing to share with Jean Blake but not my father. This troubled me. This was a lesson I was learning about a man and a woman who supposedly loved one another. There was more than a hint of betrayal in it. Of failure.

I began to know that my father didn't care very much for Jean Blake. Up until now he'd considered her a diversion in my mother's life rather than an enhancement. He trivialized her. But after their phone conversations about truth began, whenever her name was mentioned my father's face seemed to gray. In some vague way he'd begun to think of Jean Blake as a threat.

My mother had never suffered from a lack of strong identity. She wasn't particularly restless or malleable, and so I don't think my father should have feared any sort of *conversion* on her part. Yet he assumed a puzzling, competitive bluster whenever Jean's name came up. The smallest allusion to her and my father bristled and fended off her influence with a disparaging remark. He was as jealous of Jean Blake as if she were a man. I think he probably wished she was a man. He seemed to be boxing at a shadow.

Once, when Jean called, he answered the phone and without a trace of humor in his voice he called across the room to my mother, "It's Svengali."

I didn't know who Svengali was, but I remember feeling relieved that the caller was a person named Svengali and not Jean Blake. For once there wouldn't be anything for my parents to argue about when my mother hung up.

For a while it was a bad time between my parents. Not unredeemably bad—volatile and cruel—but injured feeling, remiss, full of lapses and adjustments that are made to accommodate new loyalties. Any satisfactions between them felt tentative and were not articulated.

An Ingmar Bergman film came to town, very hush-hush and explicit, an *art* film, as they were called then. There was a to-do outside the movie theatre one night; some people picketed the movie because of male nudity. It made the newspaper.

My mother and Jean Blake devised the plan that they would go to the movie wearing paper bag masks. I suppose it was a whimsical kind of statement, poking fun at everybody's pretense. They giggled all afternoon together, cutting and pasting. I thought they acted silly, yet watching them made me feel glad. They sat Indian-style on the kitchen floor, their faces rosy with merriment. They were acting out the sort of camaraderie that Girl Scouts always made me want to feel but never did because of all the duty involved.

My father came home and seemed amused, watching them work. I saw admiration flicker in his eyes. My mother even cajoled him into agreeing to join them at the movies. Then, when he saw the finished masks, he refused. They'd made caricatures out of their husbands.

He walked down the hall to his study and quietly closed the door. "Don't act so old!" my mother cried heartlessly after him. But that wasn't the issue and she knew it. She slunk into their bedroom as if scolded and threw herself across the bed. He had no such friend as Jean Blake, and if he had, my mother couldn't have stood it.

Then, in the middle of one night, I remember waking to the sound of somebody crying. A welter of desperate, pleading adult voices came from the foyer. I heard my father say calmly, "Best to go on home now, Jean."

I slid from my bed and hurried into the hallway to crouch and spy down through the stairwell. Below me Jean Blake, wearing her red kimono, was crumpled against my mother, sobbing. My father, with an air of stern formality, stood apart from them, his hand on the doorknob.

I couldn't guess what had happened, though I tried. If tragedy had befallen Leonard or their daughters—say a fatal automobile accident—I couldn't imagine that my father, no matter how much he disliked her, would send Jean Blake back into the night alone. But where *was* Leonard? And why had my father involved himself at all? How had he entered the tight little circle of their friendship and taken charge? If Jean had wanted only Mother's help, wouldn't she have phoned? My father towered over them, grimly authoritative as if he'd made an important, ghastly decision for them all.

They seemed, my mother and Jean Blake, weak and muddled in spite of all their truths.

"Do you want to use the phone? Do you have your key?" my father asked. It seemed like kindness, but I heard the spurring edge in his voice, the gravity of disgust. He was the professor merely indulging an inferior student.

My brother, younger than I, appeared on the landing, rubbing his eyes. "Is it burglars, Josie?"

I felt stunned, powerless, the way you feel in nightmares, my arms and legs wispy with fear as if, indeed, there *were* burglars downstairs and something of enormous value was being stolen away right in front of me.

After that incident my father quit warring with my mother over Jean Blake. He didn't wince when her name was spoken; he was civil to her, even deferential, on the phone. Occasionally, if she'd been absent from my mother's life for very long, he'd ask after her, and not in the brusque, jeerful way he'd inquired about her before that turbulent night. His manner was as somber and downcast as if Jean Blake were dying.

I don't know what I thought had happened that night. When I was twelve I believed that adults inhabited one world and children another. If a tragedy occurred in the adult world that I was meant to know about, I trusted my parents to inform me. The next morning, when our breakfast routine proceeded normally, I felt no urgency to ask questions. I actually sensed more lightheartedness between my parents than I had in months. Any distance between them felt cleansed and airy. I watched my mother cheerfully spooning pancake batter onto the griddle. She flipped on the radio in the kitchen window, snapping her fingers to "The Early Bird Show" featuring the Big Band sounds from Woody's Uptown Elbow Room. I could hear my father singing robustly in the shower. It was life extraordinaire and to question it would have made me feel foolish and grim.

Summer vacation began soon after and Jean Blake and her daughters went away to visit Leonard's relatives in Vermont. She wrote my mother only one letter that summer on her lavender stationery. And although I saw the letter, pilfered it and read it behind my mother's back, searching for clues that would unriddle the mystery of Jean Blake, I found nothing that suggested a mystery at all. It was a plain-spoken, unsecretive letter, perky with information: where in Vermont they were traveling, who they'd visited. It described restaurant menus, a fat cousin, an uncle's farm, souvenir shops, a tedious incident involving a flat tire.

That night, after I was in bed, I heard my parents talking. "I got a letter from Jean today," Mother reported to my father.

"Oh? Is everything all right?"

There was a long, deliberate pause. "No," my mother said finally. "And nothing will ever be all right again, thank you."

I lay in my bed listening, trying to determine my father's response by the way he conducted his newspaper. The tone of its snap, as he closed it, might indicate his culpability. His manner of rattling the newspaper seemed as articulate as language and denoted a spectrum of moods: impatience, anger, a rallying argumentativeness. Sometimes there was only a pause in the shifting, papery sigh of pages—an inkling that he'd let them sag in a dispirited way. This usually meant he'd conceded, that my mother was absolutely right, no contest. He'd dropped his guard and would suffer his comeuppance manfully.

This particular night, when my mother said what she did— that nothing would ever be the same again—accusation was implicit in her tone. Afterward I only heard his brisk rising from the chair and the opening of a door. "Very well," he said. "But we'll all live through it."

The next morning, tentative, I asked my mother if Jean Blake had contracted some incurable disease.

"Why on earth would you ask such a thing?" Mother said, bristling. "Honestly, Josie!" Clearly I was not yet a confidante. She looked at me with distrust, and I blushed and fumbled. "But she's so thin," I said. "And pale."

"When did you last see her?" Mother asked. "Is she back from Vermont?"

"I saw her last May," I confessed. "Waving at the school bus."

"And you're just now mentioning this? I had a letter from her this week and everything's really quite all right."

I wanted then so much to say, "But nothing will ever be all right again, thank you." Just to torment her a bit with my half-baked knowledge, just to see if her mask could survive, just to surprise her with my eagerness to be entrusted with the Whole Truth. "Mrs. Truth," I wanted to say to her, draping her with a comradely arm, "your daughter waits." I believed that's what being an adult finally meant: access to Truth.

In September my mother and Jean Blake resumed contact. At least once a week they went out to lunch and to a matinee movie together. They loaned each other books. But there were not so many phone calls, and there was a way in which they seemed overly considerate of each other as if their friendship were newly conceived: untested and speculative. By this time I'd convinced myself that something terrible had happened between *them*, not just to Jean Blake, and that they were in the process of seeing if they could salvage something from the ruins.

That year, for Christmas, my father and Leonard Blake gave my mother and Jean tickets for the Theatre Train, which amounted to a three-day pass to New York City and reserved seats at a half-dozen Broadway shows. I thought it was an admirable, conciliatory gesture on my father's part, an attempt to make amends for whatever friction he'd caused between my mother and Jean.

My mother had long dreamed of taking the Theatre Train, and I'd often heard her and Jean planning such a weekend together, laughing girlishly. I expected my mother to jump up and down with delight, having finally received something she'd desired for so long. But when she opened the box of tickets on Christmas morning, she only nodded and said wistfully, "Better late than never, I suppose."

They left together for New York in late January. I saw them off at the Raleigh train depot with my father and brother and Leonard and his daughters. It felt as if we were all there to celebrate something. Snowflakes swirled exuberantly down the air like confetti.

I kept thinking that my mother should have looked ecstatic, but instead she looked resigned. Her mouth was set in a thin, taut line. Yet there she was, climbing onto the train in her stylish broadbrimmed hat and elbow-length kid gloves. She was dressed to attract excitement, but excitement wouldn't come.

I felt oddly sorry for her, watching her train pull out. She waved to us from her window. She looked just then as if she'd suddenly realized her life was plunging toward some destination she wholly doubted and that she needed us desperately—the very people she was leaving—to welcome her there. She was thirty-five years old, but it was a frantic homesickness I remembered seeing in her eyes.

When she returned to us, three days later on a chilly Sunday evening, she had very little to say about New York City. She talked about spending most of the weekend in her hotel room, sick with flu. She hadn't been able to see a single play. She hadn't gone to a single nice restaurant. Forget ogling the stars at Sardi's. On the way home, she'd ordered a ginger ale on the train and had paid two dollars for it, plus a tip. The whole trip had been that sort of waste, she said. "I missed you," she told my father, looking deeply into his eyes. "You'll never know how much."

The trip to New York, then, which had seemed an effort to patch up their friendship, became, in my mind, a kind of ungrand finale. After the trip they were clearly not so thick anymore, my mother and Jean Blake. They were always friendly, but with a kind of self-protective stiffness. They were never the deep-laughter, girlish friends they had once been. So it came true: nothing was ever quite the same again.

From my child's perspective, my mother passed from the most golden era of her life into a more sensible, almost dowdy phase by comparison. She redid the house. She took sewing lessons and learned découpage. As I grew older and more balky, she seemed stricter, quick to impose curfews and censor certain of my friendships. Her stellar self winked and dimmed; she was harder to distinguish from the other mothers once again. *I* missed Jean Blake. Over the years, whenever I asked her what happened to the friendship, she would often gaze fondly in the direction of Jean's house, eventually owned by someone else, and say something like, "Oh, I suppose we just outgrew each other."

My mother stopped crying and blotted her eyes on her sleeve. She pushed her teacup aside, flattening both hands on the kitchen table as if holding open the pages of a very large and cumbersome book. "A long time ago," she said slowly, "when you were just a little girl, Josie, I rode with Jean Blake on the train, all the way to New York City to meet a man. He was not *my* man," she said quickly. "He was her lover, a man she'd loved long before she met Leonard and had never given up. I glimpsed him once at Penn Station and he *was* handsome, Josie: tall and silvery, and remote—a kind of hood ornament of a man, and I don't mean to make light. Mostly it's his name I remember. His name thrilled Jean

Blake to pieces. Listen to it: Adam Truehart. Right out of one of her books.

"I wasn't shocked, sheltered as I was. I thought of the two of them as courageous and thoroughly modern. His situation was clearly miserable—his wife was an invalid—and I knew that Jean had never been happy with Leonard—Leonard didn't like sex. Oh, it's awful what people will tell you. I hated knowing that about Leonard, but it helped me understand Jean's disloyalty. I never thought of her as being unfaithful to anything but unhappiness.

"I watched her climb from the train and run towards Adam Truehart, her red felt hat flying off her head. I watched him gather her up and crush her into himself. They kissed in an imperiled way—it was like they clung together from the edge of a cliff.

"Some dutiful young man hurried up behind them and stood waiting, awkwardly holding her hat. He'd retrieved it and only wanted to return it. But there he was, stuck, having to wait out their lifesaving.

"We had stealthily negotiated this reunion for months, wangling our legitimate weekend in New York ever since Leonard had found one of Adam Truehart's letters and thrown her out of the house. *That* was a terrible night. Your father got in on the act. She was so distraught that we couldn't keep it a secret from him. He'd always suspected Jean of being unfaithful—she was a flirt at parties and there were rumors—and he resented our alliance. That she didn't love her husband had always seemed to him possibly contaminating.

"You probably don't remember how we argued back then because we tried to be discreet, and it's been more than twenty years. But half the time, Josie, I cried myself to sleep. Half the time I wished your father would fall in love with somebody else—a young, bright student like so many of his colleagues seemed to do in mid-life—so that I wouldn't have to feel so guilty, wanting a bit of romance for myself. I only wanted romance because he was suspicious of my wanting it. I used to imagine finding a stranger's lipstick smear on his shirt as I did the laundry and saying 'Oh, well,' and letting it go. Oh, Josie, am I shocking you?''

I shrugged. ''It feels daughterly,'' I said. ''So how did she work things out with Leonard after he knew about Adam Truehart?'' I asked. ''And, by the way, I hate his name. I see a strutting peacock.''

My mother laughed a little.

''Well, she patched it up with him, made a great show of burning the letter—although there were dozens more where that one came from. She vowed and declared that Adam Truehart was dogging her, an old and truly forgotten lover who'd simply persisted. Leonard believed her. He adored her in spite of everything. When you really adore somebody like that, you believe anything they tell you, especially good news.''

''But now that Daddy knew so much, didn't he openly condemn her? Didn't he think of her as dangerous?''

''On the contrary,'' my mother said. ''He thought of her as found out and penitent. She was a known quantity and therefore disabled: a math problem solved.

''Josie, I went to New York because Jean needed me as an alibi—I went as a friend. But I think that I went looking to prove to myself that she was still a threat to your father. That he hadn't finally won me. The fact that her questioning so absorbed and involved me was a threat. I went to New York to have a secret truly apart from him. I'd reached a moment that maybe every woman reaches in a durable marriage: a moment when you know that having some burning secret is the only thing that will distinguish you from your husband once again, make you *other*.

''I sat on the train for a while until they disappeared into the crowd. Then I got my suitcase and called a taxi and went directly to the hotel.

"Our plan was that I would go alone to see all six Broadway shows, that I would save the Playbills for her to read on the train ride home. But instead of going to see *My Fair Lady* that night, I sat in the hotel bar until almost ten o'clock, trying to figure out why I felt so abandoned, so used.

"All the next day I stayed in the hotel. I watched television at night. On Sunday, after brunch, I strolled in the park and then I took a cab to the Metropolitan Museum. I kept thinking of your father and how much he had bulldozed of my heart to build his mansion of love. It was the same with Jean Blake: I let her lead and I followed. I thought of them both and how much I loved but resented them. I resented Jean most for showing me another way. Everything she said and did made me ridicule the conventions of my life—at least question them. I hadn't wanted any part of the Adam Truehart story—except the story. The rest of it rankled: Jean Blake's chattering preoccupation, the way she bit her nails on the train, the way she called him by his first and last names, both, over and over like a chant, the way she assumed that whatever was between a man like your father and me couldn't possibly be *love*, could only be an arrangement, the way, even in the passionate moment of her meeting Adam Truehart, she'd glanced back over her shoulder at the train station to see if I was watching. I thought of the boy who stood patiently behind her, a little awed, embarrassed, holding her hat. I felt I knew him well. We were, the two of us, forever abiding by the rules and regulations of other people's passions.

"I wandered through the museum for hours. I reached across the ropes and touched a Degas ballerina. I held her slipper—so much smaller than I ever dreamed. It felt cool, with a frilly roughness like lace. I was determined I would hold the slipper until a guard spotted me and told me to stop. I wanted to hold it until I embarrassed myself. I waited and people milled about me, but nobody came and told me not to touch. After a while I gave up and went back to my hotel.

"I felt detached from Jean Blake after that weekend in New York. I was no good at making up life as I went along. We stopped seeing each other except in the context of neighborliness. And I missed her. I missed our talks. I missed throwing back our heads and laughing loud. I missed having a friend I could say anything to. Only maybe I never had that, finally, or we'd have stayed friends. When you were in college, they sold their house and moved across town. I didn't see her again until she was dying in the hospital.

"I went to visit her in January, but she'd already slipped into a coma. Leonard was there—you know they stayed married. 'She's talked about you a lot lately,' Leonard told me, and maybe this was true. I sat on the edge of her bed, rubbing her cool little skin-and-bones batwing hands. She was sixty, but lying back against her pillow, her face looked smooth and youthful. She didn't have a single gray hair. I felt as if I were living inside a dream: that it was twenty-five years ago and we were best friends. She looked like a girl, yet she was dying right before my eyes. I had this overwhelming urge, even with Leonard there, to tell her all the things I ever meant to after our friendship faltered. To ask blunt questions—the kind she liked best. I leaned forward to whisper, thinking I would even confess to her that I'd faked having flu in New York, that the reason I had no Playbills to give her was that I'd betrayed her. I leaned forward to tell her that when I got home from New York, I told your father everything. That had been my way of sealing my fate quickly, of ending my romance with girlhood. I had learned that mine was a dangerous age, and I no longer wanted to be trusted.

"I leaned forward, Leonard or no Leonard, to speak the sort of truth that we had tried to honor long ago—a skewering kind of truth. And suddenly it all seemed so silly and dim. None of it seemed important or seemed like it had ever been truth at all. What *should* have happened seemed more like the truth. Leonard should have been suspicious and kept her from going to New York in the first place. Adam Truehart should have gotten flu. Jean Blake and I, despite our differences and our grudges, should have stayed friends.''

"You're torturing yourself," I said.

"I missed her long before she died," my mother said. "I missed not who we were so much as who we tried to be. I missed our naïve, silly conviction that we could get away with murder among the people who loved us best. That's how we defined love then, as something you might victimize with impunity. But look how badly we treated *each other* and who of us ever forgave?''

Neither my mother nor I talked for a while. I refilled our teacups with stone-cold tea and heated them in the microwave. But we didn't drink. We let the tea grow cold again. I stared into my cup as if it were bottomless, a wishing well. Just what would I wish for? My childish celebration of dumb luck and magic?

When the phone rang we looked at each other. "I think we should answer it," she said. "It's probably your father."

"Or Helen."

"Is there any chance," she said tentatively, "that it could be Sam?''

She would always be the mother. She would always know just a little bit more than I was ready to hear or wholly believe. "Mother," I said, "some things are really over when they're over.''

"Well, I don't believe that," she said.

When she said this, reaching for the telephone, I felt suddenly, exquisitely separate. I felt the way a young girl feels coming home from a date, shuddering from pleasure or discouragement—it doesn't matter which. She simply comes inside and closes the door. There is no place else to go. She leans against the doorframe to catch her breath. Her heart beats as if someone is stalking her, cherishing her—it is sometimes hard to tell which. Down the hall, in a moonlit bedroom, her mother sleeps contentedly beside her father. And she believes that, no matter what, she still has the rest of her life.

About the Author

☆ ♡ ☆   ☆ ♡ ☆   ☆ ♡ ☆

MARIANNE GINGHER was born on Guam but grew up in Greensboro, North Carolina, where she now lives with her husband and two sons. Her novel, *Bobby Rex's Greatest Hit*, received North Carolina's Sir Walter Raleigh Award and was named by the American Library Association as one of the Best Books for Young Adults for 1986. She currently teaches writing at the University of North Carolina in Chapel Hill.